THE WEATHER WATCHER

CLAIRE ANDERS

A CIP catalogue record for this book is available from the British Library. Published by TLC Publications Ltd

Cover Design by MiblArt

ISBN 978-1-7395389-4-1

ISBN ebook 978-1-7395389-5-8

For Marlo

THE WEATHER WATCHER

One woman. One war. A thousand skies to read before she finds her way.

Alice Peters has lived a sheltered life in her Scottish village, bound by tradition and her mother's expectations. Marriage and motherhood are the paths laid out for her.

But when war breaks out—and her mother announces a shocking engagement—Alice must decide whether to accept the future others planned for her or carve out a life of her own.

Drawn to the new village vet and guided by an unlikely friendship, Alice begins to dream of something more. Her chance comes when she joins the Women's Auxiliary Air Force, trading the safety of home for the uncertainty of war.

As a meteorology assistant, Alice learns to read the skies and aid missions that could change the course of history. But as bombs fall closer to home and the cost of war becomes personal, Alice faces a choice more difficult than any before.

The Weather Watcher is a coming-of-age story of duty, resilience, and the quiet strength it takes to chart your own course.

PART I

1

---

14 October 1939

'The HMS Royal Oak has sunk in the second major loss of life for the United Kingdom since war was declared just six weeks ago.' The BBC news announcer's voice was grave and sombre as he announced the devastating news.

Alice's hands clenched and a cold sweat broke out on her skin, chilling her despite the warmth in her living room. She perched on the edge of the sofa, leaning towards the wireless as if being physically closer could somehow lessen the impact of the words. 'Father?' she asked, hearing the tremble in her voice.

Her mother, Violet, shook her head and sank back into her armchair. 'He's not on the Royal Oak.'

That should have been a relief, but it wasn't. Alice's stomach was in knots, twisting and turning with each word. The weight of war had never felt so heavy.

The broadcast crackled and Violet turned the dial on

the wireless just a little until the static disappeared and the announcer's voice was crisp.

'It has now been confirmed that German U-boats torpedoed the HMS Royal Oak. The Admiralty has today issued the first list of survivors.'

The news wasn't a surprise. Alice had already heard the rumours. The Royal Oak had been torpedoed while it was anchored peacefully in Scapa Flow, a body of water located in the Orkney Islands. Apparently, survivors reported hearing three massive explosions. Minutes later, the battleship was sent to the bottom of Scapa Flow along with more than eight hundred of her crew. Those details weren't reported, of course. The War Office suppressed locations and casualty figures in case the Germans were listening, but word-of-mouth spread fast.

As Alice listened to the broadcast, sour bile rose in the back of her throat. She swallowed it down. Her father had spent his entire career in the Royal Navy. Perhaps that's why the danger he faced hadn't occurred to her before. But this was now the second loss for the Royal Navy, the HMS Courageous having been torpedoed only a few weeks earlier. Listening to this latest tragic broadcast, Alice realised that her father, wherever he was, was a target for the enemy. Whether he was on a ship at sea or anchored in a naval base, the people on the other side of this war were out to kill him.

Alice thought of the terror those men on the Royal Oak must have felt in their final moments. Her heart ached at the thought of them being engulfed by the cold, unforgiving waters of Scapa Flow. And she couldn't bear the possibility of the same thing happening to her father one day during this dreadful war.

Violet reached out and flicked the wireless off, abruptly

cutting off the rest of the broadcast. She stood up from her plush armchair and made her way over to the mahogany drinks cabinet in the corner of the spacious room, pouring herself a generous measure of brandy into a crystal glass. Alice watched as her mother's hand trembled slightly, the amber coloured liquid sloshing in the glass. Violet took a deep sip, leaving a trace of her signature red lipstick on the glass. She closed her eyes briefly.

The silence that followed felt heavier than the broadcast itself.

Alexander Peters was a patriot. Serving in the navy was more than a job to him. His words of duty and honour echoed in Alice's mind, and with them came a sharp stab of helplessness. Waiting and worrying, that was all she did. And she hated it. Sitting here, safe in the quiet village, listening to others report the news of death and destruction.

She wanted to do something. Not just to distract herself, but to play her part. To contribute to the war effort in any way she could.

But she wouldn't get a chance to do that in Millwood. Millwood was just an hour's drive from Edinburgh, yet it felt like a world away. The village was a peaceful haven of rolling green hills and lush farmland. Its centre was compact yet full of character with a few shops, one pub, and a thriving community centre that hosted everything from Guide meetings to social clubs. The winding streets were lined with charming cottages housing friendly locals who all knew each other.

Alice resided in the first house on Manse Lane, a four-bedroomed home surrounded by just three other dwellings. It was a quiet existence, and that quiet was beginning to suffocate her.

She turned towards her mother.

'Mother,' Alice said. 'I saw an advertisement for a clerical job. I thought I might apply. It'll be a useful distraction from this dreadful war and a way for me to contribute financially.'

Violet sat back down, and a shadow crossed her features. 'Alice, you know how I feel about you working.' Her tone was gentle yet firm. 'Your place is not behind a typewriter. And you needn't worry about providing for yourself; that's what a husband is for.'

Alice's heart sank. It was the reaction she had expected. Violet only saw a daughter who should be preparing for marriage and a life of domesticity, not one who sought a purpose beyond the confines of their home. But she could hardly blame her. Violet Peters had followed the example set by her three older sisters by moving from her father's house to her husband's house.

A few months before war broke out, Alice had been hopeful of a different reaction from her father. She'd overheard a conversation between her parents about a book-keeping position she'd hoped to apply for. Maths was one of her strongest subjects at school and she thought she'd be good at the job. Her father had been keen to allow her to apply. Violet had been dead against the idea.

'It's better than allowing her to join the women's military services,' her father had said. 'War is coming, and I won't have Alice put at unnecessary risk.'

Her mother had responded in unusually hushed tones. Alice hadn't been able to hear her, but Violet had won the argument.

Now, deflated but not defeated, Alice pressed on. 'I'm not worrying about providing for myself. I think I would be good at the job.'

Violet smoothed out a wrinkle in her burgundy skirt. 'I'm sure you would be, darling, but there's no point. You'll only have to resign your position when you marry.'

Alice tightened her grip on the arm of the sofa. 'That isn't happening any time soon, so I'd rather do something more meaningful with my time. A job might be good for me.'

Violet's lips curled into a smile, indulgent and amused. 'You're eighteen in just a few days,' she said.

'It's not my age that's the problem, it's the absence of a fiancé,' said Alice, trying to keep her voice even.

But inside, her thoughts churned.

Violet laughed and rolled her eyes. 'All in good time, darling.'

Alice sighed. She didn't just want to pass the time. She wanted a life of her own, something that belonged to her. With the country at war, everything felt sharper, more urgent. Her father was risking his life in treacherous waters, and she was stuck here, unable to shake the feeling that she was wasting away in the shadows.

If she could find work, maybe even something connected to the war effort, it wouldn't just give her purpose. It would be her way of standing beside her father, of proving she could contribute too. She didn't want to wait to be chosen by a man before she was allowed to live.

She had thought that her parents allowing her to stay in school until she turned seventeen was progress, maybe even a step towards university or a job. But clearly, the battle wasn't won.

Her eyes wandered to the window, where thick blackout curtains blocked the outside world. The dull ache in her chest deepened. She was nearly eighteen, an adult by any standard except the one in this house. And she was tired of waiting for permission.

Maybe it was time she stopped asking.

2

———

Alice awoke on the morning of her eighteenth birthday to the comforting scent of warm milk drifting up from the kitchen. She lingered under the covers for a few moments, imagining Peggy, their housekeeper, bustling around down-stairs with a pot of porridge simmering on the stove. Eventually, she slipped out of bed. The chill on the wooden floor bit at her feet. She quickly dressed in her Rangers uniform – a navy-blue skirt with a lighter blue shirt – and dragged a brush through her auburn hair before she made her way downstairs, snatching her tie off the dresser on the way.

Pausing in front of the hallway mirror, she fixed her tie around her neck and examined her reflection. Eighteen years old. It was a significant milestone that should have been marked with joy and celebration. Yet her thoughts were clouded by a heaviness she couldn't shake. The country was engulfed in war. Her heart was set on contributing to the cause, but that wasn't going to be easy. Her mother was never going to support her decision to go to work. Alice was going to have to make it happen behind her mother's back and deal with the consequences later.

As she entered the cosy kitchen, she found Violet seated at the table. Peggy, with her sleeves rolled up and her cheeks flushed from the stove's heat, ladled steaming porridge into bowls.

'Happy birthday, darling,' said Violet, springing up from her chair. Her navy-blue dress, typically reserved for the most special occasions, shimmered subtly under the morning light streaming through the window. She held out her arms and gave Alice a stiff hug.

'Thank you, Mother,' said Alice, stepping back. Her mother wasn't usually one for much physical affection, but the hug was cold, even for her. Something seemed off. 'Is everything alright?' she asked.

'Of course,' said Violet. She smoothed a hand down her already smooth hair and glanced at the clock, before turning her attention back to Alice. 'What on earth are you wearing?' she asked.

Alice looked down at her neatly pressed outfit. 'My Rangers uniform.'

'I can see that, but why? It's your birthday. And I thought your Guide meetings had been moved to a Saturday morning.'

'They have been.' The blackout and the early winter nights had proved to be an unnecessary challenge for some of the girls, particularly the younger ones, who weren't yet used to navigating the village in the dark. The whitewash the Guides had painted on the pavement edges helped a little, but it had been agreed to move the meetings to daylight hours for everyone's safety. 'We're sorting through donations today,'

Violet gave an impatient sigh. 'That's an odd way to spend your birthday.'

Alice took a seat at the kitchen table.

Peggy placed a steaming bowl of porridge in front of her. 'Happy birthday, Alice.'

Alice smiled. 'Thank you, Peggy.' She dug her spoon into the sugar bowl and sprinkled a generous helping of the white stuff onto her porridge.

'Must you use quite so much?' said Violet, retaking her seat and sliding a newspaper towards herself.

'Sorry, Mother.' But she wasn't sorry at all. She loved nothing more than a good spoonful of sugar on hot porridge. The immediate crunch in her mouth made her happy then the sweet syrup it left on top of the porridge as it melted was delicious. There wasn't much to smile about at the minute, but something hot and sweet to eat on her birthday was worth the chiding from her mother.

Alice tucked into her porridge as Violet caught up on the news and Peggy busied herself in the kitchen. She'd given Alice control over the lunch menu that day and Alice had chosen her favourite – roast beef with potatoes, carrots, and cabbage, and apple crumble with custard for pudding. The serving size of the beef had shrunk considerably in recent weeks. Everyone was being a little more conservative with their meat since war had been declared. But with rationing expected to be introduced any day now, it was hardly right to complain about a smaller portion of meat than she'd been used to.

Violet tossed the newspaper aside and Alice saw Peggy sneaking a peek over Violet's shoulder. Even from an upside-down view, the headline grabbed Alice's attention. *The First Nazi Raid on Britain: The Firth of Forth Attack.*

'What happened?' asked Alice, grabbing the newspaper and spinning it around to read the article. They were calling it an attack on the Forth Bridge, but it was the reported naval casualties that drew Alice's focus. A knot of worry twisted inside her.

'No one seems quite sure,' said Violet with a casual wave of her hand. 'But it doesn't seem too serious.'

'The first air attack on British soil. Seems quite serious to me,' said Alice, repositioning the newspaper so she and Peggy could read it. 'And it's another incident with naval casualties.' She was caught between the desire to downplay it, like her mother, and the nagging fear that this was just the beginning. The incidents and the casualties seemed destined to escalate.

'Oh, we can't focus too much on that or we'll drive ourselves to distraction.' Violet said, changing the subject.

The doorbell chimed and Violet sprung up once more. 'I'll get it,' she called out, waltzing out of the room.

Peggy shook her head and cleared away Violet's empty cup. 'Those poor families. Just sitting by the door, dreading the sound of footsteps, and wondering if today's the day the War Office sends a telegram.'

Violet returned barely a minute later, a bright smile lighting up her face. 'Your surprise is here,' she announced.

If Alice hadn't just read about German bombers over the River Forth, she might have mistaken the joy in her mother's expression for a sign that the war was already over.

Alice's heart fluttered with excitement, and she felt her pulse quicken. There was only one other occasion that would warrant such cheer. She stood up. 'Is Father home?'

'What?' Her mother shook her head. 'No, of course not.'

She clasped Alice's hands in hers, her smile returning, her eyes glistening in the sunlight that streamed through the kitchen window. 'You're engaged!' Violet announced, her voice echoing through the high-ceilinged room.

Alice furrowed her brow. 'Engaged to do what?' she asked.

Her mother laughed. 'Oh, Alice. To be married, of course.'

Alice shook her head and stepped back, prising her hands free. 'I don't know who told you that nonsense, but it isn't true.'

'The Fergusons are in the sitting room waiting for us. George has a job to get to so we had to meet at this unsociably early time so you two could meet on your special day.'

Alice sighed. 'Mother, what are you talking about?'

'Oh, Alice, do try to keep up. You're not a child anymore. Mrs Ferguson is here with George so you two can spend a little time together. It's just for a cup of tea, but that's all we can expect on a weekday morning. I would rather have waited until the weekend, but, well, it had to be today for obvious reasons. It's such a shame your father couldn't be here.' Violet's smile slipped.

Alice had always thought that she and her mother handled her father's long absences well. Now that the country was at war, his absences felt even harder to bear. Perhaps Violet talking in riddles was a sign that she too was struggling with her husband's absence.

'Are you alright?' Alice asked.

Smile restored, Violet said, 'You are in a strange mood this morning, darling. I'm sorry it's so rushed, but you can spend the entire weekend together to get to know each other properly.'

'I'm sorry, who am I spending the weekend with?'

'George Ferguson. Have you not been listening to a word I've said?'

'Why on earth would I want to spend the weekend with George Ferguson?' Alice asked.

Her mother huffed out a breath. 'Because he's your fiancé.'

It was as if her mother were speaking a foreign language, or perhaps Alice had simply slipped into an alternate reality where everything made no sense. She strained to follow Violet's continued rambling, but it was like trying to grab handfuls of smoke.

'I sincerely hope you won't be this disagreeable when we sit down to tea,' said Violet, her irritation clear to see.

'I'm not being disagreeable. I don't have a fiancé.'

'You do now, so wipe that foolish look off your face and smile.' Violet reached for the door handle and Alice thrust her hand out to push the door, keeping it firmly closed.

Alice's stomach dropped as she realised this was more than just crossed wires. 'Tell me exactly what you've done, Mother.'

'Exactly what I said I would do,' said Violet, slowing down her speech, each word drawn out like a steady drip of water. 'I have arranged for you to marry George Ferguson and invited him and his mother to tea this morning. Why are you acting as if you know nothing about this?'

'I *don't* know anything about this.'

'Alice, we discussed it.'

'When? You've been talking of a surprise for my birthday, but at no point did you say that surprise was George Ferguson.'

'The surprise was inviting George for tea this morning. We discussed the engagement at Christmas. The Fergusons were here, and they brought George. Father and I thought you two would be a good match, remember?'

Alice's fingers twitched. She let go of the door and her arm dropped to her side like a stone sinking in the ocean. She remembered. Her father had been home for a week just prior to Christmas and Violet had arranged a party. Any excuse. George Ferguson was tall, with thick dark hair that curled at the edges. At first glance, most would agree he was an attractive man. Unfortunately for him, his personality quickly detracted from his good looks. He had asked her to dance and had spent two entire songs prattling on about the absurdity of having to interview for a job when he'd been recommended for the position by his father and two other well-respected contacts. Alice had made her excuses and slipped away at the beginning of the third song and had almost collided with her mother.

'You and George seem to be hitting it off,' Violet had said. 'He's charming, isn't he?'

Alice had agreed because what else was she supposed to say about the pompous, self-entitled son of her parents' friends.

'I think you two could be a good match,' Violet had added.

Alice definitely did not say yes. She remembered quite clearly not saying a word. She also remembered quite clearly her mother's next comment. 'Don't you worry. Father and I will sort it.'

At the time, Alice didn't think much of it. In fact, she hadn't given it a second thought until now. Her mind raced with questions. Did her parents truly offer her hand in marriage to a complete stranger? And if so, did he also find the idea absurd and outdated? But the most pressing question on her mind was how she was going to escape this situation. To answer that question, she had to know exactly what she was dealing with. Despite her mother's beaming smile, Alice fought the urge to flee up the stairs as Violet opened the kitchen door. Instead, she squared her shoulders and walked as confidently as she could muster into the sitting room to meet her fiancé.

3

George Ferguson stood tall and imposing, with a sharp jawline and intense blue eyes that perfectly mirrored the deep hue of his silk tie. His dark hair was slicked back, not a strand out of place, and the cut of his tailored suit was equally flawless. His gaze first landed on Violet. A smile formed on his lips, but it never reached his eyes. Then he turned to Alice, his eyes cool and assessing. She searched his eyes, hoping to catch a glimpse of her own shock mirrored back, but he gave nothing away.

Alice took a seat on the sofa beside her mother. Violet's enthusiasm was palpable despite her obvious attempts to contain it in front of Mrs Ferguson who sat rather stiffly across from them in an armchair.

George stood until the three women in the room had taken their seats. It struck Alice that the reason for this was not good manners, but rather his less-than-discreet appraisal of their living room. His eyes worked their way around every inch of the room, taking in the paintings on the walls, the books in the bookcase, and her father's whisky bottles that still adorned the top of the cabinet in the corner.

Mrs Ferguson touched a hand to her pearl necklace, perfectly matched with delicate earrings. She cleared her throat and George took a seat.

'Right, down to business,' he said.

'What exactly is your business, George?' Alice asked. She knew full well he was looking to discuss this supposed engagement, but that wasn't a topic of conversation Alice was in a hurry to get to. Despite her desire for this meeting to end swiftly.

Mrs Ferguson smoothed her hands over her classic black skirt and tossed her chin up slightly. 'George studied law at the University of St Andrews,' she declared, a glimmer of pride in her voice.

Peggy appeared with a tray of tea, setting it on the table. Alice reached forward and poured tea for everyone. 'You're a lawyer?' Alice asked.

George waved his hand dismissively. 'My firm handles legal and accountancy matters.'

'And is that a reserved occupation?'

'Alice!' her mother scolded.

'I think it's important that we know how quickly George will be heading off to war,' said Alice.

George chuckled and added three heaped spoons of sugar to his tea.

Mrs Ferguson glared at Alice. 'I'm sure this dreadful war will be finished before the government get round to calling up George,' she said.

George fidgeted in his chair and refused to meet his mother's gaze while she rambled on about the importance of men like her son keeping the country functioning.

'Tell me about yourself then, George?' Alice said, cutting over Mrs Ferguson to steer the conversation away from such a sensitive topic.

George began talking about his work. It sounded terribly boring and as he spoke Alice watched him carefully while sipping her tea. His expression never changed, and he rarely looked in her direction, speaking mostly to Violet and Mrs Ferguson instead. He held himself rigidly, barely acknowledging Alice's presence in the room even though she sat directly opposite him. His voice was monotone and there was not a hint of enthusiasm that would have suggested he was looking forward to marrying Alice. In fact, he made no mention at all of their engagement, and Alice wondered if this had been sprung on him the way it had been sprung on her.

'Perhaps George and I should have a few minutes alone to chat,' said Alice.

Mrs Ferguson rolled her eyes at the suggestion and Alice was lost as to why. It seemed a perfectly reasonable request given the circumstances.

'I think George has to get to work,' said Violet. 'But you two can have plenty of time to talk at the weekend. I expect you're eager to start planning the wedding. There's really no point in delaying matters, especially not these days.'

George sprang up as though Violet had given him the perfect opportunity to escape this awkward nightmare. Perhaps she had more in common with George than she realised.

'I do have to get to work,' he said. 'It was good to see you all again.'

Mrs Ferguson followed her son's lead and Peggy appeared in the doorway with their coats. Alice tried to catch George's eye hoping to glean a hint of how he really felt about this situation. He turned his back to her and opened the front door. Alice really hoped her instincts were right and he was just as perturbed as she was. That would make it so much easier to put a stop to this nonsense.

With a determined stride, George and his mother exited the house. Alice stepped outside waiting for them to get out of earshot before she laid into her mother. She was equal parts confused, angry, and hungry, having never got to finish her porridge.

As she stood on the doorstep trying to work out where best to begin her rant, her friend Beatrice arrived carrying a potted fern. George stepped off the pavement to allow Beatrice to pass and she turned her head to look back at him.

'Happy birthday,' sung Beatrice when she reached the house. She handed the plant to Alice, its leaves vibrant and lush. 'Who was that?' she asked, nodding after George and his mother as they marched away from Alice's house.

Violet looked at Alice, raising her eyebrows to beckon her to speak. When she didn't, Violet filled the silence. 'That was George Ferguson, Alice's fiancé.'

Beatrice shrieked and her hands flew to her face, pressing against her plump rosy cheeks. 'Oh my goodness! You kept that one quiet.' She flung her arms around Alice and squeezed her, her dark curls bouncing around her head. 'Congratulations!'

'Watch the plant.' Was all Alice could think to say.

Violet tutted, no doubt frustrated by her daughter's ungratefulness, and stalked back into the house. Alice brushed her fingers over the leaves of the plant, straightening them back up.

Alice pulled the door closed, leaving herself and Beatrice standing in the cold on the doorstep.

'Have I come at a bad time?' Beatrice asked.

'Let's just say the engagement came as something of a surprise to me. I barely know the man.'

Beatrice's eyes widened. 'Did you say yes?'

'No, I did not.' Alice looked down. 'But I also didn't say no. This is all my mother's doing. I have to figure out how to get out of this without denting her pride. She'd never forgive me if I make her look bad in front of her snooty friends.'

Beatrice glanced behind her. 'Or you can consider what it would be like to say yes.'

Alice scoffed. 'You're joking, right?'

'Maybe not. Mr Ferguson is certainly easy on the eye. What else do you know about him?'

'He lives in Alderbrae. He's a lawyer. At least I think he is. His mother was very happy to tell me he studied law at the University of St Andrews, but he was very cagey when I asked about his profession and then he chatted on about the work that his firm was involved in. He didn't actually confirm that it was also the work *he* was involved in.'

'What else?' asked Beatrice.

'Literally nothing.' Alice pushed her front door open. A cool breeze swept in behind her. 'Thank you for the plant. Let me pop it inside then we can head off.'

Alice placed the fern on the sunny windowsill in the kitchen and poured a little water into its roots. With a sigh, she grabbed her coat and an extra spoonful of porridge, the weight of her mother's actions still fizzing in her chest. She headed out with Beatrice.

'I'm starving,' said Alice. She dug her gloves out of her pocket and thrust her hands into them. 'I didn't have time to finish breakfast before my mother ambushed me with George Ferguson.'

Beatrice linked her arm with Alice's as they strolled along the path. 'Well, you can fill up on birthday cake soon.'

'Birthday cake?'

Beatrice winced. 'Oh dear, I wasn't supposed to tell you that. Act surprised when we get to the village hall. Please.'

Alice nodded, a faint smile breaking through her foul mood. 'I will. And can you please keep quiet about my news for now?'

'What news?' came a voice from behind, startling Alice.

Alice whipped around and came face-to-face with her Guide Captain, Kathleen. Her long blonde hair had been pulled back into a tight bun and the canvas bag strapped across her body was bulging at the seams.

'Alice's engagement,' Beatrice blurted out, before clamping her hand across her mouth. 'I'm sorry,' she mumbled through her fingers, her cheeks pink. 'I can't keep secrets.'

'Why on earth is that a secret?' asked Kathleen. She took a hold of Alice's shoulders and gave her a warm embrace.

'My mother arranged it,' said Alice, a note of resignation in her voice. She kicked at a tuft of grass along the edge of the pavement, watching as a beetle scurried into the undergrowth.

'Ah,' said Kathleen. 'How terribly old-fashioned.'

Alice's shoulders sank down. 'It is, isn't it?'

'Yes,' said Beatrice. 'But that doesn't mean it's a bad thing. Look at Kitty and Henry. They were practically betrothed at birth, and they've had a beautiful life.'

'Kitty and Henry are fictional characters,' said Alice. Beatrice's bookshelves were overflowing with tattered copies of fairy tale romances. She loved nothing more than getting lost in a story of passionate love and perfect endings. And she was always first in the queue at the library when the latest *Mills and Boon* books arrived.

'All of the best fiction draws on real life for inspiration,' said Beatrice, with a dreamy smile on her face, her words soft and melodic.

Kathleen turned to Alice and smiled. 'Ignore this one. She's a hopeless romantic. In fiction, and in life.' She clasped Alice's hands in hers, her grip firm with a quiet strength. 'We won't breathe a word of this to anyone.' Kathleen glared at Beatrice, whose eyes flickered with uncertainty. 'Take all the time you need to sort out your feelings. If you are engaged to be married, we'll celebrate with you. And if not, we'll still stand by you and support your decision.'

'Thank you,' said Alice. 'I only wish my mother had said something similar. Instead, she's at home probably planning a wedding and giving my opinion no consideration whatsoever.'

Beatrice leaned towards Kathleen. 'You might have a different view if you'd seen him. He looks like Clark Gable.'

Alice laughed for the first time that morning. 'He does not. Dark hair is, I'm certain, the only similarity.'

4

―――――

THE FOLLOWING DAY, ALICE WAS NOT FEELING ANY BETTER about her surprise engagement. She marched downstairs ready to confront her mother and demand a proper conversation about it.

Violet was in the hallway.

'You're going to Guides again?' she asked, seeing Alice coming down the stairs in her Rangers uniform.

Alice nodded. 'Just to sort out some donations.'

Violet huffed out a breath and pouted as she touched up her red lipstick in the hallway mirror. 'You need to leave the Girl Guides. You're not a girl anymore.'

She held the lipstick out towards Alice, who shook her head.

'And do what, Mother? At least in the Guides, I can be useful. Honestly, what was the point of allowing me to continue school if you now won't allow me to do anything with my education?'

Violet slipped the tube of lipstick into her handbag and plucked her coat from a hook on the wall. 'Fetch the parcel from the dining room, will you? It's for your father. He's in somewhat dire need of new socks.'

'You've heard from him?' Alice asked.

'Of course.'

Excitement bubbled up within Alice at news from her father. 'How is he? Where is he?'

Violet buttoned up her coat and hooked her handbag over her arm. 'Oh, darling, you know your father. He's as quiet in a letter as he is when he's in the same room as you. And I don't know where he is. They're very careful about writing things like that down.'

Alice walked into the dining room. She couldn't help but feel a pang of sadness as she looked at the empty chair at the head of the table. Her father had always been a quiet man, but his absence seemed to make his presence even more pronounced.

She retrieved the parcel off the sideboard in the dining room and stared down at her mother's handwriting. It was some bland military address that gave away nothing.

Violet was standing in front of the hallway mirror, examining herself one last time when Alice came back.

'Mother, we need to talk about George,' said Alice, setting the parcel down on the table.

'Come. Walk with me,' instructed Violet.

Alice slipped her coat on, grabbed the parcel, and followed her mother out of the house.

They were met by Mr Dale, who was standing on the corner of their street smoking a cigarette. Alice took in his General Post Office cap with its distinctive insignia and his navy jacket adorned with brass buttons that could do with a good polish. 'How does it feel to be back in uniform, Mr Dale?' she asked.

Mr Dale gave a hearty laugh and wiped his hand down

the front of his jacket. 'It's not too bad on a day like today but ask me again when it's raining, and I might not be so cheerful.' He rummaged in his bag. 'I've got a letter in here for you, Alice, if you want it now.'

Mr Dale's postal worker son had joined the army when war broke out and Mr Dale had come out of retirement to cover the job. Or at least a part of the job. Mr Dale only seemed to deliver mail within the village and, given he knew most people, he was often seen just handing out piles of letters in the street rather than posting them through letterboxes.

'Ah, here it is,' he said, holding out an envelope towards Alice.

'Thank you,' said Alice, taking the envelope.

'That's quite alright,' said Mr Dale. He caught sight of someone behind Alice and called out. 'Oh, Agnes, I've got something for Bill. Will you give it to him?' he asked, wandering away.

'What do you have there?' asked Violet.

Alice looked down at the envelope. 'I don't know.' She tore open the envelope and unfolded the contents to reveal an elegant invitation written in cursive script.

Violet's eyes sparkled with excitement as she scanned the contents, a triumphant smile playing on her lips. 'A dinner party at the Elliot's, how splendid!'

Alice's heart plummeted. 'Please don't say it's an engagement party.' The finely scripted words swirled on the cream-coloured paper. The Fergusons were known for hosting lavish and extravagant parties. Her parents had attended a few and Violet had described them as sophisticated affairs with complicated hairstyles and uncomfortable dresses.

'Good heavens, no,' said Violet, with a dismissive wave.

As they walked, Violet wittered on about the importance of making a good impression.

'This is unlikely to be a mere social gathering, or I would have been invited too,' she said. 'I suspect it's a dinner for George's work colleagues. Your role is to make George look good by talking about how much he enjoys his work and how committed he is to the firm. Events like these are essential for securing a prosperous future for your husband,' said Violet.

'What about *my* future, Mother? I don't want to marry George,' Alice blurted out, her voice cracking with frustration.

Violet stopped in her tracks, her eyes wide with shock as she scanned the street around them. 'Alice, this is all about *your* future. George is a fine young man from a very respectable family. He will make an excellent husband for you.'

'But I don't know him,' Alice insisted. 'How can I agree to marry someone I don't even know?'

Violet raised an eyebrow, her lips pursed in disapproval. 'All I'm asking is that you give him a chance.'

Alice felt the frustration bubbling inside her. How could her mother be so blind to her feelings? She took a deep breath, fighting back the tears stinging her eyes. Arguing was futile; her mother's mind was as rigid as steel. She would attend the dinner party, but only because it offered her another opportunity to talk to George. Surely, he was as eager as she was to end this charade.

As they neared the post office, Violet straightened her hat and adjusted her gloves, exuding an air of haughty confidence that made Alice feel small in comparison. Alice followed her mother inside and handed over the parcel. The small, quaint post office was a hub of activity as several women were clustered around the worn wooden counter. They chatted with Mrs Crow, the friendly postmistress, leaning in closer to hear each other's news.

Mrs Crow gestured towards the old noticeboard hanging on the wall, adorned with colourful flyers and announcements. 'Do you see they're advertising for more women to volunteer? I pinned the poster up myself this morning. It won't be long before conscription for women comes.'

Alice's ears perked up at this. If she was conscripted, her parents would not be able to say no to her taking up employment.

'I heard that conscription will only apply to women between the ages of twenty and thirty years old,' said one of the other women.

'That takes us out of the equation then,' another said.

'Only just, of course, ladies,' said Violet. Her friends chuckled at this as Violet stood in the middle of them relishing the attention.

A strand of Mrs Crow's neatly pinned back hair fell loose across her forehead. She reached up and tucked it behind her ear. 'Did you hear about Susan?' she asked.

'Hmm, what do you make of that?' replied Violet, unusually timid about sharing her opinion. Alice suspected her mother had no idea what the story was regarding Susan, but she didn't want to admit that something was going on she wasn't aware of.

Alice turned away, leaving the women to their gossip and browsed the posters on the noticeboard. There was the usual dig for victory posters featuring beaming women holding cabbages and cauliflowers, and another showing a smiling woman repairing a dress. Make do and mend wasn't likely something Alice would ever have to do. Her wardrobe was bursting with clothes. Another poster caught her eye featuring a woman in a smart blue uniform, hand to her hat in a salute. Join the Wrens, it said – the Women's Royal Naval Service. Alice had always been fond of a uniform. It was one of the reasons she valued her time with the Guides. When she put on her uniform and looked in the mirror, a young woman with a purpose stared back at her, not a girl living in her parents' house waiting for someone to marry her.

She looked at the poster again and smiled, recalling how terribly sick she'd been the one and only time her father had taken her out on a boat. Besides, she'd heard that the Wrens was hard to get into unless you had a relative already in the Navy. There was no way her father would support her application. But the final poster was for the Women's Auxiliary Air Force. They had a nice uniform too and her father likely wouldn't have any influence with the WAAFs.

Alice took the pin out of the poster and returned to her mother's side. 'I just can't believe that she thought that was an appropriate thing to say in the circumstances,' said Violet.

'My thoughts exactly,' said another woman.

Violet flicked her gaze to the poster in Alice's hand. 'Good heavens, darling, don't even think about it. Isn't it enough that your father is at war?'

Violet said goodbye to her friends. She took the poster from Alice's hand and pinned it back on the board. 'Get that nonsense out of your head. I don't want to have to worry about you too. Besides, it's unnecessary. It's something for single girls and you're not single any more. Now, we need to stop off at the butchers before we head home.'

As they were leaving the post office, Mr Dale was arriving.

'Oh, Alice,' he said, rooting around in his bag. He held a

small parcel out towards her. 'I've just heard your news. Congratulations. Could you deliver this to Mrs Ferguson?'

Alice hesitated. 'Mrs Ferguson?'

'Aye,' said Mr Dale. 'Up on the farm. I hear you're about to become family.' He nudged Alice's hand with the parcel. 'If you don't mind, Alice. Saves me the hike.'

Alice took the parcel, tucking it in her bag. George and his mother lived in Alderbrae, a larger village only a few miles away. His grandmother, also Mrs Ferguson, owned a farm on the outskirts of Millwood. The location was all Alice knew. George's mother seemingly didn't like to talk about her husband's farming roots. Rumour was the two Mrs Fergusons didn't get along.

Mr Dale shuffled into the post office and Alice glared at Violet. 'Is the news all over the village already?' she asked.

'Why shouldn't it be?' Violet asked. 'With everything going on, it's nice to have some good news to share for a change.' She reached over and brushed a speck of lint off Alice's coat. 'Don't assume that Mrs Ferguson knows who you are. There's every chance she doesn't,' she said, her coat swirling around her as she twirled away and waltzed off, head held high.

Alice sighed and set off in the direction of the farm, wondering if this Mrs Ferguson was going to be just as haughty as the other one.

5

———

It took only ten minutes for Alice to reach Mrs Ferguson's farm. Nestled in the rolling hills, it had an air of rustic simplicity. A large barn dominated the space in front of Alice, its aged wooden planks worn and weathered. Wide double doors with red paint, faded and chipped, hinted at an era of care and maintenance that was well in the past. An old rusty truck sat near the house.

Beyond the barn lay a patchwork of fields, each one cultivated with rows of crops stretching towards the horizon.

A woman – Mrs Ferguson, Alice presumed – was standing at the far edge of the driveway, overlooking the fields, staring at the sky. Her arms were outstretched at her sides, palms raised. The breeze tugged gently at her grey skirt, but she remained unmoving. Dark grey hair snaked down the woman's back in a perfect pleat.

Alice waited, not wanting to interrupt. After a long minute, the woman lowered her hands to her sides and spun around, coming face to face with Alice.

'Oh,' she said, blinking as if startled to find someone

watching. 'Who are you?' Her gruff tone immediately put Alice on edge.

Alice straightened instinctively. 'I'm Alice Peters.' She waited for some hint of recognition to cross the woman's features. But nothing. 'I hope I didn't startle you. I didn't want to interrupt.'

The woman waved a dismissive hand, the gesture brisk. 'You didn't. What can I do for you?'

Alice pulled the parcel from her bag and held it out for Mrs Ferguson to take. 'Mr Dale asked me to deliver this to you.'

The woman leaned in just enough to examine the label, her eyes scanning the slanted handwriting. 'What is it?' she asked, her brows arching.

Alice shook her head. 'I don't know. Mr Dale just asked me to deliver it since...'

Since what? Alice really did not want to introduce herself as George's fiancée. 'I'm a friend of George's,' she settled on, lifting her chin.

Mrs Ferguson narrowed her eyes, taking in Alice more fully than before.

'Are you the fiancée?' Mrs Ferguson asked, the question landing heavy in the space between them.

Alice's shoulders dropped before she could stop them. She forced a thin smile onto her face, hoping it looked more genuine than it felt. 'I suppose so.'

Mrs Ferguson held her stare for a beat longer, then turned abruptly. 'Come inside,' she said, already striding towards the house.

Alice hesitated, then followed, the parcel still clutched in her hands.

Despite the beauty around her, Alice could see at least one reason that might have prompted George's mother to distance herself from her mother-in-law. Mrs Ferguson's home wasn't the grandest in Millwood. The guttering wrapped around the house was rusty and the once white walls were stained with evidence of leaks that had gone unchecked for some time. The side door, once painted to match the red barn doors, now only had small patches of peeling paint left clinging to it. Blackout blinds still covered the windows from the night before. Or perhaps Mrs Ferguson was one of those people who had accepted a life of darkness until the war ended and saw no point in opening them each morning.

It was certainly not in keeping with the image the Fergusons liked to present to the world.

The side door led directly into the kitchen. Mrs Ferguson took the parcel and tossed it on the large wooden table that dominated the room. She picked up a kettle from the stove and filled it with water.

'Sit,' she ordered.

Alice took a seat, uncertain whether she was about to be welcomed or given a grilling.

A knock on the door stopped her from her wondering further. Mrs Ferguson flicked her fingers between Alice and the door, a gesture Alice took to be an instruction.

Alice stood and opened the door. The man on the other side looked momentarily surprised. His dark blond hair hung loosely across his forehead and framed his green eyes. His lips curled into a charming smile and an inexplicable heat rushed to Alice's cheeks. She swung the door open wider, hoping the fresh air from outside would cool her flushed face.

'Who is it?' asked an impatient sounding Mrs Ferguson.

'Tom Cameron,' the man said, extending his hand towards Alice.

Alice shook his hand, and her pulse quickened.

Mrs Ferguson's sharp voice cut in. 'Well?'

Alice swallowed. 'It's Tom,' she said.

'Who the hell is Tom?' Mrs Ferguson barked.

Tom flashed a playful smile, his eyes dancing with amusement. With a fluid, unhurried motion, he stepped around Alice and into the kitchen. Alice watched him go, then spun on her heel and quickly closed the door behind him.

'Hello. Mrs Ferguson, I presume,' said Tom, his voice smooth as he surveyed the room. 'You called for a vet?'

Mrs Ferguson scowled, wiping her hands on a dishtowel with sharp, agitated movements. She cast a wary glance at Tom, eyeing him from head to toe. 'I did. Where is he?' she snapped.

Tom's smile didn't waver. He stepped forward, his hands loosely clasped behind his back. 'I'm the vet.'

Mrs Ferguson's frown deepened, her lips pursing. 'You're not the vet. Besides, you're still a boy.'

Tom chuckled, his confidence unshaken. 'I can assure you I'm fully qualified.' He extended his hand towards Mrs Ferguson, but she didn't flinch. He smiled and lowered his arm, unfazed. 'I'm Thomas Cameron. Tom,' he added, with a slight nod, his tone warm and unassuming.

Mrs Ferguson's eyes narrowed as she twisted the dishtowel between her hands. 'Any relation to Angus Cameron?' she asked.

Tom stood a little straighter. 'Yes. He's my father.'

That answer grabbed Mrs Ferguson's attention, and she looked Tom up and down again. Alice felt herself holding her breath, waiting to see if the vet's parentage was going to be enough. Alice knew Angus Cameron to look at. His practice was in Alderbrae, but he was the closest vet and spent a fair amount of time going between the farms surrounding the village.

'When did you graduate?' asked Mrs Ferguson.

'Five months ago,' Tom said with a confidence that Alice admired. He could have said five years ago given the self-assurance in his voice.

Mrs Ferguson shook her head. 'Well come on then. Jocelyn has an infected hoof, and I expect you to fix it.' She stalked out of the farmhouse, snatching a coat off one of the hooks on the wall as she exited.

The vet scanned the room. He turned to Alice as if he was about to ask something, but seemingly thought better of it.

He gave a quick nod then he waltzed off after Mrs Ferguson.

Alice had barely unbuttoned her coat when Mrs Ferguson returned.

'I should keep an eye on him,' Mrs Ferguson said to Alice. 'Can you come back tomorrow?'

'Oh, it's alright,' said Alice. 'I only really came to deliver the parcel.'

'About ten o'clock,' said Mrs Ferguson. She turned the tap on and soaped her hands under the running water. She paused and glanced out of the window in front of her. 'And make sure you're wearing a raincoat, or you'll get drenched.'

Alice offered a polite smile. 'I'll see you tomorrow then.'

She left the kitchen, unsure exactly why she was coming back the following day, but she found the woman intriguing, which was a lot more interesting than she found George or the other Mrs Ferguson.

Outside, Alice stopped, seeing the barn straight ahead of her. Its door was swinging gently on the hinges with Tom Cameron busy inside doing whatever it was veterinarians did. A loud moo echoed through the air, a deep and guttural bellow. Alice stepped towards the barn and peered through the open doorway. She'd intended to just sneak a peek at Tom and then leave, but a gust of wind slammed the door against her side.

'Are you alright there?' Tom called out.

Alice looked up, feeling silly. 'I'm fine, yes,' she said.

'Come on in,' he said.

She took a deep breath and stepped inside the barn.

Tom knelt in front of a massive cow, his shirt sleeves rolled up, and his hands sloshing an orange liquid over its front hoof. The animal towered over him, muscles rippling under its shiny brown coat. It looked capable of flattening Tom with one swift kick, but Tom didn't appear nervous at all. That confidence again. Alice so admired it.

Alice straightened up and pushed her shoulders back, trying to channel some of his confidence. The nerves in her stomach were making it hard to get words out. 'So that's Jocelyn?' she finally said.

'This is Jocelyn. There you go, girl,' he said, rising to his feet and patting the cow's side. 'You'll be back to normal again in no time. Well, sort of.'

'Is there a problem?' Alice asked, fidgeting with the bottom of her tie.

Tom screwed the lid onto the bottle he held in his hand and smiled. 'Depends on your perspective,' he said.

He knelt once more and softly brushed his hand over the cow's belly. He pressed his hand firmly against its abdomen. 'She's pregnant.'

Standing up, he ran his fingers through his hair, leaving

a trail of sticky orange liquid behind. He paused for a moment, examining his hands covered in the same substance he'd used to treat the cow's infected hoof. Reaching into a nearby bag, he pulled out a rag and wiped his hands clean.

'Do you think Mrs Ferguson knows?' Alice asked.

Tom dug a notebook out of his bag and flicked through it, his fingers brushing quickly over the worn pages. 'I don't think so,' he said. A crease formed between his eyes and his lips twitched as he silently read, his brow furrowing deeper with each line. He snapped the book shut and stashed it back in his bag.

'What's your uniform?' he asked.

'Rangers.' Seeing the blank look on his face, Alice added, 'Girl Guides. Rangers is what the older girls are called.'

Now that she seemed able to get her words out again, Alice would have very much liked to stay talking to Tom Cameron, but she was mindful that Mrs Ferguson would likely return at any minute and, technically, she was engaged to Mrs Ferguson's grandson.

'I better go,' said Alice, moving towards the door.

Tom stepped towards her, his green eyes sparkling. She'd never seen such green eyes, only the occasional murky green that were really a mixture of pale green with flecks of brown. There was nothing murky about Tom's eyes though.

'I have my car if you'd like a lift somewhere,' said Tom, following her out of the barn.

Alice buttoned up her coat. 'Thank you, but I'll be fine,' she said. 'You best go and give Mrs Ferguson the good news about her cow.'

Tom scratched the back of his neck with his hand. 'Let's hope Mrs Ferguson also thinks it's good news.'

Alice glanced around. 'Does she run this farm on her own?

'She does,' said Tom. 'But the farm is much smaller now. She's sold bits of it off over the years and cut her herd. There's only a handful of cows and some chickens left. Waifs and strays, my father calls them. How do you know her?' he asked.

Alice shook her head. 'I don't. This is the first time I've met her.'

Tom watched her as if waiting for a further explanation.

'I'm a friend of her grandson's,' Alice added.

Her mouth felt dry.

'Goodbye, then,' she said, striding away before he could ask her anything else.

6

―――

AT TEN O'CLOCK THE FOLLOWING MORNING, ALICE ARRIVED AT Mrs Ferguson's farm. Tom Cameron's car was sitting in the driveway. Her stomach fluttered at the thought of seeing him again. She had embarrassed herself the day before, seemingly unable to form coherent sentences around the man, but still, the thought of seeing him again made her smile.

She wore black trousers and an earthy green jumper that she knew complemented her auburn hair. Following Mrs Ferguson's suggestion, she'd brought her raincoat, and she cast a glance towards the sky. It was dominated by thick clouds, but they were white and fluffy, not the grey she usually associated with rain. The door into the kitchen was open and Alice knocked, hovering in the doorway.

Mrs Ferguson yanked a metal tea kettle off the stove and poured scorching hot tea with surprising precision into three mugs lined up along the countertop.

'Come on in,' said Mrs Ferguson.

Alice stepped inside. 'Can I give you a hand?' she asked.

Clouds of steam rose up from the mismatched mugs, each one bearing its own unique chip or crack.

Mrs Ferguson shook her head and stopped pouring.

'How's Jocelyn?' Alice asked hesitantly, unsure how Mrs Ferguson had taken the news of Tom's discovery the day before.

'Pregnant,' said Mrs Ferguson, thumping the kettle back down on top of the stove. 'I warned Nobleman that something like this would happen. His bull keeps escaping thanks to that bloody big gap in his fencing, but do you think he'll get it fixed? The man needs to spend less time in the pub and more time keeping his bull under control.'

'When will the baby arrive?' Alice asked.

'The calf,' said Mrs Ferguson, her correction laced with a note of disapproval. 'Maybe six months, Tom thinks. I don't know how I missed it. Just wasn't looking for a pregnancy I suppose.'

Abandoning the tea, Mrs Ferguson took a seat at the kitchen table and gestured to Alice to do the same. 'So, you're engaged to George,' she said. 'That's a surprise.'

'It was to me, too,' said Alice. She slipped her raincoat off and draped it over the back of her chair.

Mrs Ferguson's eyes narrowed, and she slid a finger around the collar of her cream shirt, loosening it. 'In what way?'

Alice shifted uncomfortably in her seat, feeling the weight of curious eyes on her. She didn't want to come across as though she was complaining about Mrs Ferguson's family.

'Um, well,' Alice stammered. 'It was unexpected.'

Mrs Ferguson leaned in. 'Unexpected or orchestrated?'

Alice hesitated. Orchestrated seemed like the right word, but again she was hesitant to be too critical. 'It was more of a misunderstanding that got out of hand,' she finally managed to say, avoiding Mrs Ferguson's gaze. Her shoulders sagged.

Mrs Ferguson raised an eyebrow. 'Alice, are you happy about this engagement?'

'I... I haven't quite sorted out my feelings yet,' said Alice. She forced a small smile, hoping to mask her inner turmoil. She had to talk to George again without their mothers listening in.

Mrs Ferguson stood up, dropped a sugar cube into each tea and stirred violently along the line of mugs. She slid one of the mugs along the worktop. 'You can take this out to Tom,' she said.

Heat rushed to Alice's cheeks under Mrs Ferguson's gaze. She wrapped her hands around the one for Tom and plucked it from the counter.

'Best take your own one, too,' she said. 'No point in it getting cold while you're out there.'

Alice briefly considered arguing and saying she would only be gone for a minute, but when she turned and saw Mrs Ferguson's raised eyebrows and the smirk on her face, she snatched up another mug and rushed out of the kitchen.

The barn door hung open by a crack. Alice glanced down at the two mugs in her hands, making sure not to spill their contents. She shouldn't have brought hers. Tom must be busy. She would simply drop off his mug of tea and make a quick exit. With a deep breath, she squeezed through the narrow opening of the door.

Tom Cameron sat on a bale of hay twisting a strand of

hay around the tip of his finger. He jumped up as soon as he spotted Alice. She clocked him taking in her outfit and she pursed her lips, trying to contain her smile.

'Hello,' he said.

'Hello.' Alice held the mug of tea towards him, and he reached out, balancing the base of the mug on his palm then skimming her fingers with his other hand when he took the mug's handle.

'Thank you.' He gulped down a mouthful and wrapped both hands around the mug, just as she had done inside. 'Mrs Ferguson said you might stop by.'

Alice took a sip of her own tea. 'Is that so?'

Tom smiled. 'I asked.'

Alice swallowed, not quite knowing what to say about that. 'I better leave you to work,' she said.

'I've finished, actually.' Tom patted his closed bag on the hay bale. 'I'm going to drink this tea and then I'm off to see Mr Nobleman. I'm hoping to persuade him to fix his fence before Mrs Ferguson next sees him.'

Alice laughed. 'Yes, she seems quite mad about that. Understandable, I suppose.'

Tom nodded, but he stared into the space in front of him and Alice could tell his thoughts were somewhere else.

'Is Jocelyn OK?' she asked after what felt like a full minute had passed.

Tom turned his head sharply to look at her. 'Yes, sorry. She'll be fine. I was just thinking.'

'About what?'

He took another gulp of his tea. 'The war.'

Alice shivered, wishing she'd thought to put her coat on before she left the warmth of the kitchen. She took another sip of her tea, grateful for the comforting warmth that seeped through her body. 'Yes. There's not much else to think about right now.'

Tom sank back down onto the hay bale. 'I sometimes wonder if staying here to bathe the feet of cows was the right choice.'

'Was there another choice?' Alice asked.

Tom moved his bag off the hay and patted the space beside him. Alice hesitated, picturing Mrs Ferguson's face if she opened the barn door and saw the woman engaged to her grandson sitting so close to another man. She stepped towards Tom and sat beside him anyway.

'Some of the boys I trained with have signed up. I'm here treating infected hooves and they're fighting for my country's freedom. It doesn't seem right.'

'My father is in the Navy,' said Alice. 'I would rather he was a vet and didn't have to go off to war.'

Tom nodded. 'I'm sorry.' He gazed into blank space again. 'My father is sixty-four years old. Too old to go to war. That's something of a relief. But he only stopped working so much because I was here to take over.'

'And if you join the army, he'll return to work?' Alice asked.

'He would. He still treats the small animals back at the practice, but driving around the countryside and working with farm animals is heavy going. Honestly, I think it would kill him. I know so many classmates who are struggling to get a job. I could find someone to take over from me, but Dad doesn't trust people easily. He'd gone through so many vets before I qualified. Plus, he thinks I'd be throwing away my education – and possibly my life – if I sign up.'

It was hard to argue with that. 'It sounds as though you've given this a lot of thought.'

'I've thought of very little else since war was declared.

Staying here feels cowardly. But leaving... my dad.' Tom sighed and stood up abruptly. 'But enough about that. I'm sure you've got other things you'd rather be doing.'

She didn't. It had been nice sitting beside Tom without making a fool of herself. She hadn't been able to offer him much help with his worries, but she liked to think just listening to his inner monologue had helped at least a little.

Alice reached out to take his now-empty mug. She pointed towards the cow's orange hoof, freshly doused in disinfectant. 'You keep farm animals healthy, so our soldiers and civilians are well fed. You keep beloved pets healthy to bring comfort and joy to people during the darkest of days. What's cowardly about that?'

She could see on his face that her words hadn't convinced him he'd made the right decision. Her father had been gone for two months already by the time war had been declared. Alice was used to him being gone for long periods of time, but she wasn't used to him being gone while the country was at war. She understood Tom's father's desire to keep his son at home.

7

———

Back in the kitchen, Alice washed up the mugs as Tom and Mrs Ferguson stood huddled in the corner discussing Jocelyn.

'Alice, Tom will give you a lift home,' said Mrs Ferguson.

'Oh, I can walk,' said Alice. 'It's not far.'

'No, it's not,' said Mrs Ferguson. 'But you'll get soaked. Rain will be here any minute.'

Alice glanced out of the window. She'd felt a chill in the air when she'd been in the barn, but the sky was still bright enough.

'I'm happy to give you a lift,' said Tom, walking passed Alice to scrub his hands in the kitchen sink.

Alice's attention was drawn to a brass clock attached to a polished wooden base.

'That's a barometer, right?' she asked. She crossed the room towards the sideboard, tilting her head as she studied the numbers on the barometer's face. It looked like a clock but felt more mysterious, its two hands pointing at something other than time. Her father had one at home, but it sat untouched in her father's office, more ornament than tool.

'That's right,' said Mrs Ferguson.

'And is this telling you it's going to rain?' Alice asked.

Mrs Ferguson glanced at the barometer. 'It's not telling me anything right now.'

Alice frowned. 'It measures air pressure, right?'

'It does. But that isn't really the point.'

Alice turned back to the instrument, running her fingers lightly over the cool metal. 'What is the point then?'

'The point is to capture the change in air pressure over time. If you want to know the weather now, just look out of the window. The barometer tells you if the pressure is rising or falling and how fast. That helps you to predict what's coming next. In farming, the value is always in predicting what the weather will do next because that drives action. Or inaction.' She leaned forward, her gaze steady as she studied the barometer. 'Both have merit, depending on the situation.'

Alice nodded slowly, absorbing the explanation. 'Both hands are at 30.4 right now,' she said.

Mrs Ferguson gestured towards the instrument. 'Turn the dial in the middle.'

Alice hesitated, then grasped the tiny metal ball in the centre of the barometer's face. She twisted it gently, feeling a slight resistance before one of the hands moved.

'Tap on the glass,' Mrs Ferguson instructed. 'That releases any built-up air pressure inside. Now position the needle back to 30.4.'

Alice rapped the glass lightly with her knuckles, watching as the needle quivered and then settled. She repositioned the needle.

'That's the air pressure now,' Mrs Ferguson continued. 'On its own, it doesn't tell us much. But when I check later, I'll see if the pressure is rising or falling, and how quickly.'

Alice's brow furrowed. 'And pressure that rises?'

'Rising pressure means more settled weather, less chance of rain. Falling pressure means more chance of rain. If the needle moves quickly or significantly, this means the pressure is changing fast. A weather system is coming in quickly, and that usually means high winds or stormy conditions.'

Alice glanced back at the barometer. 'I have one of these at home, but I'm not sure it's working.'

'A barometer always works,' Mrs Ferguson said matter-of-factly. 'Just tap the glass and line up the needles. Check it in the morning and in the afternoon, and you'll soon see it changing along with the weather.'

Alice nodded, her fingers lingering on the brass instrument a moment longer. Maybe it wasn't just an old relic on her father's shelf after all.

'I'm ready if you are,' said Tom, drying his hands and folding the towel.

'Maybe I'll see you another day,' said Mrs Ferguson.

Alice smiled. 'I'd like that.'

She retrieved her raincoat from the back of the chair, said goodbye, and left the farmhouse.

'You really don't have to drive me home,' said Alice. 'I don't mind getting wet and don't you need to go and see Mr Nobleman?'

'I do,' said Tom. He smiled and opened his car door for her. 'But I'm happy to take you home first.'

'Thank you,' said Alice. She slipped inside.

Tom closed her door and took his own seat.

As they drove along the bumpy dirt road, Alice winced and gripped the handle on the passenger side door as Tom's old car jolted over every pothole and bump. Each time it hit a particularly large hole, she was nearly thrown off the hard, worn seat and had to brace herself for the next one. She leaned forward and looked towards the sky.

'Checking for rain?' Tom asked.

Alice smiled. 'Yes. Mrs Ferguson seemed certain it was coming.'

'When I arrived at the farm today, she was standing at the far end of her driveway, staring at the sky, palms raised.'

'She was doing the same thing yesterday,' said Alice.

Tom pointed to a raindrop that landed on his windscreen. 'Here it comes.'

By the time they arrived at the village, the raindrops had turned into a torrent and the windscreen wipers were having to work hard to keep up.

'Maybe I'll wait until tomorrow before I see Mr Nobleman about his fence,' said Tom.

Alice gave him directions to her house and Tom pulled up outside. Despite Alice's protestations, he pulled his coat off the back seat and stepped out of the car. He held his coat up, covering her head with it as she got out of the vehicle and ran towards her front door. He ran beside her keeping his coat in place until she was on her top step.

'Thank you,' said Alice.

'You're welcome,' Tom said. 'Perhaps I'll see you tomorrow. Up at the farm. If you'll be there. I mean, I'll be there at some point.'

Alice detected a hint of uncertainty in Tom's voice that she hadn't heard earlier, and his stilted sentences reminded her of her own babbling when she'd first spoken to him.

'Perhaps,' she said. She turned and Tom hurried back to his car.

Once inside, Alice closed the door and touched a hand to her warm cheeks. She grinned. Could it possibly be that Tom liked her too?

'Who was that?' Her mother's voice came like a cold gust of wind that caused Alice to jump.

Alice turned to see Violet standing in the hallway with her arms folded across her chest.

'Thomas Cameron, the vet. He was at Mrs Ferguson's farm and offered me a lift home because of the rain.'

Alice headed straight for her father's office and picked up his barometer on the shelf.

Violet followed her. 'I don't think that old thing works,' she said.

'A barometer always works,' Alice said, repeating Mrs Ferguson's words.

She tapped the glass to release the pressure and waited for the needles to stop quivering before she lined them up.

Turning around, a satisfied smile on her face, she said, 'I can't wait for tomorrow.'

She plucked a notebook and pencil off her father's desk and moved the barometer onto the table in their hallway.

Violet grinned. 'Me too, darling, me too.'

Alice placed the notepad and pencil beside the barometer. 'I was talking about the change in air pressure.'

Violet laughed. 'You haven't forgotten it's George's dinner tomorrow, surely? It's going to be so exciting for you, darling! You'll be mingling with the elite, sipping champagne, and engaging in sparkling conversation.'

Alice felt a flutter inside her stomach as she imagined herself amidst the grandeur of the Fergusons' dinner party, but it wasn't excitement. It wasn't even nerves. It felt more like dread.

8

THE FOLLOWING MORNING, ALICE WOKE WITH NOTHING BUT thoughts of Tom Cameron and air pressure on her mind. She rolled over in bed and squinted at her clock. A little after eight. She slid out of bed and washed before dressing in her crisp Rangers uniform, its fabric familiar and reassuring against her skin. Kathleen had asked for help sorting through piles of donations in the village hall, a task Alice was more than willing to help with given she had little else to do.

She closed her wardrobe door, only to pause and open it again. Her eyes scanned the array of garments hanging neatly within. Her fingers brushed the different fabrics as she flicked through her clothing and pulled a few jumpers free that she hadn't worn in a while.

With the jumpers folded and packed into a bag to donate, she bounded downstairs, heading straight for the barometer in the hallway and stared at the needles. They'd moved, just barely. The pressure had fallen, which, if she'd understood Mrs Ferguson correctly, meant that the inclement weather was here to stay for a bit yet.

Her mother glided into the hallway with a cup of tea balanced on its matching floral saucer. She took a sip and set the cup back down with a soft clink.

'Well?' asked Violet, nodding at the barometer. 'What's it telling you?'

Alice jotted down the reading in her notebook and shrugged. 'More rain. Maybe.'

Violet leaned back and peered into the dining room. 'I told you it doesn't work. The sky is bright blue.'

Alice placed her palms on either side of the barometer and stared at its reading. She wanted to compare her reading with Mrs Ferguson's, but it seemed inappropriate just to drop by. And then there was Tom. He'd said he'd be there today. Just thinking of him sent a warm rush to her cheeks. She touched a hand to her warm skin and smiled.

A knock on the front door cut through her thoughts.

'Who could that be at this hour?' asked Violet.

Alice crossed the hall and opened the door to find a telegram boy standing on the doorstep. His navy uniform, trimmed with red, hung awkwardly off his narrow frame. A bicycle lay toppled at the foot of the stairs.

Before Alice could speak, there was a sudden crash behind her. She spun around to see her mother had dropped the teacup and saucer she'd been holding. The delicate china lay shattered on the floor in a puddle of tea.

'Are you alright?' Alice asked.

Violet's skin was pale and her eyes wide as she stared past Alice, her gaze fixed only on the telegram boy.

The boy touched a hand to his pillbox hat and looked at the letter in his hand.

'I have a telegram for Mrs Newbury,' the boy said.

Alice blinked. 'You have the wrong house,' she said. 'Mrs

Newbury lives two doors down. The house on the end with the red door.'

The boy touched a hand to his hat again. 'I'm sorry to trouble you,' he said, already retreating.

'It's no trouble,' Alice called after him, but he was back on his bicycle, pedalling away.

Alice closed the door and knelt beside her mother. Violet didn't move at first, just stared at the mess. Her hands shook as she began to gather the shards into a tidy pile.

Alice touched her mother's arm. 'Are you sure you're alright?'

'Of course, darling,' said Violet, refusing to meet Alice's eye. 'The handle must have snapped off.'

Peggy appeared with a dustpan and brush. 'I'll take care of it,' she said gently.

Violet stood, smoothing out the folds in her skirt. 'Thank you, Peggy,' she said, before stepping into the dining room and closing the door behind her.

Alice picked up one of the fragments – the handle, still intact, and still firmly attached to the cup's broken body.

'What was that about?' Alice whispered, straightening up.

Peggy tugged a cloth free from the waistband of her apron and handed it to Alice. 'I expect she thought the telegram boy was bringing bad news,' she murmured, sweeping the broken china into the dustpan.

Alice knelt again and pressed the cloth to the floor, blotting up the spilt tea. It occurred to her that everyone was living their own war. Even her mother, it seemed, who lived in fear of the telegram boy stopping at her front door.

After breakfast, Alice slipped on her coat and picked up the bag she'd packed earlier. She made her way to Mrs Ferguson's farm. The upcoming dinner party provided the perfect excuse to pop by. Alice felt that Mrs Ferguson's advice on how to handle herself at the dinner party would be more helpful than Violet's.

The smell of hay and manure filled her nose as she approached the farmhouse. Tom's banged up old car was in the driveway and the man himself was wiping the car's windows with a cloth. He hadn't yet spotted her, and Alice crept up behind him.

'Good morning!' she said, startling him.

Tom jumped and spun around, grinning at her. 'Good morning to you, too,' he said. He walked around to the driver's side of his car and retrieved a small paper bag. He handed it to Alice.

'What's this?' she asked.

'I heard it was your birthday recently,' said Tom. His cheeks flushed a little and his eyes darted between Alice and the ground.

Alice smiled at his rare awkwardness. She peered inside the bag, her smile widening as she placed her hand inside and pulled out a Chocolate Orange.

'Oh, I love these,' she said. She put her nose to the box and sniffed trying to smell the sweet yet citrusy scent. 'Thank you. And this is so special. I heard they're turning the chocolate factory into one that makes aeroplane parts. We might never see Chocolate Oranges again.'

A warm glow filled her heart at Tom's thoughtful gesture. She slipped the gift inside her bag.

Tom rolled up the sleeves of his blue woollen jumper and unbuttoned the cuffs of his shirt sleeves, sliding them

up his arms. 'I'd best go and disinfect Jocelyn's hoof,' he
said.

9

<hr>

Tom disappeared into the barn leaving Alice standing alone in the middle of the gravel driveway. She glanced around, the vast openness making her feel small, before tilting her head back and raising her palms towards the sky, mimicking the gesture she and Tom had seen Mrs Ferguson doing. Above her, the sky stretched out in a vibrant canvas of blue with white fluffy clouds arranged in a neat pattern. It looked like a fleecy blanket draped across the heavens.

'What on earth are you doing?'

Alice spun around at the sound of Mrs Ferguson's voice. She blinked several times to clear her blurred vision as her eyes adjusted from the glare of the bright sky.

Mrs Ferguson stood in the doorway of the farmhouse staring at her. Her cheeks were rosy, and her apron splattered in whatever it was she'd been cooking.

Alice smiled. 'I was trying to see what you see,' she said. 'The weather that is. You knew exactly when the rain was going to start yesterday. How did you do that?'

Mrs Ferguson shrugged, brushing a stray wisp of hair from her face. 'I just pay attention.'

'To what?' Alice asked.

Mrs Ferguson paused, a faint smile pulling at the corners of her lips. 'To everything. My mother's family were farmers going back as far as I know. She taught me to observe the subtle signs that nature gives us: the way animals react when they sense a change in air pressure, the scent in the air, even the direction of the wind.'

She slipped her apron over her head, stashing it just inside the kitchen door, and joined Alice on the driveway. Lifting her chin, she gestured towards the rolling clouds above them. 'She showed me how to read the colours in the sky, and the clouds, and how to interpret the behaviour of smoke when you light a fire. Nature has a way of speaking to those who are willing to listen.'

Alice's eyes widened with curiosity. She glanced around, as if expecting to suddenly notice all the signs she had never thought to look for. 'The only thing I know about weather is that a red sky at night means shepherd's delight.'

Mrs Ferguson laughed, her eyes crinkling with amusement.

'Oh no,' said Alice, groaning playfully. 'You're about to tell me that's not true, aren't you?'

Mrs Ferguson brushed her hands together and a puff of flour floated into the air. 'No, actually, there is some truth to that one,' she said. 'Keep looking up. You'll notice that a red sky at night usually means a dry day to follow. A red sky in the morning means we've had the best of the weather and rain is on the way.'

'What about cows lying down before it rains?' Alice asked.

Mrs Ferguson laughed. 'A cow lies down because it's tired, not because it's sensing rain.'

A sudden gust of wind whipped past them, carrying the scent of damp soil and something else earthy.

Alice wrapped her arms around herself and studied Mrs Ferguson. 'Can someone learn what you know?' she asked. 'I mean, I know we have meteorologists, but do they all have centuries of farming in their blood?'

After a moment of contemplation, Mrs Ferguson said, 'I don't know. It takes patience, dedication, and a keen eye for details that most people overlook. And weather is a fickle thing. It doesn't always do what you expect it to do. But generally, you just ask yourself if your environment looks stable or unstable. That usually tells you all you need to know.'

'And stability is good weather, right? It must be so exciting,' Alice said, feeling a buzz of energy that made her almost bounce on the balls of her feet like an excited child. 'Like predicting the future.'

Mrs Ferguson nodded towards the sky. 'What do you see?' she asked.

Alice looked up again, her eyes adjusting once more to the brightness. 'A bright blue sky with strips of white clouds.'

'And what do the clouds look like?'

Alice thought for a moment, trying to see something in the clouds like she did when she was a child. 'Like a blanket. Or pillows laid out in a row.'

'What about the colour?' asked Mrs Ferguson.

'White,' said Alice. 'But shiny too. Glossy almost.'

'It's called a mackerel sky,' said Mrs Ferguson. 'Likely named by fishermen who figured out that the beautiful pattern indicated a change in weather was coming.'

Alice smiled and looked back at Mrs Ferguson. 'It does look like silvery fish scales. So, if a change in weather is coming, does that mean dry weather since it rained yesterday?'

Mrs Ferguson shook her head. 'It's been dry all week. Yesterday's rain was isolated. A short burst of turbulence that settled quickly.' She pointed to the sky. 'The clouds in a mackerel sky are not rain clouds or storm clouds. There's moisture in the air, but it will take time for that moisture to turn to rain. Not tonight, tomorrow morning maybe.'

Alice looked up again. 'Fascinating,' she whispered to herself.

Mrs Ferguson cleared her throat. 'I suppose I could teach you a thing or two about the weather,' she said. 'If you're interested, I mean.'

Alice grinned. 'Really? I would love that.'

Mrs Ferguson nodded. 'Given we might be seeing a lot more of each other anyway.'

She watched Alice carefully, as if expecting Alice to correct her.

'Yes, about that,' said Alice. 'That's why I'm here. I'm invited to a dinner party with George this evening. It's at his house. A work thing, my mother thinks. Any advice?'

Mrs Ferguson shrugged. 'My daughter-in-law is stubborn. She gets what she wants. Usually.'

Alice's heart sank.

'That wasn't what you wanted to hear.'

'Not exactly,' said Alice, fidgeting with the end of her tie.

'George is...' began Mrs Ferguson. 'Well, there's a heart in there somewhere. He just hides it well.'

Alice smiled. 'Thanks.'

'I'm going to have a look at Jocelyn,' said Mrs Ferguson. 'Come by on Monday morning if you're free and we can watch the weather.'

She strode into the barn and Alice wandered towards the field, stopping at its edge and shielding her eyes from the bright sky. She wondered what George would make of his grandmother spending time with Alice. He wouldn't like it, Alice suspected. She sat down on the bench and gazed up at the clouds. A mackerel sky. It was a pattern she'd seen many times before but hadn't ever thought to wonder what it signified.

Tom appeared at her side, scuffing the ground with his shoe and sending up a puff of dust. 'Can I join you?' he asked.

Alice looked up, a soft smile forming on her lips. 'Please,' she said, patting the space beside her.

He sat down, resting his still bare arms on his knees, and gazed out at the landscape. 'You're deep in thought. Anything you want to share?'

Alice hesitated, her fingers tracing a pattern on her coat. 'Do you know much about the Women's Auxiliary Air Force?'

Tom shifted, leaning back slightly. 'Not really,' he said. 'Why?'

'I'm thinking of joining.'

Tom turned to face her fully. 'Is that so? And what does your fiancé think of that?' His voice hinted at curiosity and maybe just a bit of mischief, one eyebrow raised as he studied her reaction.

Alice sighed. So he knew about that. Mrs Ferguson must have told him.

Her gaze wandered over the potato fields in front of them. 'I don't think he'd like it very much,' she said. 'But given I barely know the man, I've nothing to base that assumption on.'

Tom chuckled and leaned back on the bench, crossing

his arms over his chest. 'Tell me about the WAAF. What do they do?'

Alice crinkled up her forehead, brushing a loose strand of hair behind her ear. 'Honestly, I'm not sure. I think it's mainly clerical work, but women who do well are trained up for other duties. It all seems a bit secretive so I'm thinking that might mean covert communications and code breaking. Maybe.'

She turned to look at Tom, waiting for him to laugh at her. He looked back, his face straight. His gaze held steady, giving nothing away.

'And does that type of work interest you?' he asked.

Alice furrowed her brow, her fingers fidgeting with the hem of her coat. 'You're not laughing at me.'

A gentle smile crossed Tom's face, and he tilted his head slightly. 'Why would I laugh at you?'

Alice let out a soft sigh and shrugged, looking down at her shoes. 'Certain others think it's absurd that I would want to join the Services.'

Tom nodded, his eyes narrowing as if piecing together a puzzle. He shifted on the bench, leaning forward. 'It's not the fiancé since he doesn't know, which means it's your mother who thinks that.'

Alice sank down further onto the bench, her shoulders slumping as if the weight of her words were too heavy to bear. 'Yes. My life sounds so small. I have a fiancé who is a stranger to me and an overbearing mother. There's not a lot else going on for me, is there?'

Tom's expression softened as he leaned closer to her. 'I wouldn't say that at all.' His eyes sparkled with the mischief she'd heard in his voice a few moments ago. 'In fact, I think there's a lot more to you than meets the eye, Alice Peters.'

Alice felt a heat rise to her cheeks. It wasn't just his dark blond hair and green eyes that she found attractive, it was the fact that he listened to her. She could say what was on her mind without him dismissing her thoughts immediately or laughing at her naivety. In that moment she wished so much that Tom Cameron was the man she was engaged to. His face was inches from hers and his warm breath tickled her skin. If he was her fiancé, she could close the gap between them and kiss him.

Someone cleared their throat behind the bench and Alice jumped up. 'Mrs Ferguson, we were just...' Alice's attempt to make up an excuse stalled when she took a closer look at Mrs Ferguson.

The woman had two dead pheasants tied together and hanging over her shoulder.

'Do you know how to drive?' Mrs Ferguson asked.

'Me?' asked Alice.

Mrs Ferguson sighed, a hint of impatience in her tone. 'Yes, you. He can drive, I already know that.'

Alice shook her head.

Mrs Ferguson dug in the pocket of her skirt and pulled out the keys to her truck. 'You can drive me to the pharmacy.'

Alice shook her head again. 'I can't drive.'

Mrs Ferguson tapped her foot against the dirt path. 'Why not?' she asked.

'I don't know how.'

'Now is a good time to learn. A woman with skills is useful. And when you're useful, you have choices.' Mrs Ferguson tossed Alice the keys to the truck and she caught them in one hand. 'That's a good start. Now come along, Ms Peters. It's time you learned to drive.'

Alice froze, feeling a surge of anxiety at the thought of driving a truck on a public road. She took a deep breath and let it out slowly as she watched Mrs Ferguson striding towards the truck. As she replayed the woman's words in her mind, a small smile tugged at the corners of her lips. '... *when you're useful, you have choices'*. She looked down at Tom who had been observing their exchange from the bench. His grin was wide and, unless she was mistaken, there was a glimmer of pride in his eyes.

'You can do this,' he said.

Alice squeezed his shoulder. He reached up and covered her hand with his. As their skin brushed against each other, she felt a flash of guilt. She snatched her hand back and hurried after Mrs Ferguson.

'You start it up,' Mrs Ferguson called out. 'I'll put these birds in the house. I'm going to cook them when I get back.'

Alice climbed into the driver's seat of the truck and forced herself to think of her disgust at the thought of plucking feathers from a dead bird. Anything to take her mind off Tom and the deep desire she felt for him. It was wrong to think of him that way. For now, she was engaged to another man. Until George's dinner party, at least. But for a second, she wondered what would have happened on that bench had she not been engaged. A tingling warmth spread throughout her body. She took a deep breath and started the engine, grateful that no one was there to see her blushing again.

10

Mrs Ferguson climbed into the passenger seat of her truck. 'Start her up then.'

Alice turned the key in the ignition and felt the truck rumble to life beneath her. The engine purred smoothly despite the trucks obvious age. It was reassuring and bolstered Alice's confidence.

Once Mrs Ferguson had given Alice a rundown of the pedals and gears, Alice shifted the truck into first gear and lightly pressed the accelerator as she released her foot on the clutch. The truck lurched forward, the engine stalling.

'I hope you're not in a hurry,' said Alice, deflated. 'It might take us a while to get off the driveway.'

'It takes as long as it takes,' said Mrs Ferguson with a patience that surprised Alice.

She turned the key in the ignition again, her hands sweating as she gripped the steering wheel. She took another breath to steady her nerves and focused on her feet as she worked the pedals. The truck rolled forward, and she pressed harder on the accelerator, increasing the speed to keep the momentum going.

At the end of the driveway, Alice shifted her foot to the brake pedal, pressing down. Alice and Mrs Ferguson shot forward in their seats.

'A little lighter on the brake next time,' said Mrs Ferguson, scanning the road in front of them.

Alice glanced in one direction and then the other. 'It looks clear to me,' she said.

Mrs Ferguson nodded. 'It usually is. Unless Nobleman is making his way to or from the pub in the village. But you only need to watch out for him on the way back. He can't walk a straight line with a drink in him never mind drive one.'

Alice turned the truck onto the road, the steering wheel slipping through her hands as she straightened it back up. Her knuckles were pale against the worn leather, but her grip slowly eased.

The hum of the engine and the gentle sway of the truck became a comforting rhythm as Alice gained more confidence. She glanced briefly at the hedgerows she'd walked past earlier, then back to the road, a flicker of pride tugging at the corners of her mouth.

'Just pull into that space straight ahead of you, Alice, and hit the brake,' said Mrs Ferguson, pointing to a clear patch of road in front of the village hall. Her hand hovered just above the centre of the dashboard, as though ready to grab the wheel if needed.

Alice nodded, brow furrowed in concentration. She hit the brake, a little too forcefully once again, and the truck lurched to a stop.

'Not bad at all,' said Mrs Ferguson, her hand settling on the dashboard.

'Really?' asked Alice, pulling on the handbrake with a quick jerk.

'Your steering was excellent. Next time we'll work on your speed.'

Alice screwed up her face and turned to Mrs Ferguson. 'Why? What speed was I doing?'

Mrs Ferguson smiled, the creases around her eyes deepening. 'Thirteen miles per hour.'

Alice laughed. 'Oh dear. But you said next time?'

Mrs Ferguson smiled. She shifted in her seat, the fabric of her skirt rustling, as she turned to face Alice. 'Listen. You might have to bite your tongue a lot this evening. I know that's hard. You can still say what needs to be said. There's just sometimes a better time or place to say it.'

Alice reached for the keys but hesitated, letting her fingers rest by the ignition for a moment longer than necessary. Her jaw tightened.

'I'll see you on Monday.'

'You will,' said Alice, taking a deep breath and willing the weekend to be over already.

They both exited the car, Alice handing over the keys as Mrs Ferguson took her place in the driver's seat and reversed the truck back onto the main road. She beeped her horn as she drove off.

Beatrice and Kathleen walked towards Alice. Despite their coats, it was obvious neither of them was wearing their Rangers' uniform. Alice suddenly felt overdressed for sorting through boxes of donated clothing.

'Did we just see you driving a truck?' Beatrice asked.

'You did,' said Alice, grinning widely. She had survived her first driving lesson and hadn't crashed Mrs Ferguson's truck. It felt like an achievement.

'How did that happen?' Kathleen asked.

'That's George's grandmother,' said Alice. 'She's teaching me how to drive.'

Beatrice clapped her hands together. 'Does that mean you're feeling better about your surprise engagement?'

Alice huffed out a deep breath. 'Not exactly.'

'Maybe we can help,' said Kathleen, with a sudden burst of enthusiasm. She pushed open the heavy door to the hall, its hinges groaning. 'Let's get inside.'

The wooden floors creaked softly under their footsteps amplifying the unusual silence that filled the room.

Alice exchanged a puzzled glance with Beatrice and Kathleen. 'Is it just us?' she asked, her voice echoing in the near-empty space.

'Today's meeting,' Kathleen started, her eyes twinkling mischievously, 'was arranged for the sole purpose of helping you get ready for tonight.'

Beatrice clasped her hands together in front of her chest. 'I do hope you don't mind,' she said. Her cheeks were slightly flushed. 'I know you're nervous, and I thought we could help by getting you ready.'

Alice cast her gaze across the hall, taking in the table covered in a jumble of hairbrushes, combs, and rollers. Next to it sat an assortment of makeup products in various shades, including half a dozen different lip colours. On the clothing rack, which was typically used for displaying donated items, hung three dresses.

'The dresses are just for fun,' said Kathleen. 'I'm sure you already have something in mind you'd rather wear.'

'Although this one is fabulous,' said Beatrice, stroking the shimmering ruby fabric on one of the dresses.

'What do you say?' asked Kathleen. 'Will you let us help?'

Alice laughed and removed her coat. 'OK. But I reserve the right to remove all makeup before I leave here if things get out of hand.'

Beatrice clapped her hands together, beaming. 'Then come and take a seat in my salon.' She grabbed a brush and a pack of rollers and guided Alice to a chair.

Over the next hour, Beatrice transformed Alice's auburn hair into a cascade of loose curls that framed her face delicately.

Kathleen skilfully applied makeup, enhancing Alice's beauty without overpowering her natural features. While she worked, Beatrice raided the clothing donation box and emerged wearing an array of outrageously mismatched outfits. She pranced around the hall, striking dramatic poses and giggling uncontrollably.

Alice laughed so hard Kathleen scolded her for smudging her eye makeup with her tears.

When they were done, Alice looked at her reflection. She couldn't help but feel a surge of confidence wash over her. She had been dreading the party, but perhaps she and George would manage to sneak away for a few minutes, and she would finally learn how he really feels about their engagement.

Alice stood up and twirled around, showing off her new look.

'You look beautiful,' said Beatrice. 'Are you certain you want to wear your own clothes? I think I presented some excellent alternatives worthy of consideration.'

Alice laughed. 'Yes, you did. But I have a dress in mind. Seriously, thank you. This has been such fun and I feel amazing.'

Beatrice stepped forward with Alice's coat and helped her to put it on.

'I know you don't think this engagement with George is a good idea,' said Beatrice, 'but try to keep an open mind this evening. Maybe he'll surprise you.'

Alice gave her friend a warm hug then headed home to get dressed. Her thoughts turned to Tom Cameron. Oh, how she wished it was him taking her on a romantic date instead. She pressed her fingertips to her temples, massaging the skin as she tried to push thoughts of Tom out of her mind, for tonight at least.

11

IN HER BEDROOM, ALICE SLIPPED INTO A SIMPLE YET ELEGANT dress in a deep midnight blue that complemented her blue eyes. The fabric cascaded gracefully down her body. For the first time, Alice glimpsed the woman that she was becoming.

'Alice, are you ready?' Violet called up.

Nerves fluttered in Alice's stomach as she thought about the conversation she needed to have with George. She couldn't shake off the concern that he might want to go ahead with their engagement. And he didn't seem the type to take rejection easily, so it likely wasn't going to be an easy conversation.

'One step at a time,' Alice mumbled to herself.

She swung open her wardrobe and sifted through her collection of coats. Mrs Ferguson had assured her that it wouldn't rain this evening. She selected a long velvet jacket and walked downstairs, joining her mother in the hallway.

Violet's eyes lit up with joy and she clasped her hands together as she took in Alice's appearance.

'Perfect,' said Violet. She smoothed a hand down the

sleeve of Alice's jacket. 'I know you had your reservations about this, darling, but after tonight, you'll see why your father and I think this is the right path for you.'

Alice pasted a smile onto her face and checked the pressure reading on her father's barometer. She noted down the reading next to the one she'd taken that morning and smiled. Falling pressure, but only just. She had no doubt that Mrs Ferguson was right again. Rain was coming, but not tonight.

As she arrived at the Fergusons' house, a woman who introduced herself as Mrs Winston, the housekeeper, opened the door. Madeline, another Ferguson family employee, took Alice's coat and showed her to a crowded dining room where flickering candles and soft music created a welcoming atmosphere for guests. But Alice's mind was preoccupied.

She searched the room and finally spotted George by the fireplace with a whisky in his hand and surrounded by a group of men she presumed were work colleagues. George's mother stood at the centre of a circle of women, her perfectly coiffed hair and sparkling jewellery commanding attention. As they chatted and laughed, Mrs Ferguson raised a hand, silencing them as she began to speak.

George caught her eye, and he waved her over to join him.

'Gentlemen,' he said with a charming smile on his face, 'allow me to introduce you to Alice Peters, my fiancée.'

A knot tightened in Alice's stomach at the word fiancée. The term felt foreign to her, like a pair of shoes that didn't quite fit right. And it seemed to be a sign that George was not as reluctant as she was to embrace their mothers' matchmaking.

One of the men, tall and well-dressed in a perfectly tailored suit, shook Alice's hand. The others clinked their glasses together with a collective *congratulations*. Meanwhile, George stood tall with a confident grin on his face, basking in the admiration from his colleagues as they took it in turns to pat him on the back. George hadn't bothered to introduce anyone to her; however, Violet had established through her social network that her first instincts had been correct, George was indeed hosting a dinner for his work colleagues and their wives.

'When is the wedding?' one of the men asked.

'Oh, we haven't discussed that yet,' said Alice.

A shadow seemed to cross George's face, just for a moment, and Alice sensed she'd said the wrong thing.

'I believe dinner is about to be served,' George announced. 'Shall we take our seats?'

The two groups dispersed and took seats around the long dining table. George placed a hand on Alice's elbow and steered her towards a chair. George was at the head of the table, his mother on one side and Alice on the other.

'You know, Alice,' he whispered, his grip tightening and his breath sending a chill through her, 'this engagement is supposed to be good news. You might start acting like it.'

Alice was taken aback by his words, and she sank into her seat, watching George ease himself into the chair at the head of the table. The crystal chandelier above cast a warm glow over the elegant dining room as the guests settled in for dinner. The clink of silverware against fine china echoed through the room as the sumptuous meal was served, accompanied by red wine in sparkling glass goblets.

Throughout dinner, George dominated the conversation, his booming voice drowning out any attempts by others to speak. He regaled the guests with stories of his firm's latest business successes. Alice noted that he rarely mentioned his direct contributions, instead focusing on the achievements of several of the other men in the room.

'And Arnold here,' said George, 'brought in one of the firm's biggest accounts to date just this week.'

Arnold, whoever he was, puffed his chest out with pride as the others followed George's lead and raised their wine glasses to toast Mr Arnold.

'That's quite an achievement, darling,' said the woman Alice presumed was Mrs Arnold. 'Is that the–'

'And thanks to Arnold here,' said George, seeming to not notice Mrs Arnold was speaking.

'Oh, George,' said Alice, placing her hand on the table in front of George. 'I'm sorry, but I don't think Mrs Arnold was quite finished speaking.'

George waved away Alice's interruption and gave her a patronising pat on the hand. 'As I was saying,' continued George, his glass of red wine still raised. 'Thanks to Arnold here, the firm successfully gained old man Butterworth's business, too.'

'You'll have to tell me how you finally did it,' said one of the other men. 'I've been after Butterworth's business for twenty years.'

Mr Arnold chuckled and gave his colleague a friendly wink. 'Just my exceptional powers of persuasion,' he said.

Mrs Arnold caught Alice's eye and gave her a sympathetic smile, which Alice returned, gratefully. She scanned the faces of the guests gathered around the table, noting that all the men were considerably older than George and likely higher up in the company. She couldn't help but wonder if this dinner was a calculated move on George's part to secure a promotion by stroking the egos of those in charge. And it seemed to be working. Mr Arnold, with his chest still puffed out in self-importance, didn't seem to mind George disregarding his wife so easily.

Alice bristled at the blatant arrogance and entitlement on display around the table, but she maintained a composed facade with downcast eyes as she picked at her food.

Just when Alice thought she couldn't bear it any longer, Madeline appeared to clear the dessert plates and serve coffee. The end was in sight.

'Thank you,' said Alice, as Madeline poured steaming dark coffee into the delicate china cup in front of her.

George glared at Alice as though her small note of thanks had derailed his train of thought. He carried on speaking and Alice rolled her eyes. It was hard to believe that the man wasn't tired of his own voice by now.

Just then, Mrs Ferguson cleared her throat and Alice glanced at her, registering the disapproving look on her face. Heat rose to Alice's cheeks. She quickly grabbed her coffee and took a sip, using the cup to shield her flushed face.

One of the men at the other end of the table pushed his chair back abruptly, causing it to screech against the floor. All eyes turned to him as he stood up.

'Shall we take our coffee somewhere else, gents?' the man said.

George's face turned pale, and his eyes darted around the room before his mother leaned in and whispered something in his ear. His hands fidgeted with his napkin as he listened, his nervous gaze shifting between his mother and the other men leaving the table. Alice was pleased to see a glimmer of vulnerability in him, no matter how tiny. It suggested his domineering behaviour was just a cover for his insecurities and he wasn't truly as awful as he seemed.

'Yes, quite right,' George said to his mother. He stood up and squared his shoulders. 'Let's head to the drawing room, gents,' he said.

As the men filed out of the room, George's eyes landed on Alice, still seated. He put a hand on the table and leaned in close, his voice dripping with condescension. 'You know, Alice, a woman's role is to support her husband, not to meddle in affairs beyond her comprehension.'

Alice's mouth fell open at his insult. She had barely said a word all evening, except for politely calling out his rude treatment of one of his guests. She clenched her fists, trying to contain the anger bubbling inside of her.

As George followed behind his colleagues, Alice turned to Mrs Ferguson who gave her a subtle smirk of satisfaction. Good manners were the only thing stopping Alice from storming out. She glanced at the carriage clock in the centre of the mantelpiece. That and the fact that the car Violet had arranged wasn't scheduled to collect her for another hour.

12

THE MONDAY AFTER GEORGE'S DINNER PARTY, ALICE HAD
spent the entire day at his grandmother's farm. It was a
welcome distraction from the stress of the party, which had
consumed her thoughts over the weekend. She hadn't been
able to get George alone, his mother had made sure of that,
and Violet had forbidden her from going to his house on
Sunday morning, insisting that Alice calm down before
making any impulsive decisions.

Now, as Alice arrived home and closed her front door,
she ran her hands up and down her face. Her day had been
fun, but also exhausting. Mrs Ferguson and Alice had talked
about the weather for hours. They'd even lit a fire in a small
metal bucket on the driveway to observe the smoke. Mrs
Ferguson said smoke that hovered near the ground meant
rain. She hadn't been sure exactly why but had guessed the
smoke was absorbing moisture from the air making it
denser and slower to disperse. The smoke from their fire
had risen steadily, a sign that air pressure was increasing
and, with it, more stable weather.

'Alice?' Violet called from the living room. 'Is that you?'

'Yes,' said Alice, checking the reading on her barometer and noting down the rise in air pressure from that morning's reading. She grinned. The smoke theory seemed correct. Their smoke had risen, and so had the air pressure.

Alice hung up her coat and poked her head into the living room, a big grin still on her face. Her cheerful disposition soon faded when she saw George sitting in her father's plush armchair.

'Hello, Alice,' George said as she entered the room.

Violet stood up and smiled at George. 'I'll leave you two alone. Please, finish the wine.'

A half empty bottle of red wine was opened on the table with two glasses. Her mother must have been entertaining George for quite some time. Nothing good could come from that.

Peggy entered the room bringing with her another wine glass. She handed Alice the glass, her expression softening with what Alice thought was a hint of sympathy.

'You're lucky you still have her,' said George. 'Our housekeeper, Mrs Winston, has just announced her retirement at the end of the month. Her two assistants resigned last week to take up posts in the munitions factory. That just left Madeline, our scullery maid, who now says she's leaving to join the ATS. This war is changing people. It's quite literally sending them mad.'

Alice took a seat on the sofa opposite George. 'Perhaps they want to contribute what they can to ensure Hitler never reaches our shores.' *Or perhaps they'll do anything to get out of working for the Ferguson family.* She poured a little wine into her glass. It was just for show. Even the tiniest sip of wine made her feel lightheaded and she needed to maintain her composure so she could finally break things off with George.

'Madeline has some foolish notion that she'll be serving alongside her boyfriend. The boyfriend has been sent to France. She'll certainly not be sent there, and she'll be lucky if the boyfriend comes back.'

'George, that's a terrible thing to say.' Her good manners forced her to top up George's glass before she set the wine bottle back on the table.

George shrugged and took a sip of his wine. 'It's true. These men think they're on a just crusade when they're merely cannon fodder.'

Alice's eyes widened in shock and disgust at his callousness. His eyes flickered over her face, mistaking her horrified expression for concern towards himself.

'You don't need to worry,' he said. 'My father says they are highly unlikely to call up people like me.'

Alice was stunned into silence.

'Anyway, my point was, thanks to Mrs Winston's untimely retirement, and Madeline and her delusions, my mother has no one left. And with rationing on the way, it's only going to get more challenging. My mother had to queue for the butchers yesterday.'

'That's dreadful,' said Alice.

'Yes,' agreed George, oblivious to Alice's sarcasm. 'But it's only temporary. Once we're married, you'll be there to help her.'

Alice leaned forward a little. 'To help her?'

'Yes. That's the role of a daughter-in-law, isn't it?' George took another sip of his wine, swirling it around in his mouth before swallowing.

'Is it?' Alice asked. She wasn't sure what was expected of a daughter-in-law, but she highly doubted it included taking on the role of domestic help. She reached for her glass of wine and hesitated, wondering if downing the contents would ease the tightness forming in her chest.

George must have seen the worry on Alice's face because he quickly added, 'I don't mean you must do everything that our staff did. I just mean that you'll be there to help my mother out with whatever she needs, a little shopping, maybe some assistance in the kitchen or with laundry duties. It's all things you'll be doing anyway so it won't be any extra work for you.'

Alice suddenly had a terrible feeling that Mrs Ferguson had sent George here to hasten their wedding so she could replace her domestic staff with a helpful daughter-in-law. It was probably a plan she had concocted while waiting in line at the butchers. And George's attempt to reassure Alice otherwise only made her more certain that he expected her to step into the role of domestic help and take care of the household duties for both him and his mother.

The thought filled her with dread. She wasn't cut out for such a role. She had her own ambitions, even if she didn't quite know what they were yet, and she planned to pursue them. Even after marriage.

'The thing is George,' she said. 'I might not be here either. I've been thinking about joining the Women's Auxiliary Air Force.'

His eyebrows shot up, eyes wide with disbelief. 'What on earth for? That's something for women who have no prospects of marriage. You have me.'

His reaction wasn't exactly a shock. And it was on the opposite end of the scale from Tom Cameron's supportive comments.

'George,' she said, 'do you actually want to marry me?'

George laughed and Alice wanted to throw her glass at him. Instead, she replaced it, untouched, on the table.

'What kind of question is that?' he snapped.

'A very pertinent question, I would have thought,' Alice fired back. She surprised herself with her forcefulness, but they were alone. No mothers. No work colleagues. No reason to continue playing along with this charade.

George leaned back in her father's chair, his hand gripping the armrest tightly. His brow furrowed and a look of apprehension flashed in his eyes. 'Of course I want to marry you.'

Alice raised an eyebrow. 'Why do you want to marry me?'

The creases on his forehead deepened, and he stared at her as if struggling to understand her question.

'You don't love me,' said Alice. 'So why do you want to marry me?'

He laughed. 'No one marries for love in our world, Alice. People get married to maintain their position in society. They want safety and security. Love comes later.'

Alice gave him a look that was equal parts pity and disappointment. She stood up. 'I think love is important from the beginning. When people get married, it's because they want to make a life with someone they share a deep connection with. We don't have that connection. I'm sorry, George, but I can't marry you.'

'Don't be so naive, Alice. This is happening.'

'Have you ever been in love, George?' Her words floated through the air like a soft summer breeze.

George's stern expression softened, and a small smile played across his lips. His eyes grew slightly distant, as if lost in thought. But the moment passed quickly as he shook his head and stood up. He placed his wine glass on the table.

Surprising her, he took her hands in his. 'This is all very

sudden,' he said. 'I know that. But you will learn to love me, Alice.'

Alice wiggled her hands free from his. 'No, George,' she said. 'I can't marry you. I'm sorry, but I just can't.'

He glanced at his watch. 'I have somewhere to be. But this is happening, Alice. Feel free to start making plans for the wedding. Our mothers certainly seem keen to get on with it, so I'm sure you'll have plenty of help.'

George reached for his glass again, lifting it to his lips and taking a deep gulp, draining the crimson liquid in one large mouthful. His eyes closed as he savoured the taste before setting the empty glass down with a thud on the table. He gave a curt nod and then disappeared out of the door.

Alice's expression felt frozen, her lips parted in disbelief. She hadn't expected him to refuse to take no for an answer. Tears welled up in her eyes, threatening to spill down her cheeks. She leaned forward and sucked in a deep breath to quell the surge of panic rising within her. It was going to be trickier to get out of this engagement than she thought. As much as she hated to admit it, she was going to have to get Violet on her side, which right now felt impossible. The Fergusons were held in such high regard in her mother's social circle. Breaking off the engagement could cause a scandal, and Violet would not allow her daughter to be at the centre of it.

Alice blinked rapidly, trying to hold back her tears. George had seemed very certain that she would learn to love him. He hadn't, however, given her any indication that he hoped to love her too. That wasn't a life she was prepared to sign up for.

The clanging of the kettle hitting the stove caught her

attention and Alice straightened up. Her panic and disbelief turned to fury, and she gathered up the wine glasses before storming off to find her mother. Perhaps George wasn't listening to her, but this time Alice would make sure that Violet heard her.

13

———

ALICE FLUNG OPEN THE KITCHEN DOOR TO SEE HER MOTHER unwrapping a platter of sandwiches. Steam from the tea kettle on the stove rose in gentle wisps around her.

'I won't marry him, Mother,' Alice announced, no longer caring to be tactful. She placed the wine glasses in the sink and washed them under the hot tap. 'George wants me to be his mother's domestic help since their staff have resigned to take up war work and their housekeeper is retiring.'

Violet maintained her composure, setting out two teacups as if entirely unsurprised by her daughter's announcement. 'There's a war going on, darling. We're all having to make sacrifices.' She waved her hands around the kitchen as if pointing to the evidence of her own sacrifice.

Alice glanced around. Making her own pot of tea and having sandwiches for dinner could hardly be considered a sacrifice.

'Marriage shouldn't be a sacrifice,' said Alice. She dried her hands and took the platter of sandwiches, placing it on the kitchen table.

Violet gave a haughty laugh. 'A marriage is between two people,' she said, her voice laced with superiority. 'There are inevitably sacrifices to be made.'

'I think the word you're looking for is compromises,' said Alice. 'That has an entirely different meaning, Mother.'

Violet's sigh echoed through the kitchen, a heavy and drawn out exhale filled with irritation. 'Shall I make us an appointment with the dressmaker. I hear she's had a rush of orders with brides keen to have their weddings before their men leave for the war. Mrs Ferguson is as keen as I am for the wedding to take place, so I don't see any reason for delaying.'

'I bet she is,' Alice muttered under her breath, rolling her eyes.

Violet raised an eyebrow. 'The dressmaker?' she asked.

Alice crossed her arms over her chest. She was close to stamping her foot but stopped herself because it felt like a childish action. 'No, because I'm not getting married.'

A gentle hiss of steam escaped from the kettle, and Violet turned off the flame beneath it.

'Alice, your father and I have already agreed to this so it's happening.'

As Violet echoed George's words, Alice couldn't help but feel like she was at the heart of a conspiracy. Her father was usually her route for escalation when Alice and her mother couldn't agree. Albeit *"Just go along with whatever your mother wants. It will make both of our lives easier,"* was his usual contribution to the debate.

'Doesn't my opinion matter?' Alice asked, quieter now. It was a question, but also a plea for understanding, for a voice in a situation that seemed to have no room for her thoughts or feelings.

Violet reached out and patted Alice on the top of the arm. 'Of course it matters, darling. But you're clearly not thinking rationally. George Ferguson is a perfect match for you. He comes from a good family and has the financial means to take care of you. Plus, he's handsome, isn't he?'

He was a lot less handsome the more Alice got to know him.

'Can we talk about this more when father comes home?' Alice asked, hoping that at least one of her parents would see it from her point of view.

'Of course,' said Violet, picking up the kettle.

Alice felt a glimmer of hope. Her father could be away for months, so it bought her time to figure out another way out of this ridiculous situation.

Violet tipped up the kettle and the boiling water poured into the teapot with a soft gurgle. 'But in the meantime,' added Violet, 'I'll make the appointment with the dressmaker. It takes time to make a beautiful dress.'

The weight of her mother's expectations settled on Alice's shoulders once again. She crossed the kitchen and slumped down into a chair, feeling defeated.

As Violet reached for a second cup and poured another tea, Alice sat a little straighter in her chair. A tiny seed of brilliance had just sprung from nowhere. She knew three girls who had rushed to get married before their fiancés had gone off to war. Two of them had been eager to start their married lives, but one of them, according to the village gossip, was already pregnant given the size of her belly only weeks after her new husband had left.

'I have to say, Mother,' said Alice, 'I'm surprised you are so keen for the wedding to take place quickly.'

'Why is that?' Violet asked.

'If the wedding takes place too soon, isn't there a danger that people will gossip about *us*.' Alice emphasised the word us. 'I'm not like those other girls rushing ahead with a wedding before their fiancés ship out to war. Everyone knows George hasn't been conscripted. People might think we're rushing the wedding because your daughter is in the family way.'

Violet picked up the milk jug, but her hand hovered above her teacup. Alice could almost hear the cogs turning in her mother's mind. Violet loved to know the gossip. She did not want to be the one being gossiped about. Her aversion to scandal might be more helpful than Alice had first thought.

Violet sploshed a drop of milk into each cup and brought them over to the table. 'Perhaps it is unfair to ask you to make wedding plans when this is all still so new to you,' she said. 'We should give you a little time to get used to the idea of being engaged. You'll see for yourself that it's for the best. Then we can make wedding plans when you're truly excited about it.'

'That's a good idea,' said Alice. She took a sip of her tea, holding the cup to her mouth and hoping it covered the grin on her face from successfully manipulating Violet. Without her mother pestering her to make wedding arrangements, Alice would have time to come up with a way out of the wedding altogether. Simply saying no was evidently not enough. She needed a plan that saved both Violet and George from any embarrassment.

Suddenly, the shrill, piercing wail of the air raid siren sliced through the silence.

Alice sprung up from her seat, her heart pounding in her chest. In contrast, Violet, unfazed, stood up, retrieved a

Thermos flask from the cupboard, and steadily poured the contents of the teapot into it.

'Alice, scoop up the sandwiches, will you?' Violet called over her shoulder.

'Honestly, mother!' said Alice, her voice tinged with exasperation. 'You'd rather see us die than let a pot of tea go cold.'

Violet poured milk into the Thermos and screwed the lid on, her movements deliberate and unhurried. 'I've spent too many hours sitting in that damp cellar and not a single bomb has landed near us. Not that I'm complaining about that, of course, but unless we hear the drone of an aircraft with that blasted siren, we have enough time to pack up our tea. No point wasting good rations.'

'We don't have rationing, Mother.'

'Not yet. You mark my words, it's coming.'

Alice snatched up the plate of sandwiches and darted towards the cellar, Violet's footsteps echoing on the wooden floor as she followed.

No enemy aircraft had been spotted close to Millwood. And while some people had taken to calling it the Phoney Way, the village's proximity to the capital city and the nearby RAF base in Drem, meant the people of Millwood took air raid warnings seriously. Most people did anyway.

Once inside the cellar, Alice flicked on the overhead light, casting a warm glow over the cosy space. She settled onto the wooden bench that stretched along one wall, its surface softened by the addition of floral cushions Violet had added after their first night in the cellar. As air raid shelters went, this one felt almost luxurious, a small haven against the threat from above.

Violet set down a tray holding the Thermos and both cups of tea onto a nearby table. She took a seat beside Alice.

Alice reached for one of the cups and took a sip, the hot tea providing a comforting distraction from the eerie wailing outside. Her mind drifted back to her conversation with George. If it came down to choosing between working for Mrs Ferguson or signing up for military service, Alice knew exactly which path she'd prefer to choose.

14

———

THREE WEEKS AND THREE AIR RAID SIRENS LATER AND ALICE was on her way to Mrs Ferguson's farm. Each of the sirens had proved to be nothing more than a talking point for the villagers. Since the bombing on the Firth of Forth, they hadn't heard of any significant German activity over Scotland's airspace. However, the Germans had sunk another Navy ship near the Faroe Islands with the loss of more than two hundred lives. Now in the depths of winter, it felt as though the war was inching closer to Scotland by the day.

Alice's footsteps fell heavily on the gravel path leading to Mrs Ferguson's farmhouse. She paused at the back of the truck and stared up into the sky. It was a fine day for a farmers' market. Cold, but the sky was bright with only a few fluffy clouds.

Mrs Ferguson bustled out of her house carrying three trays of eggs stacked on top of each other. Alice had offered to help her sell her wares at the weekly market in Alderbrae.

'Do you think this weather will hold?' Alice asked.

Mrs Ferguson placed the eggs carefully in the back of her truck alongside another three trays, two crates of milk in glass bottles, and two baskets of winter vegetables. 'Do *you* think this weather will hold?' Mrs Ferguson asked.

Alice smiled. Mrs Ferguson had taught her to analyse not only the shape and colour of clouds, but their height and how smooth or otherwise their edges were. Low clouds meant rising humidity, a sign of inclement weather. Rough, jagged edges were also a sign of instability and worsening weather.

Alice looked up again. 'I don't see anything that makes me think it won't. Steady air pressure overnight. It's early, but the sky looks stable.'

'Then that's good enough for now.' Mrs Ferguson patted the pockets of her coat, her eyes scanning the bed of the truck. 'Grab the keys to the truck, will you? I've left them on the mantlepiece in the living room.'

Alice hesitated, biting her lip. Mrs Ferguson let out a light laugh, lines of age creasing around her eyes. 'Don't worry, I'll drive there. But you're driving home.'

Alice smiled and headed into the farmhouse, opening the living room door.

The keys were resting above the fireplace next to a collection of silver photo frames. There was a photograph of George there. It was clearly taken a few years ago. Nothing more recent. She picked another frame up, her gaze lingering on the image. It took her a time to recognise Mrs Ferguson in her younger years. But she immediately recognised the village church in the background. Its sturdy wooden doors and five concrete steps made it a popular spot for wedding pictures. In the photo, a grinning Mrs Ferguson wore a step-skimming dress with what Alice's mother would describe as a daring neckline. She clutched a bouquet of flowers and stood next to her handsome groom, who was too preoccupied with his beautiful bride to look at the camera. Alice brushed her finger along the bottom of the frame, representing two lives full of joy and dreams for the future.

She turned her gaze to the photograph beside it. With a gentle hand, she lifted the frame up. In it, a young man stood in crisp military uniform. His face was youthful, barely old enough to be in the army.

A sudden noise from behind made Alice jump, and she turned to see Mrs Ferguson entering the room, a stern expression on her face.

'I'm sorry,' said Alice, feeling her cheeks flush. She returned the photograph to its spot on the mantle. 'I didn't mean to intrude.'

Mrs Ferguson shook her head, her lips pressed together in a sharp line. 'Did you find the keys?' she asked.

Alice nodded. She held the keys out in the palm of her hand like a peace offering. But her curiosity couldn't be contained. 'Is that your husband?' she blurted out.

Mrs Ferguson's expression hardened, and she tore the keys from Alice's hands. 'It is,' she said in a low voice, before turning on her heel and stalking away.

She heard the truck's engine rumble to life, and she dashed out, taking care to shut the living room door fully behind her.

Mrs Ferguson navigated the truck down the winding roads towards Alderbrae's farmers' market. Alice sat in the passenger seat, still mortified at having been caught snooping.

'I'm sorry I looked at your photographs,' said Alice. She'd already apologised once but felt the need to say it again before they had to work side by side at the market.

'Family can be tricky sometimes,' said Mrs Ferguson. She let out an exasperated breath. 'My son, George's father, made it quite clear from the moment he could talk that he had no interest in farming. When my husband died, he tried to push me to sell the farm. I wouldn't and he didn't like that. Eventually I had to, but I made sure to do it in small increments. It caused a lot of friction, let's just say.'

'I'm sorry to hear that,' said Alice. 'Do you mind me asking when your husband died?'

'In January, it'll be twenty years,' said Mrs Ferguson.

'And your relationship with your son has been tense all of that time?' Alice asked.

Mrs Ferguson nodded. 'Give everyone a few weeks to calm down, you say. But that few weeks turns into a few months. Before you know it, twenty years have gone by and you're still unhappy with each other.'

'So you don't see your son anymore?'

'Oh, I do,' said Mrs Ferguson. 'I get the obligatory visits on birthdays and Christmas, but not much else. I'm not complaining. I'm just as bad as he is.'

Mrs Ferguson slowed down as they approached Alderbrae town park and carefully parked near the entrance. The market had taken over the park, which had been decorated with a vibrant sea of colourful paper flags fluttering in the breeze.

They stepped out of the truck and were greeted by two women at the entrance. The women wore matching long dark green dresses beneath black unbuttoned coats. Their hair was neatly pinned back, framing their welcoming smiles. Their attire wasn't a conventional uniform, but they still looked styled to match each other.

'Welcome!' said one of the women, her voice filled with warmth. 'The market opens shortly. Once you've unloaded, please enjoy the complimentary refreshments on the far side of the park.'

Alice joined Mrs Ferguson at the back of her truck and slid one of the crates of milk bottles towards her. She hoisted it off the truck and headed into the market to find their allocated sales pitch.

They sold out within only half an hour, crowds of people keen to get their hands on some eggs and fresh milk.

Mrs Ferguson headed off to collect drinks for them both. Once Alice had packed up their stall, she stood idly, twirling a strand of hair between her fingers and gazing out into the crowds. Suddenly, she spotted George strolling towards her. She didn't know why she was so shocked. Alderbrae was, after all, his hometown. It's just that George didn't strike her as the kind of person who would attend a farmers' market.

This was the first time she'd seen him in weeks. She'd heard from Peggy that Mrs Winston had managed to find someone to take over as housekeeper for the Fergusons. With Mrs Ferguson having someone to look after her house and Violet keen to avoid the scandalous suggestion that her daughter might be pregnant, the pressure to make wedding plans had evaporated.

George was accompanied by a red-headed young woman and a well-dressed older man with a stern expression on his face. Her heart raced as she considered darting behind a nearby tree, but that thought seemed ludicrous. Instead, she stood rooted to the spot, awaiting his arrival.

As George drew closer, Alice saw the shock register on his face as their eyes met. His steps faltered slightly, and he stumbled over his words. 'Oh, Alice, what a surprise to see you here,' he managed to say, his eyes widening with astonishment.

He turned to his companions and gestured towards Alice. 'This is Alice,' he said, neglecting to mention that she was his fiancée, an omission Alice noted but wasn't in a hurry to correct.

Alice offered a polite smile. The red-headed woman regarded Alice curiously before slipping off a green velvet glove and extending her hand in greeting. 'I'm Dorothy James,' she said, introducing herself warmly. 'And this is Mr Paggett.'

Alice shook Dorothy's hand. 'Pleased to meet you,' she said. She extended her hand towards Mr Paggett, whom she was certain pretended not to see it, his eyes fixed on something behind her.

'Pleasure to meet you, Alice,' said Mr Paggett, his tone stuffy and insincere.

George cleared his throat, shifting nervously from one foot to the other. 'The firm has sponsored this event,' he said, gesturing towards the bustling crowds and colourful decorations surrounding them. 'It's always good to champion small businesses.'

Alice nodded, understanding dawning on her. That explained his presence. 'That's wonderful,' said Alice. 'Your generosity is truly making a difference to these local producers.'

'Yes, yes,' muttered Mr Paggett before strolling off, his eyes seemingly locked on another man a few paces away. Alice watched as he reached the man and slapped him on the back, shaking his hand enthusiastically.

She turned back to George and Dorothy.

'I'm here with your grandmother,' said Alice. 'She'll be back in a minute or two. I know she'd love to see you.'

George lifted his arm, his eyes fixed on where a watch would normally sit, but the skin was bare. With a slight frown, he swept his other hand across the fabric of his sleeve, as if wiping away invisible dust. 'We really must be going,' he said.

He hurried off after his colleague, not sparing a glance back at Alice, as he disappeared into the throng of people.

Dorothy gave Alice a small shrug and arched her eyebrows just enough to convey a quiet disapproval. She leaned in closer to Alice and sighed. 'I'm sorry,' she said under her breath. 'It was very lovely to meet you, Alice.'

'Lovely to meet you too, Dorothy,' said Alice.

Dorothy drifted off after George and Mr Paggett leaving behind the scent of her jasmine perfume mingling in the air.

When Mrs Ferguson returned, Alice decided against telling her that George was here. It could only hurt to know that he had passed by but wouldn't stay to say hello.

'Did you see anyone from Millwood?' Alice asked.

Mrs Ferguson shook her head. 'One or two only.'

'Why doesn't Millwood have its own farmers' market?' Alice asked. 'It seems to me that there are lots of small farms on the outskirts of the village. It might also be a useful event for friends and neighbours to swap their own homegrown produce. We've got so many Brussels sprouts this year. I planted far too many seedlings in the spring and poor Peggy has been cooking them for weeks now. Everyone who visits leaves with a stalk of sprouts.'

'That seems like a marvellous idea, Alice,' said Mrs Ferguson. 'Perhaps you should organise something.'

Alice nodded. Perhaps she would.

She glanced in the direction George had gone. A whirlwind of feelings swirled within her. Despite the unexpected encounter with George, his failure to introduce her as his fiancée gave her a glimmer of hope that she could still convince him to end their arranged engagement.

15

In January, Violet had been proven right and rationing was introduced. People were worried about food shortages, although shortages hadn't yet materialised. Alice had roped in her fellow Guides to help realise her vision for a Millwood farmers' market. They'd decided to call it the Millwood Community Market to make it clear that everyone was welcome. Farmers, neighbours with extra produce, and Guides who would use the market to distribute the donated clothes and shoes they'd collected.

Alice was sat on the floor of her living room pairing up boxes of children's shoes when Violet threw open the living room door with a gleeful grin on her face.

'There's a gentleman here to see you,' she announced.

Alice stood and brushed her hands down her skirt to knock out the creases that had formed. Violet stepped aside and George came into view, filling the doorframe. His sharp suit was a familiar sight, but his tie hung loosely around his neck. The top button on his white shirt was undone.

'George?' said Alice, quickly putting on a polite smile to greet him. 'What a nice surprise,' she said, with forced cheeriness. Her mind raced, wondering why he was here and what he wanted.

George stepped into the room and Violet pulled at the door handle. 'I'll leave you two alone.' She glared at Alice as she closed the door. A look which Alice took to mean "don't say anything stupid".

George held a letter out towards Alice.

'What's this?' she asked, taking the letter and quickly scanning it. A soft gasp escaped her lips. 'You've been conscripted?'

George nodded. 'I've to report for duty on the nine-teenth.' She could see the fear etched on his face. For all his bravado about the war, joining those fighting for the country had not been in his plans.

A lump formed in her throat, telling her to keep quiet and wish him the best of luck. She ignored it. Her heart wouldn't allow him to leave still thinking that they would be married when he returned.

With a nervous laugh, he reached for her hand. 'Alice, I think we should get married on the Saturday before I go,' he said.

Alice froze, unable to believe what she was hearing. 'Why?' she managed to choke out.

His grip on her hand tightened. 'We need to get married before I leave. It's what everyone does.'

Alice stared at him, her mind racing but her mouth unable to form any coherent words to respond. But George's conscription changed everything. She couldn't dither any more or hope that he would come to his senses. She had to be the brave one. The one to stand up to her mother since it appeared George had no intention of standing up to his.

Alice clasped his hand between both of hers and

straightened her shoulders. 'George,' she said, 'I'm sorry. I'm so very sorry, but I can't marry you.'

His eyes widened and his jaw slackened, and for once his arrogance remained hidden. He paced around the room, his steps faltering as he processed her words. Alice was certain that George did not want to marry her. The man was weighed down by expectations and the added burden of conscription looming over him. He collapsed into her father's armchair, conflicting emotions written all over his face.

'Neither of us know how long you'll be gone,' Alice continued, 'but I think you need something to fight for. A life with a woman whom you don't love is not it.' He opened his mouth as if to argue back, but Alice raised her hand to stop him. 'A future full of possibilities must be better than a marriage to a woman you barely know. Don't you want to come home from war and find a woman who loves you, someone you can love with your whole heart, and it will have been worth the wait for you.'

A flicker of something crossed his face and Alice suspected he already had someone in mind. A look she recognised from the last time she had mentioned love to him.

'There's someone you love already, isn't there?' She kept her voice calm and even.

George looked at his feet. 'Yes,' he admitted.

Alice laughed. 'Then why on earth did you want to marry me?'

He shrugged. 'We're a good match,' he said.

Alice shook her head. He was just as snobby as Violet. And he could be pressured by his mother into doing something he didn't want to do. Much like herself.

Alice could see George wrestling with his own thoughts.

He held up the conscription papers. 'Receiving this made me think about how short life might turn out to be.'

She knelt beside him and touched her hand to his conscription papers. 'Receiving this shouldn't make you think about how short life could be. It should make you think about what you want in your life. And *who* you want in your life? It's OK for you to prioritise your happiness over family obligations or whatever it is that's holding you back.'

George's shoulders slumped as if he'd been holding tension there all day that he'd finally been able to let go off. A smile creased the corners of his mouth. His exhale was a deep sigh of relief, followed by a low chuckle that grew into a laugh, a deep and genuine laugh that echoed off the walls.

'Thank you, Alice,' he said, still chuckling.

Alice laughed now, too. 'What would you have done if I'd agreed to marry you on Saturday?'

'I would have married you.'

'There's still time for you to marry someone else,' Alice said.

His grin faded. 'I'm not sure that's what she wants.'

'You won't know until you ask. Love matters, George. It matters more than someone's background, or their status, or whether our parents approve of them. Fight for her and the future you'll have together when you return.'

George smiled again and stood up. For the first time since meeting him, his smile wasn't a smirk. It was genuine and his eyes flooded with an emotion she hadn't thought him capable of feeling let alone displaying. She held her arms out and he stepped into her hug. It was the closest they'd ever come to intimacy throughout their engagement. Neither of them should be trapped in a loveless marriage and she certainly didn't want to be married to someone who would inevitably end up sneaking off with another woman.

Alice closed her eyes as he held her against his chest. It was the right decision.

Alice pulled back. 'Can I ask you for one thing?'

George nodded hesitantly.

'Please go and see your grandmother before you leave,' said Alice. 'She misses you terribly.'

George ran a hand through his hair. 'That's complicated,' he said.

'I know,' said Alice. 'But it doesn't have to be.'

Once George had gone, Violet wasted no time, barging into the living room. She stared down at Alice who was now back on the floor repacking a box of school shoes. 'Well?' she asked.

Alice paused, looking up at her mother. 'I'm no longer engaged to be married.'

Violet's eyebrows shot up her forehead, her hands fluttering helplessly. 'Oh, Alice! What did you do?'

'I've given George my blessing to marry the woman he loves. That woman is not me.'

For a long moment, Violet simply stared, speechless. Then she sank onto the sofa with a harsh, jagged exhale, fingers digging into the cushions. 'What am I going to do with you?'

Alice got off the floor and sat beside her mother. 'You're going to do nothing. I'm eighteen years old. You've done your bit. Where I go from here is up to me.'

'And where is it you want to go?' Violet asked.

Alice hesitated.

'Exactly,' said Violet. 'One of us has to have a plan.'

With that her mother sprang off the sofa and stalked from the room.

16

———

THE EARLY MORNING SUN CAST A DEEP RED GLOW OVER THE farm as Alice arrived. Where once Alice might have marvelled at the beautiful colours, she now recognised those rich colours as a sign that the good weather had passed, and a wet and windy low-pressure system was on the way.

Mrs Ferguson stood at her kitchen door, silhouetted against the morning light. 'Good morning,' she said as Alice approached. 'You're up and about early.'

Alice glanced at Mrs Ferguson's apron. The stiff fabric was speckled with soft brown and white feathers, which Alice told herself had attached to the apron when Mrs Ferguson had been collecting eggs rather than anything more unsavoury.

She shoved her hands deep into her coat pockets. 'I came to tell you something.' Her stomach was in knots. It was ridiculous for her to be so nervous telling Mrs Ferguson she and George were no longer engaged. But she'd become very fond of Mrs Ferguson and was worried that this would change things between them.

'George and I ended our engagement,' she blurted out.

Mrs Ferguson nodded. 'I know.'

'You do?' Alice asked. 'How?'

'George came to see me yesterday,' Mrs Ferguson said. There was a hint of a smile on her face, but she seemed to be trying to keep it in check.

Alice grinned, pulling her hands from her pockets and clasping them in front of her. 'He did? Oh, I'm so pleased.'

Mrs Ferguson allowed her smile to fill her face. 'I suspected it was your idea.' She reached forward and clasped Alice's hands in hers. 'Thank you.'

Alice nodded. She turned around to take in the view and the peaceful surroundings, breathing out a sigh. 'I'm going to miss it up here.'

'What's to miss?' asked Mrs Ferguson.

'Well, if I'm no longer engaged to George...'

'What does that matter?'

Alice grinned at the not-so-subtle invitation to continue visiting the farm. 'Are you by any chance free next Sunday?'

Mrs Ferguson narrowed her eyes. 'Probably. Why?'

'That's the date of the first Millwood Community Market,' she said enthusiastically. 'I finally got the village councillor's agreement. He said we could use the space around the village hall. He even agreed we could use the hall itself if it rained. As long as we cleaned up afterwards and, in his words, we didn't leave the place smelling of manure.'

Mrs Ferguson laughed. 'What on earth does he think we'd be selling?'

Alice smiled. 'Exactly. The Guides are going to help spread the word. And we're organising a stall with donated children's clothes, shoes, and toys so we can distribute them to anyone who needs them.'

Mrs Ferguson smiled at Alice. 'That's a lovely idea.'

Tyres on gravel crunched behind them. Alice turned to see Tom's car pulling up, sunlight glinting off its dusty windshield.

'Is Jocelyn alright?' Alice asked.

Mrs Ferguson rolled her eyes. 'She's the best cared for pregnant cow in Scotland, I expect.'

Tom strolled over to join them beside the house, flashing them both a grin. 'I was dealing with an emergency nearby.'

'Oh,' said Alice. 'I hope everything was alright.'

He nodded. 'The so-called emergency turned out to be a goose with a cough. The noise it was making sounded perfectly goose-like to me, but I've given the owner a syrup to feed it. It's useless really, but people feel better if they at least think they are helping in some way. But I'll just check on Jocelyn since I'm here.'

'I'll put the kettle on,' said Mrs Ferguson. She stepped back into the house as Tom headed towards the barn.

Alice wandered over to the old wooden bench that over-looked the fields. She took a seat and admired the green fields, still vibrant despite the winter weather. She was glad that Mrs Ferguson was still happy for her to visit, despite everything that had happened with George.

'Can I join you?' Tom asked, appearing over her shoulder.

Alice smiled and gestured for him to sit. They sat side by side in companionable silence, each lost in their own thoughts.

She was happy George had visited. Mrs Ferguson must have been delighted. But the breakup weighed heavier on her mind than she had expected it to. Her initial newfound sense of freedom with endless possibilities had waned, and now, she felt adrift, unsure of which path to take next. A chill in the air nipped at her cheeks. She shivered and pulled her coat closer around her, appreciating the warmth of the fabric against her skin.

'What has you so lost in thought today?' Tom asked.

Alice hesitated for a moment. She took a deep breath and turned to face him fully. 'I ended my engagement with George,' she said.

Tom's eyes filled with concern and something else that she couldn't quite place. 'I don't know what the right thing is to say, Alice, given the circumstances. But I'm sorry if you're upset.'

Alice nodded. 'Thank you. I'm not upset. Not really.'

Tom reached out and squeezed her hand in comfort. 'You're allowed to be. The end of a relationship is always difficult even when you know it's not right for you.'

Alice tilted her head down and dragged her gaze along the ground at their feet. 'It's not that. What I had with George could hardly be described as a relationship. It's just, where do I go from here? That's the question I need to answer.' She sighed.

'You and I have some things in common,' said Tom. 'You're agonising over what the future holds for you and I'm agonising over my decision not to go to war.'

She looked up at him now. 'That's not really your decision,' she said. 'You're a veterinary surgeon. That's a reserved occupation for a reason. You're needed in this country. Who does it benefit sending you off with a gun in your hand and leaving the country's livestock to fend for themselves?'

'The army need veterinary surgeons too.'

Alice closed her eyes. 'Please don't tell me why. It's bad enough thinking of men on a battlefield. I don't want any other images in my mind.'

'My point is that we're both at a crossroads in our lives. We're both struggling to find our place in this world, and we're both searching for something worthwhile to do with our lives.'

Alice nodded, her gaze dropping once more to the ground. 'Yes, that's true. But at least you have a purpose. You have a profession, a skill that you can use to help others. I feel like I have nothing to offer.'

Tom leaned back slightly, a crease forming between his brows as he studied her. 'That's not true,' he said, his voice soft but firm. 'There are many things you would excel at. And you've got a kind heart, Alice.' He tilted his head slightly, offering her a small, reassuring smile. 'That's something that's sorely needed in this world.'

Alice blushed at the compliment, her fingers fidgeting with the edge of her sleeve.

He leaned forward, his eyes burning with an intensity Alice hadn't ever seen in them. 'I'm glad you're no longer engaged. You're not someone's possession to be given away against your will.' His voice had a quiet, steady passion that sent a shiver down Alice's spine. 'You're a person with dreams and aspirations and, if you'll forgive me for being so bold, you should be with someone who supports those dreams.' He hesitated for just a fraction of a second before continuing, his voice barely a whisper. 'Someone who sees you as you truly are and supports you no matter what.'

Alice stared at Tom, her heart beating faster, her breath quickening as his words sank in. She had never heard anyone speak about her like that before. She swallowed, her chest tightening with a strange mix of hope and fear. For the first time in a long time, Alice felt excited about her future. She was only eighteen years old. She hadn't missed her chance. Her palm grazed the rough grain of the wooden bench as she reached down and placed her hand on top of Tom's. The warmth of his skin sent a thrill through her, and when their fingers intertwined, she felt a connection she hadn't expected, but desperately needed.

'Thank you,' she said softly, although her words sounded so inadequate in the moment.

Tom gave her hand a gentle squeeze. 'You're welcome,' he said. 'Now, sadly, I have to go. I'm covering the practice for my dad this morning.'

They strolled back to the farmhouse, and, after a quick cup of tea and a scone, Tom headed off.

Alice walked him out and watched him drive away, her heart fluttering at the thought of him. With a sigh, she turned back towards the house to see Mrs Ferguson standing in the doorway, a knowing glint in her eye. 'You two still dancing around each other then?'

A small, mischievous smile played on her lips, making Alice blush furiously.

17

A week later and Alice stood nervously at the doors of the village hall greeting the arrivals to Millwood's very first community market. Rain lashed off the ground and splashed up Alice's trouser legs as she welcomed the very soggy villagers into the hall.

'Aren't you glad you arranged the hall as a contingency?' asked Beatrice, standing beside her, sheltering from the rain under the overhang of the roof.

Alice glanced behind her into the hall. The walls were lined with local farmers hoping to sell their produce. So far, only a few potential buyers were milling around. 'I think the rain is putting people off.'

Beatrice held her palm out from under the shelter. 'It's so frustrating that weather forecasts have been banned. I don't see what's so secretive about the weather. I hope it stops soon.'

'It will,' said Alice.

Beatrice leaned forward to look up at the sky. 'I don't know. It's still pretty cloudy.'

It was cloudy. But the clouds had been shrinking

throughout the morning. A sure sign the weather was stabilising.

Alice's forecast had been right, and, within the hour, rays of sunlight had broken through the clouds and bathed the village hall in bright yellow light. A steady stream of people now shopped for extras to supplement their weekly rations.

Farmers had taken up most of the space inside the hall but villagers with homegrown produce to spare milled about outside, trading cabbages for leeks and broccoli for beetroot. Even Peggy had turned up with a basket of sprouts.

Once the rain had stopped, Beatrice and a few of her fellow Guides had dragged two tables outside covered them with boxes of clothes, shoes, and toys. There was now a queue of children waiting to have their feet measured so they could go home with a pair of preloved shoes.

When the arrivals slowed down, Alice took a few minutes to say hello to her mother who had appeared, accompanied by their neighbour, Mrs Scott.

Mrs Scott gave Alice a warm smile as she approached. 'You've done a fabulous job, Alice,' she said.

'Hasn't she just,' echoed Violet, basking in the praise being doled out to her daughter.

A vibrant blue umbrella was hooked across Violet's arm, the fabric glistening with raindrops that hadn't yet dried. Alice smiled. It took something special to get her mother outside on a rainy day.

Mrs Scott leaned into the centre of their little group. 'Don't look now, but here comes Mrs Ferguson.'

Alice turned around. Her face fell. It wasn't the Mrs Ferguson she was expecting to see. George's mother was striding towards them, her long coat billowing behind her, and a small, elegant handbag clutched in her hand. Alice braced herself. She hadn't seen his mother since they ended their engagement. She could only imagine the fallout.

'Mrs Ferguson,' said Violet, getting in there first. 'How lovely of you to come all of this way to support our little event.'

Mrs Ferguson's mouth curved politely, but there was no warmth there. 'One must be charitable above all else.' She turned to Alice, tucking her bag under her arm. 'I hear you're the organiser of this event.'

'She is indeed,' said Violet, standing a little straighter suddenly.

'How quaint,' said Mrs Ferguson, her gaze scanning the clothing stall and the queue of children.

Violet's shoulders dropped as if she were deflating in front of Alice's eyes.

'Yes, it is,' said Alice. She widened her grin. 'All of this is thanks to the farmers of Millwood and the generosity of the people who live here. And the generosity of your mother-in-law who's providing refreshments. Her own home-cooked stovies. They're quite delicious. But I expect you know that. You must have been treated to them before.'

'Quite,' said Mrs Ferguson. 'Alderbrae, as you know, has a weekly farmers' market. We have business sponsors, which is why we were able to put on such an elaborate event.'

Alice looked around. Her event offered everything that Alderbrae's had, just on a smaller scale. And elaborate wasn't a word she would have used to describe the Alderbrac market.

'Of course,' added Mrs Ferguson, her lips settling into a thin, sneering line, 'if you hadn't treated my George the way you did then I'm sure he could have arranged for his firm to sponsor your little event too.'

Alice opened her mouth to defend herself against Mrs Ferguson's insinuation but was stopped by a firm squeeze to her arm from her mother.

'How is George?' asked Mrs Scott. 'I hear he's engaged again.'

'Well,' sputtered Mrs Ferguson. 'The boy is terribly confused. Broken-hearted,' she said, glaring at Alice, 'and then he was conscripted. A dreadful combination.'

'Oh,' said Mrs Scott. 'I'd heard that George was very happy with his new love. Remind me of her name. Dorothy James, isn't it?'

A small gasp escaped Violet's mouth. Mrs Ferguson's cheeks turned a light shade of pink, and she looked to the side, avoiding Alice's eye.

'Well, that's what war does for you,' said Mrs Ferguson. She turned to Alice, but Violet put her hands on her hips and shook her head.

'Dorothy James,' said Violet, almost under her breath. She glanced behind her and then leaned towards Mrs Ferguson. 'I'm so sorry.'

Mrs Ferguson squared her shoulders. 'Well, enjoy your little event,' she said, before turning on her heel and marching away.

Violet folded her arms, watching Mrs Ferguson retreating. 'I hadn't heard about that,' she said in a rare acknowledgement that there was a sliver of gossip she didn't know.

'What's the big deal?' asked Alice.

Violet turned to her. 'Oh, you don't know Dorothy James.'

Alice nodded. 'I met her, actually. She was at the Alderbrae market with George.'

Violet and Mrs Scott exchanged a glance, eyebrows shooting up towards their perfectly groomed hairlines.

'Dorothy James is,' Violet glanced around her again, 'divorced,' she said with a whisper.

Alice laughed. 'Divorced. Why are we whispering about that?'

'George cannot marry a divorcee,' added Violet.

'The scandal will bump Mrs Ferguson's social status down by a considerable margin,' added Mrs Scott. 'And I heard that she was the one who petitioned for divorce. Mrs Ferguson will not like that.'

A lightness settled in Alice's chest, and she felt a twitch on her lips with a smile she couldn't contain.

'Why are you looking so pleased with yourself?' asked Violet.

Alice shrugged. 'I liked Dorothy,' she said. 'She'll be good for George. I'm very happy for them both.'

Divorce was rare, but it was no longer considered a scandal. Not outside of Violet's social circle anyway. And if Dorothy was the one who instigated the divorce, then that was a sign that she wasn't the type of woman who would allow the Fergusons to walk all over her. And for George to have publicly announced his plans to marry Dorothy despite his mother's objections, that showed growth.

Alice decided to leave her mother to gossip about this latest development. She spun around and came face to face with Tom Cameron. He offered his arm and Alice took it, slipping her arm through his.

'Well, Alice, I have two things to say,' started Tom. He nodded behind them. 'Firstly, I'm glad you're not marrying George. You do not belong in that world.'

Alice laughed, her fingers dancing over the fabric of Tom's coat. 'Of that I have no doubt.'

'Secondly, you've achieved something quite wonderful here.' His eyes seemed to sparkle with pride. He stopped walking, planted both hands on Alice's shoulders and guided her body around. 'Just look at what you've done.'

Alice glanced over at the makeshift stalls she had set up for that morning, feeling a swell of pride at what she had accomplished. The second-hand clothing stall was proving to be a hit, with boys and girls eagerly picking out garments that caught their eye. Shoes clacked against the dirt path as children tried on different pairs, their faces lighting up with joy at finding something that fit just right.

Beatrice and Kathleen were leading a group of children in noughts and crosses using chalk and the wooden walls of the hall, their voices filled with encouragement and laughter as they cheered on the participants. The sound of gleeful shouts blended harmoniously with the tinkling laughter of younger children exploring the toy stall.

Alice spotted the other Mrs Ferguson who was serving paper cups of stovies from a picnic table near the main door. The savoury aroma of the stew wafted through the air, making Alice's stomach rumble. Alice smiled. Her engagement to George hadn't all been bad.

18

Alice woke to the sound of aircraft droning in the distance. Her bedsheets felt rough against her skin as she lay motionless, trying to decide if she'd dreamt the noise. She wiped at her eyes. Each passing moment brought with it an increasing unease, a tension that seemed to reverberate through her bones. The sound was faint, but it was growing louder.

Her pulse quickened and she launched herself out of bed, grabbing her robe from the back of a chair. She opened her bedroom door and squinted into the gloomy hallway. Her mother's bedroom door was still closed. The ticking of the grandfather clock downstairs echoed in the dark of the night. There was no air raid siren, and the droning had faded to a distant growl, like a beast retreating in the darkness.

Alice closed her bedroom door and went to the window. She pulled back the thick blackout curtains just enough to see outside. The sky was a deep shade of grey, with heavy clouds obscuring the stars. But amid the gloom, the full moon cast a blurred silvery glow over everything. Alice couldn't remember the last time she had seen a full moon. She was usually inside before nightfall with the blackout curtains firmly in place.

She pressed the heavy curtains back into place, and let her robe slide off before she crawled back under her bedcovers. It was a British fighter plane from nearby RAF Drem, she told herself, the drone of its engine having been carried on the wind. Yet, despite her attempts at reassurance, her body remained stiff with tension.

As the warmth of her blankets settled around her, the silence was abruptly shattered by the piercing wail of the air raid siren. A series of explosions thundered in the distance. With shaky hands, Alice threw off the covers and reached for her robe. The door to her bedroom burst open, revealing Violet, her eyes wide with urgency. Together, they hurried down the stairs. The floor trembled beneath their feet, each rumble accompanied by the menacing roar of warplanes slicing through the night sky. The vibrations pounded against Alice's chest like a caged bird desperate to flee. But there was nowhere to go. All they could do was hide.

They reached the basement and huddled together on the bench, their bodies trembling with fear as more explosions echoed through the walls. Panic coursed through Alice. Every nerve in her body was on edge. Violet stared at her, wincing as another explosion rang out.

Alice closed her eyes and silently prayed for safety amidst the deafening chaos above ground. She didn't know what else to do. She spent her days looking for ways to be helpful, but that night, she felt utterly helpless.

In the morning, Alice dressed in trousers and a jumper with flat, lace-up shoes. Something practical. She wolfed down a slice of toast with a smear of last season's rhubarb jam and followed her mother out of the front door. Whenever something happened in the village, people made their way to the village hall. It was the meeting point for those looking for gossip, but also for those wondering how they might help.

Her eyes were still bleary from lack of sleep. She rubbed them and breathed in deeply, relieved to find that her village was still standing. The air was alive with the crisp scent of dew on grass and the sweet fragrance of the first blooms of the approaching summer. It was a stark contrast to the acrid stench of burning buildings and destruction that Alice had prepared herself for.

Pale-faced neighbours and weary early morning shoppers huddled together, exchanging stories of the air raid. From overheard snippets of conversation, it seemed that most of the bombs had hit farmland and hadn't damaged their village in any way. Not physically, at least.

A few people seemed certain that their rural community had not been the intended target so there was little chance of the bombers coming back, but that didn't make Alice feel any safer. Some of the villagers were more upset that the air raid sirens had failed to sound with enough warning. It seemed that others, like herself, had heard the bombers before they'd heard the sirens.

Alice tried to shake the feeling of unease. She reminded herself that they were safe for now, but she couldn't help glancing up at the sky every few minutes. Only this time, it wasn't the clouds she was looking for.

'Don't you be digging out any waterlogged air raid shelters today,' said Violet, as they marched towards the centre of the village. 'It's not your fault if people haven't maintained their shelters properly.'

Alice knew that was a distinct possibility. Months of seeming inactivity had led to complacency. But if anyone still referred to this war as "phoney" then events of the last few weeks had quashed that. Germany had launched a full-scale invasion of Belgium, Luxembourg, and the Netherlands. They seemed well on their way to France. Neville Chamberlain had handed over the Office of the Prime Minister to Winston Churchill. And now, German bombs had once again landed on Scottish soil. There was nothing phoney about this war.

'I'll do whatever is needed,' said Alice, swinging her arms as they walked. 'It sounds like we were lucky last night. If the Germans come back, we need to make sure everyone in the village is ready.'

Violet huffed out a breath. 'You've always been too soft-hearted for your own good, Alice.'

A woman wearing a bright red coat caught Alice's attention as she approached, her brisk pace confident and with purpose. She thrust a leaflet into Alice's hand with a quick flick of her wrist. 'Just something to think about, ladies,' the woman announced in a clear, no-nonsense tone before moving swiftly along, extending another leaflet to the next passerby.

Alice stopped and looked down at the thin paper in her hand. Its corners curled in the gentle breeze and a bright-faced young woman in uniform smiled up at her. 'They've opened a temporary recruitment office in Alderbrae,' Alice said, reading the text.

Violet, standing beside her with arms crossed, raised a sceptical eyebrow. 'Well, that's as good as useless,' she said, her tone dismissive. 'Anyone who wants to sign up already has. And anyone who was still considering it, well, let's just say last night will have firmly put them off.'

Alice tightened her grip on the leaflet as she continued to scan the text. 'It says here they're also looking for ARP Wardens. That could be good for me. It would allow me to stay at home, but still do something useful,' she added, casting a hopeful glance towards her mother.

Violet snatched the leaflet from Alice's hand. 'No man wants his wife wandering through the streets in the dark of night. That's a job for men who are too old to fight.'

'Not anymore,' said Alice. She took a deep breath and turned her face towards the sun for a moment. 'Besides, there are lots of men who would understand their wives wanting to pitch in during times of war.'

Violet scoffed. 'Such as?'

'Men like Tom Cameron,' Alice mumbled under her breath.

'Don't even think about it,' Violet scolded, slipping her arm in Alice's and gripping her tight as she forced her to walk again. 'From what I know of the profession, a veterinarian does not have the financial means to care for a wife and a family in anything other than squalor.'

Alice was sure that must have been one of Violet's many exaggerations, but she wasn't about to argue. It wasn't the man's choice of profession that appealed to her, it was the man himself.

Violet had quickly got over her upset about George Ferguson when she found out about George's engagement to Dorothy, the divorcee. It had caused quite the scandal in Violet's social circle and Alice's brief engagement had all but been forgotten.

They reached the village hall and Violet released Alice's arm.

Alice nodded towards the groups of people huddled outside the hall. 'It looks as though half the village has turned out to help. Are you coming in?'

'To dig out air raid shelters?' Violet raised an eyebrow, her expression haughty. 'Besides, you know I have an appointment this morning.'

She searched her mother's face for any hint of compassion for her neighbours but found none.

Violet handed the scrunched-up flyer to Alice. 'You can bin that,' she instructed, her voice clipped. 'Be home for dinner.'

Without waiting for a response, Violet turned away, her heels clacking against the pavement as she strode towards her most important appointment – her weekly blow-dry.

Alice sighed deeply and unfolded the crumpled flyer, smoothing out its creases. As the paper flattened, her final conversation with George replayed in her mind. She had told him he needed something worth fighting for. It was good advice. And for George, that was Dorothy. She was his reason to be brave.

Alice had nothing to be passionate about, nothing to inspire her own courage. That realisation hit her like an icy gust of wind, the sting of which left her feeling hollow. Her gaze drifted to the flyer in her hand, the image of a woman in uniform smiling confidently back at her under the heading *Aircraftwoman Jones keeps them flying*. The woman seemed to beckon Alice towards a different kind of life. One filled with purpose and independence.

The future Alice wanted to fight for was not tied to the sometimes-suffocating confines of Millwood and her mother's expectations. She had to treat last night's air raid, with its wailing sirens and the ominous thrum of planes overhead, as a wake-up call. It was a clear sign that she needed to stop merely dreaming about her future and start actively crafting it.

She smiled and tucked the flyer in her pocket. *Aircraftwoman Peters*. It had a nice ring to it. But that was tomorrow's task. Today, her focus had to be the people of Millwood.

Inside the village hall, Kathleen and Beatrice stood in front of a chalkboard scribbling notes with names against each line. The Guides were always the first to turn up to help.

Kathleen's face lit up when she saw Alice approaching. 'We were just looking at how we can help with the aftermath of last night's air raid.'

Another group of girls arrived behind Alice and pulled chairs into a circle around the chalkboard.

'Thank you all for coming,' said Kathleen. 'From what I can see and hear, there were no direct hits on the village itself. They seem to have fallen on the surrounding fields. Some people, however, have realised that their air raid shelters are no longer fit for purpose. Some shelters need a good clear out having become waterlogged in the winter and never properly drained, and some are poorly stocked for anyone to spend longer than a half hour test drill in.'

Alice smiled to herself. She could picture her mother standing with her hands on her hips and an I-told-you-so expression on her face.

'We can definitely make sure everyone is safe and secure if another air raid were to happen,' Alice said. She and some of the others had helped to assemble many air raid shelters so carrying out a little maintenance on them shouldn't be a problem. 'We can start taking inventory of what supplies we have and what we need to restock then we can reach out to the community to see what's needed.'

Kathleen smiled, clearly pleased with Alice's initiative. 'That's a great start.'

Alice, Beatrice, and a couple of other girls worked diligently, taking stock of what long life food, bedding, and first aid supplies they had on hand. This was the first time the villagers had spent any length of time in their shelters, so they probably hadn't thought about practical ways to make them more comfortable and keep any little ones entertained. Alice also prepared a system for tracking which shelters needed additional stocks only and which ones needed a bit of repair or maintenance.

Once they'd finished, the girls dispersed and set off into the village to see who needed help. Alice's first stop was going to be the farm to check on Mrs Ferguson and her animals.

She headed straight there. As she neared, she scanned the horizon for any signs of damage from the air raid. To her immense relief, the farm appeared unscathed. The old stone farmhouse and the barn were just as she had last seen them.

Tom's car was in the driveway, and she spotted him talking to Mrs Ferguson, his back turned towards her. Her heart fluttered in her chest, and she smiled, feeling for the flyer in her pocket. She was eager to share her decision to apply for the Women's Auxiliary Air Force. She wanted the first time she spoke the words aloud to be with someone supportive, someone who would see the excitement in her eyes and mirror it back to her.

Tom turned at the sound of her footsteps, a mix of surprise and relief crossing his face as he saw her.

'Alice,' he greeted her warmly, stepping closer to her. 'I'm glad to see you're safe.'

'You too,' said Alice, glancing around at the undamaged surroundings. 'Is everyone OK?' she asked Mrs Ferguson.

Mrs Ferguson nodded. 'We have drama of a different kind going on right now.'

'Oh,' said Alice, her forehead creasing with curiosity.

'Jocelyn is in labour,' said Tom.

19

———

While Tom headed into the barn to check on Jocelyn, Alice followed Mrs Ferguson into the kitchen.

'How can I help?' she asked.

Mrs Ferguson stopped at the sink, her weathered hands gripping the handle of a large steel bucket as water poured into it from the tap. She cut the flow off abruptly, heaved the bucket out of the sink, and placed it on the floor at her feet.

'Take this water to Tom,' she said. 'And don't forget the soap.'

Alice scooped up the bar of soap sitting beside the sink and carried it along with the bucket out to the barn.

Tom stood in front of Jocelyn who shifted and scraped her hooves along the barn floor, her discomfort obvious. Tom's coat and jumper had been tossed on a nearby hay bale.

'Ah, good,' said Tom. He stroked Jocelyn's head then retrieved the bucket from Alice. He wasted no time sticking his arms in the bucket and splashing water up his bare forearms. 'Ever seen a calf being born?'

Alice shook her head.

'Stick around if you like,' he said.

She closed the barn door to keep any drafts out while Tom took the soap and cleaned both of his arms, dropping the bar into the bucket and rinsing the lather away with handfuls of the water.

Alice removed her coat, rolled up the sleeve of her jumper and scooped the bar of soap out of the bucket, laying it on the barn floor. Soap was becoming increasingly scarce. No point wasting any by allowing it to disintegrate at the bottom of the bucket. She dried her hand on the side of her coat and watched in part awe part disgust as Tom's hand disappeared into Jocelyn's back end.

The poor creature let out a cry that sounded like pain, but she stood motionless, almost as if she knew Tom was there to help her.

'Should I stroke her head like you were doing earlier?' Alice asked, keen to help if she could.

'No,' said Tom. 'Just stay back. She's calm so far, but it won't take much for her to kick out.'

'Is she going to be OK? Is the baby OK? Sorry, the calf,' Alice added, remembering Mrs Ferguson correcting her terminology when she'd previously called the calf a baby.

Tom's face screwed up in concentration and Alice kept quiet, allowing him to work. Whatever he was doing with his hand deep inside the cow, it was clearly hard work. Sweat glistened on his forehead and his feet were digging in so hard to the floor for leverage that she could see his thigh muscles straining through his trousers.

It seemed like an eternity, but it couldn't have been more than a few minutes when Tom gently pulled his arm out of the cow, a satisfied smile on his face. He then grabbed a length of rope that Alice hadn't noticed on the floor and inserted it, along with his arm, inside Jocelyn. After several more minutes of intense work, Tom released a relieved sigh and slid his arm out.

'Come around this side,' said Tom, gesturing with his head for Alice to get closer.

She positioned herself just behind Tom. His breath heaved in his chest. Poor Jocelyn's fur was matted with dirt and streaks of blood, her body trembling with exhaustion. The stench brought tears to Alice's eyes and clung to her skin like a pungent perfume.

Tom's hand tightened on the rope, and he leaned back with a slow, steady pull. The cow strained, and little by little a pair of hooves appeared, then two legs, until at last the calf slid free and landed on the straw-covered floor with a wet thud. The calf lay motionless. Tom snatched a handful of hay and wiped blood and mucus from the animal's face. Alice held her breath.

A few seconds later, one of the calf's front legs twitched. Then another leg moved and finally its eyelids flickered open, and it gave a sharp intake of breath. Tom quickly dragged the bloodied and gunky animal towards its mother who immediately began licking it clean.

Alice let out a happy laugh. She couldn't tear her eyes away from the scene as the bond between mother and baby was ignited. While Tom disappeared around the back of the cow to tend to whatever else his job required, Alice took a seat on the nearby bale of hay.

Once Tom had finished, he washed his arms as best he could with the bucket of water and joined Alice on the hay bale to watch the animals bonding. They sat in comfortable silence. Alice could feel the exhaustion radiating off Tom. She understood why he felt like he couldn't leave this job. It took so much physical strength and endurance, more than she ever would have guessed. It wasn't a task for a sixty-four-year-old man, and Alice could see why Tom felt responsible for keeping his father from having to take on this work again.

Alice turned to him, seeing the weariness etched on his face. 'You did an amazing job,' she said, her voice filled with admiration.

Tom smiled, the lines of his face softening. 'Thank you.' His voice was hoarse. 'The calf was breech. She wouldn't have been able to deliver him on her own.'

'Him?'

Tom nodded and looked towards the calf. 'It's a boy.'

Alice felt a rush of affection for Tom as she watched him gazing at the mother and calf. When he turned back to her, there was something in his smile that she hadn't noticed before. A longing, but also an uncertainty.

'I made a decision today,' he said. 'I've enlisted. My dad is going to deal with the small animals, and I've found a student vet who is going to help him with the bigger ones.'

Alice's hand trembled as she reached for his, her fingers entwining with his in a tight grasp. She would not pull away this time.

'I made a decision, too. I'm applying to join the Women's Auxiliary Air Force. A recruitment office has opened in Alderbrae and I'm going tomorrow.'

Tom's smile widened revealing a dimple on his left cheek that she hadn't noticed before. Her heart pounded in her chest. The air around them seemed charged by the undeniable attraction that had simmered between them for too long.

Tom's thumb caressed the back of her hand, his touch gentle yet electrifying. He slowly leaned towards her, their eyes locked in a moment of shared vulnerability. It was as if the world had fallen away and left only the two of them in this small corner of the barn. And she wanted nothing more than to capture Tom's lips with her own.

Their lips met and a spark ignited deep inside of her. His kiss was tender and sweet yet filled with an intensity that made her shiver with desire.

The rustle of straw broke her trance and Alice bounced up from the hay bale. Her eyes darted towards the barn door expecting to see Mrs Ferguson standing there, but the door was still closed. Tom reached up from his seat and, with a gentle touch, nudged her chin, turning her head towards the calf. The animal's legs splayed out as he battled against himself in his attempts to stand up. He crashed to the ground, resting for only a second before Jocelyn bent her head towards him and encouraged him to try again. The little calf straightened his back legs and leaned forward, rocking unsteadily as he attempted to get up onto all fours. With a final push, he stood upright. He trembled as he attempted to keep his balance, but he was up.

'Yes!' said Alice. She clasped her hands together with the excitement of it all.

Tom stood up to join her. Her breath caught in her throat as she exchanged a nervous glance with him. What did this mean? The kiss should have opened up a world of possibilities between them, but the reality of their situation loomed overhead like a dark cloud. Tom was leaving. And so, she hoped, was she.

'I have something for you,' said Tom. He rummaged in his bag and pulled out a long green box, passing it to Alice.

She took the box and ran her finger along the painted wood. She opened it to reveal three pens, shiny metal, without a scratch or fingerprint.

'I'm hoping you'll write to me,' said Tom.

Alice smiled. 'I will. I promise.'

Tom took Alice's hands in his. 'I know this probably seems complicated to you.'

She nodded. 'A little.'

'For me,' he continued. 'It's very easy. I care for you a great deal, Alice, and I think you care for me too.'

'I do.'

Tom grinned, his dimple returning. 'Then we will figure this out. Whatever happens, we will find a way to be together. Even if that's not right now.'

She wanted to find solace in Tom's words, but this war was showing no signs of being over. Neither of them knew what the future held.

'I suppose I should go inside and tell Mrs Ferguson the calf is here,' said Alice, suddenly deflated.

Tom nodded. 'In a minute,' he said, kicking at some straw with his feet. 'There's something I'd like to do one more time.'

'Oh, and what's that?' said Alice, her tone more playful.

He reached forward, his fingers gently curling around her waist, and drew her close until there was scarcely any space between them. She allowed her body to melt against his. Tilting her head back, she surrendered to the moment and allowed his lips to find hers with a tender and lingering touch that sent a shiver down her spine.

Alice stepped into the farmhouse, picking stray bits of hay from her sleeves. The scent of warm toast and strong tea filled the kitchen.

Mrs Ferguson, who had been sipping her tea at the kitchen table, set her cup down with a soft clink. 'All good?' she asked.

Alice grinned. 'It's a boy.'

Mrs Ferguson stood slowly, just a hint of a smile on her face. 'I think I'll call him Bernie.' She adjusted her apron, her sharp eyes narrowing with curiosity. 'What's the matter with you?' she asked.

'Nothing,' said Alice, her voice unusually high-pitched.

'Something happened in that barn, and it wasn't just a birth,' said Mrs Ferguson, crossing her arms.

Alice sensed she wasn't going to get away with saying nothing happened. She touched her chin, wondering if Tom's stubbled jawline had left a mark on her.

She met Mrs Ferguson's gaze. 'I have decided to apply to the Women's Auxiliary Air Force,' Alice announced, her voice steady now.

There was a moment of silence as Mrs Ferguson processed Alice's words. Her serious demeanour softened ever so slightly, and a flicker of something akin to pride flashed across her features before she quickly composed herself.

'They'll be lucky to have you, Alice,' Mrs Ferguson finally said, her voice betraying a hint of emotion that caught Alice off guard.

'Thank you,' said Alice. 'I might not even get in, but I've got to try. They're recruiting now in Alderbrae so I'm going tomorrow and I'll see what happens.'

Alice followed Mrs Ferguson outside. Just before Mrs Ferguson entered the barn, she stopped and looked towards the sky. Alice followed her gaze and stared up at the rolling clouds above her, like silvery fish scales. A mackerel sky, she now knew.

Mrs Ferguson cleared her throat. 'Tomorrow, huh? Go early so you can get home before the rain starts.' She winked at Alice and headed inside to meet the new arrival.

20

ALICE STOOD OUTSIDE THE ALDERBRAE COUNCIL OFFICE, HER heart pounding in her chest. She had nothing to be nervous about. If the Women's Auxiliary Air Force turned her down, she hadn't lost anything. But if they accepted her, she'd have to tell Violet she was leaving home. That was the more nerve-wracking conversation. But it was also one of the reasons she was here. She had to get out from the influence of her mother. It was time for her to make her own way in life.

She pushed open the wrought iron gates, their ageing metal creaking in protest at being disturbed. With each step closer to the door, Alice felt the knot in her stomach tighten just a little bit more. She squared her shoulders and stepped inside the building. The air indoors was tinged with the smell of old books and polished wood, a comforting scent that wrapped around her like a familiar blanket and Alice wondered if that was the intention.

'Good morning,' said the woman sitting behind a sleek oak desk, adjusting the glasses perched on the bridge of her nose. 'Are you looking for the recruitment office?'

Alice approached the desk and cleared her throat. 'Yes,' she began, her voice wavering slightly. 'I'm here to apply to the Women's Auxiliary Air Force.'

The woman set aside a stack of neatly arranged papers and offered Alice a reassuring smile. She reached for a bundle of forms and slid them across the polished oak counter. 'Just fill this out, dear,' she said, tapping the top sheet with a pen. 'You can take a seat over there if you want to do it now.'

Alice nodded, clutching the forms as though they might disappear if she let go. She turned and made her way to a seat in the corner of the room, near a large, bright window. Sunlight spilled across the wooden floorboards, casting warm patterns over her lap. She placed her bag at her feet. There was no sign of the rain Mrs Ferguson had told her to prepare for. But it would come. She was certain of that.

Forcing herself to steady her hands, Alice smoothed the first page against her knee. As she filled out the application, a sense of anticipation slowly replaced her nerves. The questions were straightforward, asking for her personal details, work experience, and her reasons for wanting to join the WAAF. Alice made sure to include that she was a competent driver and held a provisional driving licence. Thanks to Mrs Ferguson, she was now quite adept at driving a truck. It was just frustrating that driving tests had been suspended because of the war so she'd likely be stuck with a provisional licence for some time yet.

With each answer Alice penned down, her strokes became firmer, more assured. She was no longer just toying with an idea. This was real. And she really wanted it.

Application completed, Alice stacked the papers neatly and pressed them together. Excitement bubbled within her as she returned the forms to the front desk.

The woman behind the counter took them and gave Alice a warm smile. She added the papers to a neat stack behind her. 'You'll be contacted shortly for an interview and assessment,' she said. 'Keep an eye on your post.'

Alice hesitated, gripping the strap of her bag. 'Will I definitely get an interview?' she asked, unable to keep the hopeful edge from her voice.

The woman picked up Alice's forms, flipping through them with a practiced eye. 'I don't see why not.'

Alice's heart lifted. A grin spread across her face. 'Thank you,' she said.

Alice practically floated out of the recruitment office. As she headed towards the bus stop, her thoughts were a whirlwind of the possibilities that lay ahead. This was her chance to make a real impact, to contribute to the war effort in a meaningful way. The small bus that connected Millwood to its neighbouring towns pulled up. Alice climbed aboard and settled into a seat towards the back. Her newfound enthusiasm was tempered by the fact she still had to tell her mother.

Violet was standing at the dining table arranging a bouquet of flowers for the centrepiece when Alice arrived home. During the bus ride, Alice had rehearsed her words, occasionally muttering them aloud and drawing curious glances from other passengers. Waiting for an interview date to be confirmed was pointless; Violet would likely see the letter first and it would only make matters more difficult if Alice hadn't already told her about it.

She crept into the dining room and took a seat at the

table, smoothing her skirt to give her trembling fingers something to do. 'Mother,' Alice began.

Violet picked up her scissors and snipped the bottom off a stem of lilacs, the petals quivering from the sudden motion.

'I went to Alderbrae today,' Alice continued, her voice steady despite the nervous flutter in her chest.

'I'm aware of that,' said Violet. She snipped another stem with sharp efficiency, and the discarded piece flew across the table, sliding to a halt in front of Alice.

Alice stared at it, momentarily thrown. She hadn't told Violet where she was going.

'Mrs Ferguson telephoned me,' Violet said coolly, adjusting a stem into place. 'She was wondering what on earth you were doing coming out of the WAAF recruitment office.'

Alice's mouth fell open. The room seemed to tilt slightly. She had rehearsed lots of possible responses from Violet, but she hadn't foreseen that George's mother might have seen her and jumped straight on the telephone to Violet.

'I...' Alice started, but she wasn't quite sure what she now wanted to say. Her fingers curled into the fabric of her skirt. 'What did you tell her?'

Violet set the scissors down for a moment and wiped her hands on a linen napkin. 'I told her that you were just making enquiries. That you were exploring the possibilities, but nothing had been decided yet.'

Alice let out a breath, her shoulders loosening. She'd expected her mother's first response to be "absolutely not", so this was better than anticipated.

'That's good,' Alice said quickly. 'I *was* just exploring the possibilities. The woman on the desk seemed certain I would get an interview, but who knows what will happen after that.'

Violet picked up another stem, snipping it with a finality that made Alice uneasy. 'Of course, you won't be going to any interview,' she said matter-of-factly, shaking loose petals into a pile.

Alice's eyebrows drew together. 'But you just said–'

'What was I supposed to say,' snapped Violet, cutting Alice off. She turned, planting both hands on the table. 'Was I supposed to tell Mrs Ferguson that I had no idea what my daughter was up to? She would love that, wouldn't she? She's still upset about George and his *divorcee* so she's looking for any opportunity to divert the gossip in someone else's direction.'

Alice shook her head incredulously. The other Mrs Ferguson had been more upset about George's choice of partner than she had been about his conscription. And it seemed that Violet was more upset about how Alice had made her look in front of Mrs Ferguson than she was about Alice applying to the WAAF behind her back.

'I'm sorry,' Alice said, her hands gripping the edge of the table. 'I'm sorry that I put you in that position with Mrs Ferguson, but I'm not sorry that I completed the application form. This will be good for me, Mother. If I get asked to attend an interview, I'm going, and I hope they see enough potential in me to give me a position.'

Violet's eyes widened in shock at Alice's outburst, and then quickly darkened with anger. 'Absolutely not, Alice!' she cried, setting down her scissors onto the table with a clatter.

There it was. The reaction Alice had expected.

'It's only a matter of time before single women get conscripted,' said Alice, repeating one of the arguments she had concocted on the bus. 'Isn't it better that I apply before conscription, so I have an element of choice over what I'll be doing?'

Violet let out a sharp breath, her fingers tightening around the stems she'd picked up. 'And whose fault is it you're a single woman?' asked Violet. 'If that's all this is about then I can find someone else for you, Alice. Then you won't have to worry about conscription at all.'

Alice scoffed, shaking her head. 'I'm not worried about conscription. At this point, I'd welcome it. I need something more in my life than marriage and babies.'

Violet blinked, her skin paling. 'You don't want to get married at all?' she asked, her voice quiet but sharp.

'Of course I do,' said Alice. 'But I want to marry someone I love.'

A long silence stretched between them. Then, Violet's gaze hardened. She straightened, smoothing out an imaginary crease in her apron. 'Is this about that vet?' she asked.

Alice felt her cheeks colour and she reached her hand forward to sweep the flower stems into a small pile to avoid her mother's questioning eye. 'It's about me,' she said.

Violet put the flowers into a glass vase already half-filled with water. 'Do you have any idea what you're doing?' Violet asked. 'The WAAF are based at RAF bases, which means you'll be putting yourself directly in harm's way. It's too dangerous. Your father would never allow it either.'

Alice took a deep breath, trying to calm her own anger. 'I'm not a child, Mother,' Alice replied, her voice firm. 'I understand the risks involved, but I am willing to take them for a chance to do something meaningful with my life.'

Violet's eyes softened and Alice thought she glimpsed a sliver of understanding. 'There's nothing more meaningful you can do than to raise a child,' said Violet.

Alice felt a pang of guilt. 'I didn't mean to suggest that marriage and babies was not meaningful. Of course it is. It's a perfectly valid choice. I just want to make a different choice, that's all. Right now, anyway.'

Tension crackled in the air between them. For once, Violet struggled to find the words to express herself. 'The war will end eventually, Alice, but the choices you make now will shape the rest of your life. There are other ways to support the war effort without putting yourself in danger.'

'I understand your concerns, Mother, but this is something I know I must do.'

Violet positioned the vase of lilac blooms in the centre of the dining table and straightened up. 'Do not expect me to support you in this reckless endeavour. If you go through with this, you'll be doing this against my wishes.'

Thunder growled in the distance and a shower of hailstones pelted against the dining room windows. Alice's shoulders dropped. She nodded slowly; her eyes filled with unshed tears. Violet spun on her heel and stormed out of the room, her footsteps pounding on the hardwood floors.

PART II

21

Alice woke up on the first day of WAAF training camp in her narrow metal bed with nineteen other women sleeping around her. She stared up at the barrack hut's corrugated iron ceiling thinking of the last conversation she'd had with her mother. Violet hadn't even been able to bring herself to wish Alice luck. She was scared, Alice understood that, but Alice was certain she'd made the right decision. Despite the nerves bouncing around in her stomach.

She rolled out of bed and smiled to the woman in the bed next to hers, wondering if she felt just as queasy. It was still dark and only a few of the women were awake. Alice padded to the washroom, another hut tacked onto the end of their sleeping quarters that had washbasins on one side of the wall and toilets on the other.

After a quick wash, Alice left the washroom and stopped dead in her tracks, distracted by the sight of one of the women in her barracks sitting on her bed, completely naked, and running her fingers through her wavy, chestnut brown hair. She felt her cheeks flush. The woman, seeing Alice's obvious embarrassment, laughed.

'Never seen anyone naked before, huh?' the woman said.

Another woman leaving the washroom bumped into Alice's back. 'Oh, I'm sorry,' she said.

'No, it's my fault,' said Alice, moving her feet again and clearing the doorway. She strode back to her bed, avoiding all eye contact.

The naked woman laughed again. 'Don't let me bother you, honey,' she said. 'I refuse to wear government issued underwear. It's bloody awful. And, besides, where I come from, plenty of folks walk around naked. It's no big deal. I'm Daphne, by the way.'

Alice looked back towards Daphne and offered her a sheepish smile. 'I'm Alice,' she said.

'What kind of place has people just wandering around naked?' one of the other women asked.

'Probably best not to say,' Daphne said, her grin faltering slightly. 'I'm here for a fresh start.'

'That's why I'm here, too,' said another woman.

'Why? Did you also have a job that required you to take your clothes off?' The judgement was clear by the woman's tone.

'No. The fresh start. The WAAF offered me accommodation and an income of my own. I left my fiancé after I caught him with another woman.'

There was a collective gasp around the barrack hut.

'Good for you,' one of the others said. 'You made the right decision. If he can't control himself before the wedding, he's not likely to control himself afterwards either.'

'That's exactly what I thought.'

'Well, I'm here to do my bit for our country,' someone said.

Everyone turned in the direction of the voice. A young blonde woman was perched on the end of her immaculately made bed with her legs crossed and her delicate hands clasped in her lap. 'I'm Betty,' she said.

Daphne cleared her throat and stood up. 'No one is here to serve their country,' she said, strolling, still naked, towards the washroom.

'I am,' Betty insisted. 'My father and brothers are all serving in the RAF. They're doing their bit, and I wanted to do my bit, too.'

'Honey,' said Daphne. 'Every single one of us in here is running from something or chasing something. You included.'

Betty opened her mouth as if to argue further, but Daphne slipped into the washroom and the conversation was over. The hut was silent, and Alice turned to face the wall, dressing with as much modesty as she could manage. Daphne was right, at least where Alice was concerned. Being given the opportunity to contribute directly to the war effort felt good, but there were so many other reasons that had driven her into the recruitment office the day she'd applied.

Alice tucked her shirt into the regulation shorts they'd been issued for Physical Training, the fabric still stiff from being new. A small smile played on her lips as she imagined what she must look like. If her mother could see her now, she would purse her lips and arch an eyebrow in that disapproving way of hers. The memory of their last conversation lingered. Violet had barely managed a stiff farewell, any words of encouragement noticeably absent. Taking a deep breath, Alice turned back around, ready to face the challenges of her first PT session.

Daphne had returned and was finally dressed. She snapped the waistband of her shorts. 'Passion killers, right?' she said.

Alice smiled as her thoughts drifted to Tom. Their relationship hadn't even begun, but saying goodbye to him had still been agony.

Her thoughts were cut short as the door to their barrack hut swung open.

The officer responsible for their day-to-day discipline and training, WAAF Sergeant Atkinson, marched in, her uniform pristine and her face serious. 'Alright, recruits, who's ready for PT?' she bellowed.

'Me,' replied Betty, springing up from her bed and looking far too enthusiastic for six o'clock in the morning.

By the afternoon, Alice felt foolish for having dressed facing the wall that morning. She'd just come back from her medical inspection, which had required all the women to strip naked in front of each other as they were marched between curtain spaces for all manner of tests and examinations. By the end of that first morning, the women knew each other more intimately than they ever would have imagined.

'We're lucky to have a washroom joined onto our barracks, you know?' Betty announced.

When no one else spoke, Alice scanned the barracks and saw Betty shifting uncomfortably beside her bed, already fully dressed in her uniform. She fidgeted with her hat, leaving it sitting at an odd angle on her head.

'Is that so,' Alice finally said to Betty's obvious relief.

Alice scanned her own uniform as best she could with no mirror. A dull, dark smudge marring the shine of her right shoe caught her eye. Bending down, she rubbed the spot vigorously with her thumb to restore the shoe's glossy finish.

'I have several friends who have already completed their training,' said Betty, focusing now entirely on Alice. 'They all warned me that the ablutions were not private and usually involved a trek outside to even get there. Sometimes past the barracks of the airmen.'

'I bet Daphne would still make her way there in the buff,' one of the other women added.

Everyone laughed, Daphne included.

After a hearty lunch, Alice and her fellow trainees headed outside to the gas room for their first gas drill, an exercise they were all dreading. Alice stared at the small brick building, breathing deeply to take in fresh air while she could.

Sergeant Atkinson stood in front of the building. 'This exercise will prepare you to work effectively in the event of a chemical attack,' she said. 'You will be locked in the gas room, your gas mask on the floor in front of you. When you hear the gas being pumped in, pick up your mask and fit it correctly to avoid being overcome by the gas. Once everyone in your group has successfully fitted their gas masks, remove your masks and wait until the door has been opened for you.'

Alice suddenly felt queasy and regretted having eaten as much as she did at lunch.

When the recruits were divided into their teams,

Sergeant Atkinson gave the command to begin. Alice stepped forward and opened the door to the gas room. She and five others stepped inside and put their masks on the floor.

Sergeant Atkinson slammed the door shut behind them. Alice squinted as her eyes adjusted to the dim light. When she heard the hiss of gas, she focused only on getting her gas mask on, securing it around her face and sucking in a deep breath as she watched the others fit their masks. When the time came to remove the mask, Alice held her breath for as long as she could. She'd heard of others stumbling out of the building with their eyes streaming and coughing to the point of falling over. Alice stood as tall as she could, her chest burning and tears stinging her eyes. Daphne stood opposite her and they locked eyes, silently urging each other to stay strong.

It was a relief when daylight flooded into the gas room and the trainees all stumbled out into the fresh air. Alice tossed her gas mask to the grass, her breath heaving in her chest. She sucked in clean air and wiped her hands across her eyes, now streaming with tears. If the point of the exercise was to extol the benefits of a gas mask, then lesson learned. She leaned forward and placed her hands on her knees, taking one ragged breath after the other.

Once she was able to stand, she looked around at her fellow recruits. Some were upright, others were still hunched over trying to find their breath.

After they'd learned how to decontaminate themselves and their equipment, they walked back towards their barracks in silence, everyone stunned and throats too raw to speak. Alice glanced over at another group of recruits huddled around a metal barrel. Flames erupted from the top of the container, while plumes of smoke lingered at head height, drifting slowly around the group as though pressed by an invisible force from above. One of the women waved the smoke away from her face with her hand. Alice glanced towards the sky.

'Looks like it'll be wet for PT tomorrow,' she said.

Her fellow recruits groaned.

22

ALICE WOKE TO THE SOUND OF RAIN PELTING AGAINST THE windows of her sleeping hut. The women dressed and made their beds. They knew the routine by now. Each bed had three thin mattresses. Biscuits, they were called, for reasons Alice hadn't quite figured out yet. Every morning, they had to fold them in half and stack them neatly at the foot of their bed frame. Their scratchy blue blankets and sheets were to be neatly folded and tucked around the biscuits.

By the time Sergeant Atkinson came in, they were all already standing at the ends of their immaculate beds ready for inspection.

As Atkinson made her way down the narrow aisle of the hut, Alice glanced down to double-check her bed. Something creamy white caught her eye. Her pulse quickened as she recognised the corner of Tom's last letter to her. She'd read it in bed and only now realised that she hadn't put it away before she'd gone to sleep.

Sergeant Atkinson's heavy boots clomped closer. Alice wondered if she had time to reach down and whip the letter away. She drew in a breath, but it was too late, Atkinson stepped towards her.

'Do you have a problem, Peters?' Sergeant Atkinson asked.

Alice snapped her head up. 'No, ma'am.'

Atkinson's sharp gaze swept the length of Alice's bed, settling on the paper poking out.

'It seems the whole of D Hut has a problem,' said Atkinson. With a swift motion, she plucked the letter free. 'This is a demerit. For everyone.'

She let the words hang in the air as the other women exchanged glances. No one dared to groan out loud, but Alice felt everyone's disappointment.

Atkinson handed her the letter and moved on to the next bed.

She stopped in front of Betty. Alice turned her head just a fraction to see Betty's cheeks colouring scarlet as Atkinson shook her head.

'Is that crease supposed to be there?' Atkinson asked.

Betty shook her head. 'No, ma'am. Sorry, ma'am.'

'Another demerit,' Atkinson barked, causing Betty to jump. 'Day two and two sanctions. Not good, D Hut. Not good at all.'

Inspection over and a collective exhale rippled through the women as they left their hut and made their way to PT.

Alice stepped out into the rain, her boots already sinking into the mud. It was not a good day for the physical training obstacle course.

'I'm sorry about that,' Betty said to the group as they walked.

'Me too,' Alice added.

A few of the women offered small hesitant smiles, but no one spoke.

Betty sidled up to Alice, as if seeking comfort from the other person who had let the side down.

Alice smiled. 'We'll do better tomorrow.'

Betty brushed rain from her forehead, her blonde hair plastered to her scalp. 'It was just so hard to drag myself out of bed this morning that I didn't leave myself enough time.'

Alice stepped into a puddle and cold water gushed through to her ankle, drenching her sock. 'Blame the gas exercise yesterday. We're all exhausted.'

Betty nudged her. 'Who was your letter from?'

Alice smiled. 'Tom.'

Betty grinned. 'Your boyfriend?'

'Sort of,' said Alice. They arrived at the obstacle course. 'It's a long story. I'll tell you later.'

Alice fell into line at the start of the muddy obstacle course, back straight, heart pounding. She took a deep breath.

Sergeant Holmes led their PT sessions. He towered over all the women as he walked along the line of recruits, his lips curled into a sneer. If he was trying to intimidate them, he was succeeding. Raindrops landed on Alice's eyelashes, and she blinked them away. Any second now, she'd have to dive onto the sopping ground and crawl her way out from beneath the heavy net in front of her. She looked to the girls either side of her.

'We can do this,' she said, trying to quell the butterflies in her stomach.

'Easy,' said Daphne, her tone carrying her usual breezy confidence.

On the other side of Alice, Betty fidgeted with the hem of her shorts, looking decidedly less certain. 'If it makes you feel any better,' she said, attempting a half-hearted smile 'I already know I'll be awful at this, so you definitely won't come last.'

'Is it a race?' asked Alice, glancing between the two of them.

Before anyone could answer, a whistle sounded, and Alice propelled herself forward. The net lay ahead of her. As she reached it, she threw herself to the ground and pulled the net up and over her head. She crawled, each movement a struggle as she slipped on the muddy ground, her arms ensnared in the ropes.

Rain hammered down on her back, tempting her to quit, but something inside her refused to surrender. She forced herself forward, inch by agonising inch.

Finally, after what felt like an eternity, Alice crawled out from under the net, covered in mud and struggling to catch her breath. But her challenge wasn't over. She sprinted towards the climbing wall, grabbed a rope, and heaved herself upwards. She quickly reached the top and hoisted herself over the wall, feeling a rush of exhilaration as she landed on the other side.

With every obstacle conquered, Alice reached the finish line, exhausted, muddy, and soaked through to her skin, but beaming. Daphne had already completed the course and was sat on the wet ground, a broad smile on her face.

Alice sank down beside her.

An anguished squeal drew Alice's attention, and she turned to see Betty crawling on her hands and knees towards the finish line. Her face was contorted with effort, and her limbs trembling with exhaustion, yet she pressed on.

'Nearly there, Betty,' Alice called out.

As she crossed the line, Betty allowed her weary body to

collapse, her cheek landing on the muddy grass, a mixture of defeat and relief washing over her features.

Daphne clapped her hands together. 'Don't you just feel so alive?' she asked.

'No,' said Betty. 'No, I don't.'

Alice reached out and gently patted Betty on the arm. 'Well done,' she said. 'We all made it.'

When their breaths came more easily, Alice, Daphne, and Betty hauled themselves to their feet. Alice's muscles protested at the movement, and she was already dreading the next day ache.

'Not bad for a first attempt, ladies,' said Sergeant Holmes, surveying the group with satisfaction. 'This challenge was both physically and mentally tough, and I'm pleased you all completed it. Go and get cleaned up, and I'll see you again tomorrow.'

Betty groaned. 'Seriously? Do we have to do this every day?' she muttered under her breath.

Daphne laughed. 'Sounds like someone is regretting keeping up with the Jones's.'

Betty wiped her dirty hands down her shorts as they walked towards their barracks. 'What's that supposed to mean?' she asked.

'That's why you're here, isn't it?' Daphne put an arm around Betty's shoulders and gave her an affectionate squeeze. 'Your friends have already signed up and you felt left out, so here you are.'

'That's not true, at all,' Betty insisted.

Daphne smiled. 'Oh no, then why are you here?'

'I...' Betty glanced around as if checking for anyone eavesdropping on their conversation. She crossed her arms and let out a sharp sigh. 'OK, fine. Everyone is saying that single women are going to be conscripted, and I didn't want to have to work in the fields.'

Alice and Daphne looked at each and then, unable to help themselves, erupted into a fit of laughter.

Betty's cheeks flushed. 'Why is that funny?'

Daphne had tears streaking down the mud on her face. 'You're here because you were scared they'd make you become a land girl?'

Betty stopped walking and put her hands on her hips. 'Yes,' she said more defiantly. 'Look at me. I'm not built for the outdoors. Making my own bed is apparently a challenge.'

'Aircraftwoman Peters!'

Hearing her name, Alice turned to see Sergeant Atkinson striding towards her, boots splashing through shallow puddles. Alice straightened up, brushing damp strands of hair from her forehead. She raised her hand in a crisp salute, tempering the pride she felt at having a formal title that was something other than Miss Peters.

'Yes, Sergeant,' said Alice.

'It looks like you successfully predicted today's rain,' said Atkinson, brushing droplets from her sleeve. 'What made you so certain it would rain?'

Alice hesitated, shifting her weight. 'Oh,' she said, feeling heat in her cheeks despite the cold. 'It was just a silly thing.'

Atkinson's expression didn't waver. 'There's nothing silly about the weather Aircraftwoman Peters.'

'No, Sergeant,' said Alice quickly. 'I didn't mean to suggest there was.'

'Then tell me, how did you know it would rain?'

Alice swallowed. 'The smoke from the fire,' she said, aware of Betty and Daphne staring at her. 'Smoke reacts differently depending on atmospheric pressure and moisture levels.'

'And?' asked Atkinson.

'Well, I noticed that the smoke from the container fire hung close to the ground. I'm not exactly sure about the science of it all. One theory is that smoke absorbs moisture in the air making it denser, thus weighing it down. And if there's moisture in the air, that means low atmospheric pressure, which typically brings rain.'

Atkinson studied her. Something shifted in her expression, but Alice couldn't decipher what it meant. 'Report to the Squadron Officer at 1500 hours.'

Alice stiffened. 'Yes, Sergeant. May I ask why, Sergeant?'

Atkinson's mouth twitched. 'Just be there,' she said, before striding away.

Betty exhaled. 'What was that about?'

Alice watched Atkinson's retreating figure disappear into the distance, her heart pounding in her chest. 'I've no idea,' she murmured, her voice barely above a whisper. The Squadron Officer oversaw the entire camp, and Alice's mind raced with possibilities. She bit her lip. 'Do you think I'm in trouble?'

Betty shook her head. 'I don't think so.'

'No,' said Daphne. 'Atkinson wasn't criticising you for anything. She looked quite impressed, actually.'

'I thought so, too,' Betty agreed.

'How do you know about atmospheric pressure?' Daphne asked as they continued walking to the barracks.

Alice smiled. 'Mrs Ferguson. A farmer friend in Millwood. She always seemed to know what the weather was about to do, so I asked her to teach me.'

Daphne stomped into a muddy puddle, splattering them

all with cold water. 'Come on then, Weather Watcher. Please tell me it's going to be dry tomorrow.'

23

It seemed predicting the rain during her training had been enough to get Alice noticed and a prized slot on the next available training programme at the Meteorology Training School, something Alice hadn't even known existed. After completing her WAAF training, Alice arrived in Dunstable, a small estate about thirty-five miles from London and surrounded by a tall, barbed wire fence.

Meteorology training took place at numerous RAF bases across the country, so Alice felt a thrill of privilege at being assigned to Dunstable – the heart of the Met Office's Central Forecasting Office. She couldn't wait to get started. She also couldn't wait to get out of the rain.

A stern-faced guard at the security entrance waved her through. She was directed to a low wooden building draped in layers of camouflage netting. Stepping inside was like being transported back to the bustling chaos of London Paddington the day Alice had arrived on the train. Streams of people, some in civilian clothes, others in neatly pressed uniforms, weaved their way around in all directions, leaving Alice standing awkwardly in the middle looking lost.

She wiped her hands down her air force blue uniform to brush away raindrops still clinging to the fabric. A woman in a plain grey skirt and crisp white shirt approached her. She held a clipboard against her chest and exuded an air of efficiency. 'Are you here for Met training?' she asked, her voice cutting through the din of people marching around.

Alice nodded. 'I guess I stand out.'

The woman smiled. 'Name, please?'

'Aircraftwoman Alice Peters.'

Alice smiled. It still gave her a buzz that she had a title.

The woman scanned down the list on her clipboard and ticked off Alice's name. 'Uniform inspection is outside in five minutes,' she said. 'Afterwards, report to room four. Just down that corridor over there.'

'Thank you,' said Alice. She straightened the collar of her uniform and tucked a loose strand of hair behind her ear. She knew that meteorology was under RAF command, but she'd somehow expected it to be less formal than her initial air force training.

Outside, Alice shivered against the cold. A military car rumbled past her, its tyres splashing through puddles on the wet road. Nearby, a cluster of WAAF women stood together. Alice tugged the bottom of her jacket down and approached the group. Her gaze settled on a petite woman with striking fiery red hair, who was wrestling with her cap, trying to tuck rebellious curls beneath it.

The woman huffed out a breath and finally yanked the cap off her head, curls bouncing free.

'Can I help?' Alice asked, stepping forward with a tentative smile.

The woman returned the smile and handed Alice her cap. 'Could you hold this for me, please? This drizzly rain is a nightmare for us curly-haired girls.'

Alice held the cap, watching as the woman slid metal pins through her hair to clamp her curls against her head with practiced precision.

'Thanks,' the woman said, extending her hand to retrieve her cap. 'I'm Iris, by the way.'

Alice returned the cap. 'I'm Alice. Are you here for meteorology training too?'

Iris nodded. 'For my sins. I applied to be a wireless operator, but here I am. What about you? Did you choose this?'

Alice shook her head. 'It was suggested to me, but honestly, I'm excited to be here. I find the weather fascinating.'

Iris grinned and took a step closer, linking her arm through Alice's. 'In that case, I have a feeling you and I are going to be great friends. I'll need all the help I can get.'

Alice laughed, feeling the warmth of burgeoning friendship spread through her despite the cold.

Their conversation was interrupted by a stern-faced flight sergeant who stepped out of the building and called the women to attention.

'Ladies, welcome to the Meteorology Training School.' Her voice was firm yet kind, her features softening once the women were in formation. 'I am Flight Sergeant Mackie. You are here because the Royal Air Force needs the brightest minds to forecast the weather.'

Flight Sergeant Mackie paced up and down the now

neat row of women giving a rundown of what they should expect over the next six weeks. The winter air was crisp and carried the scent of damp earth and engine fuel from the adjacent airfield. Despite the chill, Alice felt a surge of excitement at just being here. She had already proven herself capable and disciplined. Now she was on the brink of something even more significant. Mrs Ferguson's words replayed in her mind: *If you want to know the weather now, look out of the window. The value is always in predicting what the weather will do next.*

'There's a reason why wartime weather forecasts are classified,' said Flight Sergeant Mackie. 'Weather can determine whether a mission succeeds or fails. It can decide if the Nazis cross the Channel or not. Accurate forecasts are essential.'

The rest of Mackie's speech was drowned out as Alice felt a knot tighten in her stomach. She hadn't truly grasped what was at stake until now. Her eyes flickered nervously to the other women standing in formation. Iris was beside her, her back straight and chin held high. She exuded an air of confidence that Alice couldn't quite muster.

In an attempt to project the same composed demeanour, Alice took a deep breath, squared her shoulders, and anchored her gaze to the control tower in front of her. The stakes were high, but she'd made it this far. She just had to stay focused and learn everything she possibly could about the weather while at Dunstable.

After their welcome and uniform inspection, Alice and Iris made their way down the corridor towards room four as instructed. Their fellow trainees streamed in ahead of them just as the door opposite opened. A man marched out and Alice stepped aside to let him past. The door swung closed behind him, but it didn't shut fully. Alice heard the thrum of machinery inside and stepped forward to peer through the gap.

Rows of machines were lined up, like typewriters only larger and seemingly operating on their own. Alice had never seen anything like it. The din was like twenty high speed typists all working simultaneously. Overseeing it all were a dozen women, loading paper into the machines, or pulling out paper with newly received data.

'Teleprinters,' whispered Iris, looking through the door. 'They receive data from all over the country.'

Alice's view was obscured by a woman in the room stepping towards the door. She gave Alice a small smile and then closed the door.

'Fascinating, isn't it?' said Iris, her eyes sparkling.

They turned and headed into room four. Maps, weather charts, and coded synoptic symbols dominated the walls – a complex language of numbers and letters Alice barely recognised. The air smelled of chalk dust and damp fabric, a sign that the room had seen many trainees before her.

They slipped into two empty desks near the front and Alice pulled out her notebook and pen before tucking her bag beneath her chair. Around them, other WAAF recruits murmured, some exchanging nervous glances, others already flipping through thick manuals filled with incomprehensible equations.

The door burst open, and a group of RAF men strode in, their presence a whirlwind of boisterous energy and the sharp scent of cologne.

One of them, grinning with an easy confidence, swept

his gaze across the room. His smirk widened. 'Oh, I think I'm going to like this class,' he said.

Iris rolled her eyes.

'Pity you have a girlfriend back home, Harding,' another airman said, elbowing him before shoving him towards an empty table across the aisle from Alice. The men chuckled, their camaraderie easy and unbothered as they continued to joke around.

Alice picked up her pen, twirling it between her fingers.

'Hey, you,' said Harding.

Alice turned to find the cocky young airman staring at her. He ran a hand through his dark hair and flicked his gaze to her hands. Alice placed her pen on the table.

'No need to be nervous,' said Harding. 'We've got the hard job. You're just a secretary in a uniform.'

The sharp stomp of approaching boots silenced the room, leaving Alice no time to respond. It was probably just as well. She had no idea what to say to that. The men snapped to attention. Alice, uncertain but instinctively following their lead, scrambled to her feet.

The man who entered stopped at the front of the room and turned to face them all. He stood tall in his crisp RAF uniform, the fabric immaculately pressed and gleaming slightly at the sleeves. Three narrow, sky-blue stripes circled the cuffs of his sleeves, unmistakable markers of his rank. But it was his face that truly commanded attention. A thick wiry moustache arched above his upper lip, with a pair of bushy white eyebrows that framed eyes so sharp and calculating they looked like they'd miss nothing.

'Good morning,' he said, his voice like a boom of thunder. 'I'm Squadron Leader Davies.' He paused, his gaze swept across them. 'Ladies,' he bellowed, 'this is not a finishing school.'

A low hum of laughter rose from the men, but one sharp glance from Davies snuffed it out instantly.

'You are here because we need every able body in the air and on the ground. But let me make one thing clear. We do not lower our standards. If you don't meet the grade, you won't pass. It's as simple as that.'

Alice swallowed hard, suddenly regretting her position at the front of the classroom.

'I suspect a few girls won't last the morning,' someone said. It was Harding, of course. He caught Alice's eye and winked at her.

Alice looked towards Davies, expecting him to quickly admonish Harding. Instead, Davies turned sharply, pointing to a large poster behind him, filled with rows of cryptic weather codes. 'These symbols dictate what you record, when you record it, and how it is reported. Memorise them.'

If Davies wasn't going to put Harding in his place, then she might have to. She couldn't spend the next six weeks with Harding making jibes at her expense. She thought of Violet and Mrs Ferguson. Both would know exactly how to deal with such a person. But she'd think about that later. For now, she was here to learn.

She twisted in her seat, turning away from Harding. Her eyes locked onto the columns of letters and numbers sprawled across the poster that Davies stood beside: III CL CM WW VhNh.... The list went on and on, some letters sitting on the line, others beneath it, forming a pattern that made no immediate sense.

'By now, you will be aware that weather forecasts are classified,' Davies continued. 'That means you must learn to code every observation you make. We cannot risk the Germans intercepting our weather data. Accuracy is not optional. Timely reports are not a courtesy.'

He let the weight of his next words hang heavy in the air. 'A single miscalculation could cost lives.'

Alice's pulse kicked up a notch. The walls of the room suddenly felt closer, the air thicker. She had been so sure of herself before arriving, naively believing she already knew a thing or two about meteorology. Now, with another language plastered around the walls and the pressure of life-or-death calculations looming over her, she wasn't sure of anything at all.

Three hours later, Alice found herself squinting as sunlight streamed through the classroom window. She glanced up at the clock. Ten past eleven.

She raised her hand.

'Yes?' asked Davies.

'Sir, the saying rain before seven, fine by eleven seems to be more accurate than not. What's the science there?'

Davies snorted. 'Miss...?'

'Peters,' Alice added.

'Miss Peters, your job is to gather data. Leave the interpretation of that data to the Met Office forecasters,' he snapped.

He moved on, gravitating towards the airmen on the other side of the room. Harding caught her eye and smirked. He glanced towards Davies as if checking he was out of earshot and then leaned across his desk in Alice's direction.

'Best keep those old wives' tales to yourself or you'll become the class clown,' mumbled Harding.

'I wouldn't want to knock you off your perch,' Alice whispered back.

Harding's grin faltered ever so slightly then his smirk

reappeared. It was a low blow, and so unlike her, but she was determined to learn as much as she could during her training, and she wasn't going to let a man make her feel incapable just because he flew planes, and she didn't. She squinted again towards the sunlit window. Besides, she thought, an old wives' tale or not, the rhyme had proven itself correct. Again.

24

———

AFTER A FULL MORNING OF THEORY WITH SQUADRON LEADER Davies and a quick lunch, Alice and Iris made their way to another classroom. Harding and two of his airmen colleagues lingered in the hallway.

'My cousin is a pilot,' said Iris, as they slipped past the men and entered the room. 'They should only be here for a week or two and then they move on to flight school.'

Alice smiled. 'I can't say I'll be sorry to see them go.'

Inside, Alice glanced around her. This lesson promised more hands-on training. She perched on a stool around one of the six large wooden tables that he been pushed together. At the centre was a white slatted box. The door on the front of the box was open revealing an array of weather instruments inside. Iris sat beside her.

'So far, coding's my favourite,' said Iris.

Alice laid her notebook in front of her. Her gaze settled on the barometer inside the white wooden box. 'I think I'm going to like this class best.'

She scanned through the notes she had made that morning, her gaze drifting down the neat lists of abbreviations and their meanings. Coding was *not* Alice's favourite. She pressed her fingers to her temples, massaging the dull ache that had settled there.

Sunshine streamed in the large windows bringing a comforting heat to the afternoon. She closed her eyes.

Someone took the stool beside her, nudging her arm as they sat down. She looked up to see Harding grinning beside her.

'Pilot Officer Harding,' he said.

'Aircraftwoman Peters,' replied Alice.

Harding laughed. 'If you say so,' he said, glancing at his friends as if checking to make sure he had an audience.

Alice turned back to her notes, refusing to participate in Harding's show.

She had hoped he'd leave her alone now that she had shown she could stand up for herself, but he leaned closer and tapped a finger to her notebook.

'I hope you're not expecting the weather to behave just because you wrote it down nicely,' he said.

Alice closed her notebook. 'I hope you're not expecting to learn about the weather just because you're loud,' she said.

This earned a laugh from Harding's friends.

'I'm a pilot,' Harding declared, his voice dripping with sarcasm. 'I don't need to learn about the weather.' His words were laced with a mocking confidence, as if the very idea of studying atmospheric conditions was beneath him.

Alice turned to Iris beside her. 'I don't know what's wrong with me,' she whispered. 'I'm not usually so rude.'

Iris shook her head. 'He's the rude one.'

Harding leaned over the desk and picked up a ther-mometer, spinning it around like a cowboy spins his gun in the movies.

A delicate hand reached out and plucked the thermometer out of Harding's grip.

'Good afternoon, aircraftwomen and pilot officers,' said a woman in a sharp uniform, the thermometer resting in her open palm. Alice recognised her at once, the same flight sergeant who had inspected the women's uniforms that morning and given them an overview of what to expect during training.

'For those of you who don't know me, my name is Flight Sergeant Mackie, and it's my job to teach you how to handle these weather instruments to ensure accurate ground level forecasts. And why is accurate forecasting essential to the RAF?'

'No one likes a bumpy landing,' said Harding, his trademark smirk on his face.

Mackie placed the thermometer carefully on the table and strode to the front of the room. 'Weather reports are the backbone of every RAF operational briefing,' she said. 'The success of every training flight, every sortie, and every critical mission both at home and abroad depends on knowing the weather. It's not enough to merely understand the weather at take-off. The RAF must know the atmospheric conditions at thirty thousand feet, spanning the entire flight path, *and* upon landing eight hours later. For the pilots in the room questioning your presence here, let me be clear, if the weather forecaster predicts treacherous conditions, your aircraft is grounded. The data from these instruments, gathered by meteorology assistants, and interpreted by highly skilled forecasters, is the razor-thin line between a bumpy landing and an operational catastrophe that ends with your aircraft plunging into the icy depths of the North Sea, never to return home.'

Alice was transfixed, watching as Mackie silenced the men and commanded the room.

'Now,' said Mackie. 'Who can tell me what the box in the centre of the table is called?'

Alice raised her hand.

'A Stevenson Screen,' said Harding.

'Very good,' said Mackie.

Alice put her hand down, feeling like a child in school.

Harding smirked and Alice turned away, her face as straight as she could muster in the probably pointless hope of showing Harding he wasn't getting to her.

Mackie stepped between Alice and Harding. 'Everyone gather round,' she instructed. 'We're going to get hands on with these instruments.'

Mackie pushed a small metal and glass case into the centre of the table.

She tapped the side of the box with her knuckles. 'This,' she said, 'is a thermo-hygrograph. It records two of the most critical atmospheric readings: temperature and relative humidity.'

She opened the casing to reveal a rotating drum wrapped in graph paper, its slow turn driven by a clockwork mechanism.

'It's not enough to know what the air feels like now,' Mackie continued. 'We need to know how it's changing. Is fog building? Is a cold front moving in? Is humidity rising? This pen here tracks temperature. This one, humidity.'

Alice leaned in to examine the fine, oscillating lines. The pens quivered, as if alive with secrets. She sketched a rough image of the thermo-hygrograph as Mackie talked them through how to read the instrument. Alice was enthralled by the technology. She hung on Flight Sergeant Mackie's every word. This was why she was here. This is what mattered. Not Harding's distracting nonsense.

Once everyone had taken a turn setting and reading the thermo-hygrograph, Mackie showed them how to change the graph paper and replace the ink for the delicate pens.

Mackie looked over the group and tapped the box again. 'This is operational intelligence. If the temperature drops and the humidity climbs, what happens?'

'Fog?' Alice suggested, uncertainty in her voice.

'Yes,' said Mackie. 'Fog. Fog on the runway can ground flights and affect visibility. Any reduced visibility can obscure bombing targets, hamper visual navigation, or prevent safe landings. And cold, moist air can freeze on aircraft surfaces, causing instrument failure or even kill the engine mid-flight. Your meteorologists don't just report the weather. They predict it. And to do that, they need every scrap of data you can give them. It must be accurate, timely, and well-understood.'

Mackie stepped back from the table and allowed the trainees a few minutes to complete their notetaking.

Alice finished writing and read through her notes. Something Mackie had said replayed in her mind. *Every scrap of data.*

Hoping Mackie was more openminded than Squadron Leader Davies, Alice turned to her.

'Can I ask something, Flight Sergeant Mackie?' Alice kept her voice low. She wanted to know everything she could about meteorology, but she didn't want to be a continual target for Harding's ridicule.

'Of course,' said Mackie.

'Is there any truth to the saying *rain before seven, fine by eleven*?'

Harding leaned around Mackie and shot Alice a grin.

'You're not letting that one go, are you? Didn't Davies already tell you to keep your old wives' tales to yourself?'

Alice's cheeks flushed.

Iris leaned around her, her mouth set in a sharp line. 'Actually, I think *you* said that.'

She could have let it go, but she was here to learn. Mrs Ferguson had taught her so many forecasting techniques. They weren't based on charts or instruments, but rather instinct and theories. And more often than not, they were right. There had to be some truth behind them.

Mackie cleared her throat and stepped back from the large table. 'Predicting the weather is a science,' she said.

Harding sat up straighter on his stool, a self-satisfied smirk playing on his lips. Alice braced herself for another dismissal, like the one Davies had given her.

'However,' Mackie continued, 'like any science, we don't yet have all the answers. Perhaps we never will. Today's meteorologists build on the knowledge of sailors and farmers who, for centuries, have predicted the weather without the aid of weather instruments and mathematical equations. They relied on their instincts, and insights handed down through the generations. Science is, in a sense, playing catch up to folklore.'

Harding exhaled sharply, a dismissive breath escaping his lips like a gust of wind, carrying with it an air of impatience and indifference.

'Let's look at some elements of folklore and what the science tells us,' said Mackie. 'Aircraftwoman Peters, you asked me a question. Can you please repeat it for the class?'

Alice glanced around her, her cheeks still warm. 'I asked if there was any truth to the rhyme, rain before seven, fine by eleven.'

'Rain before seven, fine by eleven,' repeated Mackie as

she walked towards the windows. 'The early risers among you may have noticed that it was indeed raining before seven this morning. Did anyone notice what time the rain stopped?'

Harding nudged Alice, but she sat on her hands and stayed silent.

'Come on,' said Mackie. 'You're here to become weather watchers. Someone must have been paying attention.'

'Peters noticed,' said Harding.

'Aircraftwoman Peters?' prompted Mackie.

Alice fidgeted with her pen and fought the urge to shrink into herself and disappear from the glare of her classmates. Mackie stared at her expectantly and Alice had no choice but to fill the awkward silence. 'I didn't notice what time the rain stopped,' she said. 'But I did notice that the sun was shining at ten past eleven.'

'Thus, proving the rhyme,' said Mackie.

'Does it prove it though?' asked Harding. 'If I said it would rain at five o'clock, sometimes I would be right and sometimes I would be wrong.'

'Exactly,' said Mackie. 'For folklore to be useful, it must be right more often than it's wrong. So, let's look at the science. Where does our weather come from?'

Alice picked up her pen and flicked to a fresh page in her notebook. She felt her body drift forward, ready to absorb everything Mackie was about to share.

'Most of the United Kingdom's weather comes from the Atlantic Ocean,' said Mackie, moving from the window to a large map pinned to the wall. She hovered her hand over the Atlantic and swept her hand across the United Kingdom. 'A low-pressure front can sweep its way across the country in four hours. And low pressure brings rain.'

Everyone was silent, even Harding seemed to be paying attention for once.

'So, this rhyme is probably right more often than it's wrong,' Mackie continued. 'But there are many variables. Wind speed, as an example, can influence how long a weather front hangs around. Accurate forecasts don't rely on one story or one instrument or one reading. Forecasters will look at everything they have available to them and start from there. What other weather folklore stories have you heard?' asked Mackie.

Iris cleared her throat and chimed in. 'I heard that frogs can be heard croaking before a storm.'

Mackie nodded her head. 'Frogs croak before a soak. I've heard that one. Animals generally have excellent weather instincts. Frogs mate and lay eggs in bodies of freshwater, so it makes sense that they like the rain. Can they predict rain before it falls though? Not that I've ever noticed.'

The pilot next to Harding leaned forward, his elbows resting on the large desk. 'I don't know about frogs,' he said, 'but I do know that a mackerel sky means I'm probably not flying home in the same weather conditions as those I took off in.'

'Ah yes,' said Mackie. 'The beautiful altocumulus clouds. Sometimes called a mackerel sky because the rippling pattern of the clouds resemble the scales of a fish.'

Alice wrote down the word "altocumulus", adding "mackerel sky" beneath it. She sketched a few neat lines of rippled clouds. She'd been studying clouds patterns for months, focusing on their appearance and the weather that came with them. Now, she would also know their names.

'Altocumulus clouds are a sign of moisture in the air,' said Mackie. 'For the pilot at least. Weather on the ground can be stable, but the pilot will have to fly through that moisture at some point. Part of a meteorology assistant's duties is to observe clouds and take notes on the types, height, and quantity. I think this is a good time to head outside and look up.'

Alice closed her notebook and sprang up from her stool. Harding gave her a look, but she chose to ignore him. This was the most excitement she'd had in training yet, and she wasn't about to let a pilot with a superiority complex dampen her experience.

25

––––––––

If Alice ended her first day on a high, she was slammed back down to earth on day two by Squadron Leader Davies. The chalk dust hung in the air as Davies outlined a series of weather readings and observations on the blackboard – pressure systems, wind speeds, cloud formations, and temperature gradients – all noted in his neat, precise handwriting. His task for the trainees: craft a written weather forecast based on this data with appropriate recommendations for your pilots.

Alice stared at the data long after her fellow recruits started jotting down their thoughts. The winds were fierce and the low-pressure system was certain to bring rain. Her instincts were to ground all flights. But this was British weather. If flights were grounded by wind and rain, they would seldom take off. And she expected that waiting for the perfect flying conditions was a luxury that couldn't be indulged during war.

So, she composed a comprehensive weather report based on the data presented. She guessed that the strong winds would blow the low pressure clear within four hours and recommended that only experienced pilots be chosen for essential operations. Her recommendations felt naive and inadequate at best, but on day two of her training, it was the best she felt she could do.

Now, with a stern expression, Squadron Leader Davies paced the classroom, handing back their efforts with sharp critiques.

'Nowhere close,' he said, tossing a paper onto Iris's desk. Iris's face flushed with embarrassment as she quickly snatched up the paper.

Alice took a deep breath, her fingers tapping nervously on the wooden desk, and waited for her turn.

Davies stopped in front of her, his shadow looming over her as he dropped her paper onto the desk. A thick black line slashed diagonally across the page, like a wound. 'If you send your pilots out in that weather, Miss Peters, you'll be lucky if half of them make it back,' he said, his voice cutting through the tension in the room.

He moved on, handing Harding's completed paper back without a word.

Harding hunched over his desk, his eyes darting across the page.

Alice, trying to be discreet, stole a glance at Harding's paper, noting several comments in the same harsh black ink that had marred her own. She slumped back into her seat, her mind swirling with doubt and frustration. Was her forecast so far off the mark that it hadn't warranted a single written comment?

When Davies handed back the last of the papers, he strolled to the front of the classroom. 'You all failed to predict the storm. Remember this next time someone asks you to predict the weather. I'll see you all same time tomorrow,' he said.

Iris shook her head. 'That was a disaster,' she mumbled, folding her paper in half and slipping it into her bag.

Alice watched in disbelief as everyone packed up their belongings. That could not be the end of his lesson. It seemed to her that so few in the class had completed the exercise to his satisfaction that he must surely have been intending to show them how their forecasts should have been done.

She stood up, nerves fluttering in her stomach, but she felt compelled to at least ask.

'Squadron Leader Davies,' Alice called out, her voice steady despite her nerves.

Davies turned to face her, his expression unreadable. The room fell silent as all eyes turned to watch their exchange.

'Yes, Miss Peters?' he said, his tone sharp.

Alice took a slow, deliberate breath. 'I wondered if you might talk about your weather forecast and the recommendations you might have offered under those conditions, so we can improve our future forecasts.'

Davies remained silent, his eyes boring into her with an intensity that made the room feel smaller. He adjusted his uniform jacket with a tug, the fabric snapping back into place. 'You've misunderstood the point of this exercise, Miss Peters.'

Alice glanced at Iris who offered only a helpless shrug, her eyebrows knitting together in confusion that mirrored Alice's own.

'In what way, sir?' Alice asked.

Davies scanned the room, his gaze settling on Harding. 'Flight Officer Harding,' he said.

Harding leapt to his feet. 'Yes, sir.'

'Are meteorology assistants expected to predict the weather?' Davies asked.

'No, sir,' Harding replied.

'And are they expected to offer operational advice to the RAF?' Davies asked.

'No, sir,' said Harding.

Davies swept his gaze around the room again before addressing the group.

'Your role as meteorology assistants is to collect data and record it meticulously,' Davies began. He raised his hand and then slowly lowered it, signalling for everyone to retake their seats.

Alice sat down, her brow furrowed in confusion.

'Interpreting that data,' Davies went on, 'is the duty of seasoned forecasters and flight commanders. They are the ones who will analyse data, reports, pilot experience, operational objectives, and numerous other factors before finalising a weather forecast and flight plan. The weather scenario I presented was based on genuine early data from a storm that lasted eighteen hours. Some of you predicted rain, yet none of you anticipated the continuing conditions. Any civilian could have taken the same figures and accurately transcribed the wind speed and temperature. In fact, some of you even got that wrong.'

Alice straightened in her chair as she tried to process what she was hearing. 'So, the purpose of this exercise was to reveal our inadequacies,' she said.

Davies shook his head. 'Not your inadequacies. Your limitations. I see young women coming in, who may have displayed an aptitude for science or mathematics, mistakenly assume that understanding weather codes or reading synoptic charts qualifies them to predict the weather. It does not. Know your role and respect the expertise of the fore-casters.'

Alice nodded slowly, absorbing the lesson. 'So, you expected us to fail. You wanted to show us that forecasting is an entirely different skill that belongs to someone else.'

Davies nodded. 'Your role is vital, but you are operating within strict boundaries. You are here to learn timely and accurate recording, meticulous coding, and how to draw precise synoptic charts. Stay focused.'

Davies dismissed the class with a flick of his wrist, and everyone filed out of the room. Alice remained seated, lost in thought about the past day and a half. She had been so focused on turning herself into a weather forecaster that she had overlooked the importance of her actual role as a meteorology assistant. For the forecaster to excel, Alice needed to master her own responsibilities. Any greater aspirations would have to wait.

26

IRIS HAD BEEN RIGHT. THE PILOTS LEFT DUNSTABLE AFTER A week to continue their RAF training elsewhere. For the women left behind, the next few weeks were a whirlwind of lectures and paper-based exercises. Alice dived into the work with renewed focus and clarity. Her favourite part was getting hands-on with the instruments, reading barometers, thermometers, and wet and dry bulbs to measure humidity. But she no longer searched every instrument reading for its meaning. That wasn't her role.

She learned to read synoptic charts and how to draw her own. She studied cloud formations, from the wispy cirrus clouds that spread a silky sheen across the upper atmosphere to the towering cumulonimbus clouds that signalled severe weather and near-impossible flying conditions. Her notes were extensive and covered everything from sketches of the various cloud types to techniques for determining their heights and quantities.

She practiced calculating wind speeds and directions both on the ground and at twenty thousand feet in the air.

Soaking it all in when her instructors explained that even minor shifts in atmospheric pressure could influence flight paths. It was overwhelming, but also exhilarating.

She learned to launch weather balloons, watching as they ascended into the sky to capture valuable data not available to her on the ground. Each balloon carried a small instrument package called a radiosonde, which transmitted information back to the ground via radio signals. It was in those moments, standing on the windswept airfield with her gaze fixed on the drifting balloon, that she fully understood the significance of her work. Her calculations, her observations, would assist pilots in safely navigating dangerous skies.

By the end of her training, the once-daunting symbols on the weather charts made sense. She was confident at taking instrumental readings and ground-based observations. She even found herself, just for fun, predicting the next day's conditions with growing confidence and increasing accuracy. She kept those forecasts to herself, though.

In her final week, Squadron Leader Davies moved around the classroom as the trainees created yet another synoptic chart. Having spent hours practising in the evenings, Alice's hand was steady as she drew intricate patterns of isobars, weather fronts, and pressure systems on the large map spread out in front of her.

'Neat. Precise,' mumbled Davies from somewhere nearby.

Alice kept her head down and her focus on the task in front of her.

She set her pencil down to double-check her work and immediately felt a large hand patting her on the shoulder.

'Well done, Peters,' said Davies.

It was only then that Alice realised his mumbled compliments were about her work.

'Where is it you're going after training?' Davies asked.

'I'm hoping it'll be RAF Turnhouse, sir,' Alice said.

She'd requested the Edinburgh base but was still waiting for her official orders. Being closer to home was a distinct advantage, she and Tom hoped to be able to schedule leave together, but she also had a friend at Turnhouse. Betty worked the switchboard there and she and Alice were hoping they could share a billet.

Davies nodded and moved on.

Iris caught her eye. 'High praise, indeed,' she whispered.

That evening, Alice sat by the telephone in a small office, elbows on the desk in front of her as she pored over her notes. Her head ached with the strain of the day, but she was expecting a call, and she knew her headache would melt away as soon as she heard Betty's voice.

During training, there had been so few opportunities for Alice to make or receive telephone calls, but Betty had been given permission to make a few personal calls and had arranged to call Alice at eight thirty.

There was a knock at the open door, and Iris poked her head into the room, cheeks flushed with excitement.

'I've got my orders!' she announced, practically bouncing on the spot.

Alice blinked away the tiredness from her eyes. 'Where are they sending you?'

'Dunstable!' Iris beamed.

Alice hesitated. 'Oh, you're staying here? And you're not disappointed by that?'

Iris shook her head, her grin only widening. 'I can't say much,' she said, stepping inside and lowering her voice. 'But it looks as though I'm getting something close to my first choice after all.'

Alice tilted her head. She recalled their first conversation. Iris had hoped to become a wireless operator but had been assigned to meteorology instead. No one talked about what else went on at Dunstable, but everyone knew it was more than just weather reporting.

Alice smiled. 'Secret work then,' she said.

'I didn't say that,' Iris replied, lips twitching.

'No, of course not.' Alice stood and wrapped Iris in a tight hug. 'I'm so happy for you.'

When Iris left, Alice's thoughts shifted to her own future. She was on the brink of leaving her trainee days behind, stepping into the reality of a job and the weight of her own responsibilities. The idea of putting everything she had learned into practice without the safety net of her instructors was both exhilarating and terrifying.

It was almost nine by the time the phone finally rang. Alice snatched up the receiver, desperate to hear a friendly voice. 'Hello! Hello!' There was nothing but static on the line. Alice waited, her fingers crossed that the connection would clear.

'Alice, can you hear me?'

Alice leaned into the receiver. 'I can!' she said, relief flooding her voice. 'Oh Betty, it's so good to hear from you.'

'You too! Sorry for the delay. This line's been temperamental all evening.'

'It's no trouble,' Alice assured her. 'I can't believe we've managed to have a call.'

Betty laughed. 'You and me both. I had thought a nice comfortable job on the switchboard would give me telephone privileges of some sort, but no. And, between you and I, the job is not as comfortable as I had hoped.'

Alice laughed. She glanced down at the table's scratched surface, tracing one of the grooves with her fingertip. 'It's keeping you on your toes then?'

'It is,' Betty said. 'But I like it. You wouldn't *believe* the things I overhear. Not that I'd ever repeat them, of course.'

'Of course not,' Alice said, grinning as she shifted in her seat. 'You must know half the secrets of the RAF by now.'

'Actually,' said Betty, 'I do. But it's not fun when you can't tell anyone. How's it going over there in meteorology?'

'It's amazing.' Alice rested her elbow on the table. Though tempted to dive into a detailed account of everything she'd been studying, she held back. Weather reports were classified as Secret, along with their methods of collection. 'I wish I could tell you everything, Betty.'

Betty sighed down the telephone line. 'Why must everything be classified these days? It gives people nothing but food to talk about. And no one likes talking about food when there's so little of it about.'

Alice smiled at her friend's frustration. She was right about one thing; food did dominate conversations.

'I'm trying not to complain about food too much,' said Alice. 'Tom is eating little more than crackers and corned beef. He's longing for a steak dinner with roast potatoes, carrots, and green beans.'

Betty gave a soft hum that floated down the telephone line. 'What I would give for some crispy roast potatoes. Mash is the potato of choice here. Food aside, how is Tom?'

'He's good,' said Alice. She rolled the telephone wire between her fingers, twisting it into loops. 'I don't know where he is or what he's doing, but he says he's happy and that he made the right decision. Although he misses me, so he says.'

Betty sighed. 'I miss you too. Have your orders come through yet?'

Alice paused, the wire now coiled tightly around her index finger. 'Not yet.'

'They're cutting it fine,' said Betty. 'But I believe you're going to get your wish. I've already applied for a change of billet. And boy do I need it. Right now, I'm sharing a billet with Nancy Pressman. We work the switchboard together and she's hopeless. She constantly connects calls to the wrong people. On Tuesday, she accidentally disconnected the station commander's call. She was, of course, mortified, but never seems to learn. She's almost burned down our billet twice.'

Alice laughed. She could hear the frustration in Betty's voice.

'I'm not exaggerating,' Betty continued. 'Once she used our emergency candles to make the bathroom feel cosy and ended up setting the blackout curtains on fire. Last night, she put bread under the grill and promptly forgot about it.'

Alice heard Betty giving a deep sniff.

'My uniform still reeks of smoke. The woman is a hazard and I'll be glad to see the back of her. I've requested one of the houses close to the base. Just picture it, you, me, and Daphne, when she's finished her training, all living and working together.'

Alice closed her eyes for a moment, letting the image bloom in her mind. She could picture it. But who would have guessed at the beginning of their training that it would be Alice, Betty and Daphne who would have formed the closest of bonds? Daphne, having shown an aptitude for mechanical work had been packed off to mechanics training, where she was seemingly quite adept at maintaining Spitfires.

The faint creak of approaching boots made Alice open her eyes. She turned to see Flight Sergeant Mackie striding into the office. Alice immediately jumped up and saluted, holding the telephone receiver firmly in her other hand.

'At ease, Peters,' said Mackie. Her tone was warm, but brisk. 'Continue your telephone call. I just wanted to give you this before I leave for the evening.'

She handed over an envelope with Alice's name neatly typed on it.

Alice stared at it for a moment, her heart giving a small, unexpected lurch. 'Thank you, Sergeant,' she said, accepting the envelope.

Once Mackie's footsteps faded down the hallway, Alice turned back to the telephone. 'Betty, are you still there?'

'Still here. What was that about?'

'My flight sergeant just handed me something.' Alice flipped the envelope over. It was unsealed. With one hand, she slid the letter out and unfolded it, smoothing it flat on the desk in front of her.

Her eyes darted across the typewritten words, her heart racing. 'Oh my goodness, Betty,' she gasped.

'What is it?' asked Betty, her tone laced with concern.

Alice read the letter again, her fingers trembling slightly. 'I've got my orders,' she said, hardly able to contain her excitement. 'I've been posted to RAF Turnhouse!' Her voice burst with delight, and she quickly covered the telephone mouthpiece with her hand to avoid deafening Betty with her ecstatic squeals.

'Alice, that's wonderful. I knew it! I just knew it,' said Betty, her voice rising in tandem with Alice's. 'I'm so proud of you.'

Alice pressed the letter against her chest, feeling the weight of her achievement settle in. Taking a deep breath, she whispered, 'I'm proud of me, too.'

27

ALICE TURNED UP FOR HER FIRST DAY AS A METEOROLOGY assistant at RAF Turnhouse with nerves gnawing at her insides. Gone was the safety of her training instructors. Now, it was up to her to read, record, and code the weather data from the instruments held on the base. She'd expected to be met by Turnhouse's meteorology forecaster, Flight Lieutenant Elliot Sinclair, but there had been no sign of him. Instead, Betty, her friend and now housemate was showing Alice the way.

'I expect Flight Lieutenant Sinclair is busy,' Betty said.

Alice nodded. 'Of course.'

The weather on the ground was calm with light cloud cover and a gentle breeze. But Alice had learned in training that conditions on the ground sometimes bore no resemblance to conditions in the air. Flight Lieutenant Sinclair, her new boss, was probably off briefing flight crews ahead of whatever operation they had planned for that day.

'The meteorology office is separate from the main building,' said Betty, who had been posted to RAF Turnhouse right out of training. Three months as a switchboard operator and she seemed to know her way around the base.

'We're a fighter squadron base,' said Betty. 'Home to Supermarine Spitfires and Hawker Hurricanes so I'm told.'

Alice nodded. She'd been briefed in Dunstable. The pilots at RAF Turnhouse were responsible for intercepting enemy aircraft to defend key targets including Rosyth Dockyard and the Forth Bridge, the railway bridge that stood tall in the Firth of Forth. It was also home to the squadron that claimed the first Luftwaffe bomber to be shot down over the British mainland.

'This is the Mess Hall in here,' said Betty. She opened a door for Alice to peer inside.

The large room housed rows and rows of long tables and had an overwhelming odour of fried onions, coffee, and aviation fuel. A dozen airmen were seated. Some were eating and some were reading a newspaper. None of them glanced in Alice's direction.

Betty closed the Mess Hall door and continued along the corridor. 'Your office sits on the edge of the second runway. There are three runways, but I guess your office is located there because it's close to the operational briefing hut. It's also nearest to the field where your weather instruments are held.'

Alice smiled. She had loved working with the weather instruments during training and couldn't wait to get hands on with them again. Looking at a collection of numbers and interpreting what that was going to mean for the weather that day and beyond was endlessly fascinating to her.

Betty pushed open the heavy blue door at the end of the corridor and sunlight flooded in, blinding Alice as she exited the building. She blinked away the effects of the sudden brightness and looked around her in awe.

A long runway stretched out in front of her with a plane taking up the space closest to them as it prepared to take off.

'That's a Spitfire, I think,' yelled Betty, her voice straining to be heard above the roar of the plane as it trembled and then shot along the runway, taking off into the air.

Alice nodded.

In the air, the Spitfire's wings dipped from side to side and Alice closed her eyes, feeling the wind on her skin and the lift in her hair.

'That's your office over there,' said Betty.

Alice followed Betty's direction to a small one-storey building at the top edge of the runway. It was fairly nondescript from the outside. Compared to the main building and the aircraft hangars opposite, it was perhaps the most boring building on the base, but Alice didn't care. She knew that what went on inside that building was something akin to magic and she couldn't wait to be a part of it.

'Thank you, Betty,' Alice said. 'I'll take it from here.'

'Good luck,' said Betty, giving her a hug. 'I'll see you in the Mess Hall at one o'clock if you can make it.'

Alice took a moment to take in her surroundings. Planes lined up along the runway, airmen milling around, greasy-looking mechanics passing her, giving her a look. In just a few short months, she'd gone from her quiet life in Millwood to the hustle and bustle of Edinburgh's RAF base.

She brushed her hands down her uniform, straightened her collar, and headed to her new office.

The door to the meteorology office swung open harder than she had intended, and she lurched forward to slow it down, but the door clattered against the wall.

The three people inside turned towards her and Alice felt an awkward heat rise up her neck. Not exactly the professional first impression she had hoped to give.

'Good morning,' she said. 'I'm Aircraftwoman Alice Peters.'

The room was modest, its space dominated by a row of sturdy wooden tables lining one wall. Each tabletop was cleverly tilted, designed for the meteorology assistants and forecasters to better read and prepare weather charts. Maps and charts, filled with swirling lines and symbols, were scattered across the surfaces, while the soft hum of equipment filled the air.

Two men were huddled over a large desk, a map spread out in front of them. Their gazes, however, were now fixed on Alice. The only other person in the room was a woman, another WAAF going by her uniform.

'I'm the new meteorology assistant,' Alice added, when no one spoke.

One of the men, a tall, serious-looking man with glasses pointed to a cluttered desk in the corner of the room. 'You can sit over there,' he said.

Sensing that no further introductions were going to be made, Alice closed the door and took a seat at the corner desk. The woman offered Alice a polite smile then returned her attention to the notebook in front of her.

Alice slipped her bag under the desk and scanned the piles of paperwork strewn across the desk. A bundle of papers hung off the edge of the desk and she nudged them forward to stop them tumbling to the floor.

'Don't touch anything important,' the man added, not looking directly at her.

Alice sat back and clasped her hands on her lap. She tilted her head to listen to the mumbled conversation between the men but could only pick out the occasional word; storm clouds, westerly winds, thirteen hundred hours.

Finally, their conversation came to an end and the other man straightened up. He tipped his hat towards Alice and left the room, the woman following behind with a quick wave towards Alice.

Alice was now alone with the man she presumed was Flight Lieutenant Elliot Sinclair, RAF Turnhouse's lead forecaster. He was a tall man with neatly clipped reddish brown hair and thick-framed glasses that were sparklingly clean. He seemed lost in the map in front of him, oblivious to Alice's presence.

Alice cleared her throat and stood up. 'You're Flight Lieutenant Sinclair, is that right?' she asked.

The man looked up, his storm-grey eyes widening a little as if he was surprised to see her still there. 'Elliot,' he said.

'I'm Alice,' she said, expecting that he'd already forgotten her name from her earlier introduction. 'Where would you like me to start, Elliot?' she asked.

The man seemed to bristle upon hearing his name and Alice wondered if she'd made a mistake dispensing with the formalities of titles.

Elliot sighed and approached her desk. He rummaged around and pulled a hardback book out from beneath a map.

'Here,' he said, holding the book out towards her.

She reached for the book and flipped it open to the first page. Inside were columns of weather data, temperature and air pressure readings, wind speeds, cloud types, and other observations.

'Your job is to take readings every hour,' said Elliot. 'Do you know how to do that?' There was a cynicism in his voice that Alice hadn't expected to be there.

'I do, sir,' she said, springing up from her chair.

He nodded towards a map on the wall. 'That map shows

the locations of all the meteorology instruments on the base.'

Alice took a deep breath and walked across to the map. 'I'll just get on with it then, sir,' she said.

She scanned the map, searching for the meteorology office to get her bearings. It seemed like she was on her own. The least she had expected was a polite welcome, but Elliot came across as both distracted and highly sceptical of her abilities as a meteorology assistant. The only thing she could do now was her job. It was up to her to prove that she could be useful to him.

28

———

ALICE WALKED ALONG THE NARROW STRIP OF PATHWAY THAT bordered the runway. The roar of another Spitfire taking off filled the air, and she covered her ears as it flew past her and into the sky. The instrument field that Betty had pointed out to her earlier was just ahead. Alice opened the gate and stepped inside.

A sleek blackbird landed on the wooden fence. It tilted its head, fixing its beady eyes on Alice, and sang a sweet melody that floated towards her in the crisp morning air.

'Thank you for the welcome,' said Alice. 'It's the nicest one I've had today.'

She glanced around to ensure no one was nearby to overhear her talking to a bird. She was alone. The instrument enclosure was in a secluded spot, far from any buildings and trees to guarantee accurate readings.

Before her was the Stevenson Screen – a white slatted box positioned on grass and 1.2 metres off the ground, designed to shield the sensitive instruments from the very thing they were designed to measure. She wished she had brought a camera to capture her first official weather reading. Oh, if only Mrs Ferguson could see her now.

The hinges creaked as Alice opened the Stevenson Screen, revealing the array of weather instruments inside. The thermometer, the hygrometer, the barometer – they all beckoned to her. With steady hands, she carefully noted down the temperature and humidity. She tapped the glass face of the barometer and watched as the needles wavered briefly before settling into position. She noted down the low atmospheric pressure that predicted a change of weather ahead.

After recording the data from the Stevenson Screen, Alice turned to the anemometer. It spun lazily in the light breeze, whispering secrets of wind speed and direction that Alice now knew how to interpret. She made a note of its readings in the logbook and looked up into the sky. A change was coming, but it should still be smooth take-offs and landings for the next few hours at least.

Next, she inspected the sunshine recorder, a gleaming glass sphere that captured the sun's rays throughout the day. It was a thing of beauty, a testament to the wonders of nature and science intertwined. She marvelled at its design before jotting down its measurements.

Shifting her focus to the sky, she employed the most sensitive instrument of them all – the human eye. Wispy cirrus clouds filled the sky. They looked as though they were barely moving, but that was a trick of the eye. Cirrus clouds moved fast and were a useful early warning of changing weather conditions.

Once Alice had recorded all her observations, she closed the logbook, smiling at the surge of satisfaction she felt. She had just put her training into action and the data she had gathered would be used by Elliot and the forecasters in Met

HQ to shape the timing and flight paths of crucial operations. She had longed to do something valuable with her time, and this was it.

She made her way back towards the meteorology office, her mind already processing the data she had collected. Her next job was to code the data and send it by teleprinter to Met HQ where it would be received by the women in the teleprinter room that she'd sneaked a peek into during her training.

Elliot appeared to be waiting for Alice as she entered the office, his sharp gaze immediately locking onto her.

He held out his hand. 'I need to double-check your data before you send it anywhere,' he said.

Alice handed over her meticulously recorded readings, glad she had taken the time to make her notes neat as well as accurate.

Elliot's brow furrowed as he scanned through the pages.

He stalked out of the office, logbook in hand, leaving Alice standing there, deflated on her very first day.

She slumped into the chair behind the desk. She told herself not to take it personally, reasoning that naturally Elliot would want to verify her competence before entrusting her to do it on her own. But a shadow of uncertainty loomed as she considered the possibility that this might be the reality of working for Elliot Sinclair.

While she waited, Alice busied herself tidying her desk, straightening the piles of paperwork rather than organising them so as not to mess up any system that Elliot had developed in the chaos.

He returned a short time later and handed her the logbook back.

'Go ahead and submit *these* figures,' he said. He emphasised the word "these" as if to make it clear to Alice that he'd had to correct her figures.

She opened the logbook and scanned through her readings and notes. Elliot had adjusted her cloud observation notes, but otherwise her figures were unchanged.

Alice began encoding her data, but the knot of tension in her stomach was hard to ignore under Elliot's watchful gaze. She took a deep breath and forced herself to concentrate on the task in front of her. To gain Elliot's trust, she couldn't afford any mistakes.

With Alice's data meticulously coded and sent off, she settled into her task of drawing her first synoptic chart. Her role was to visually translate her collected weather data, alongside the detailed weather report Elliot had provided, into a comprehensive map for the afternoon's aircrew briefing. Elliot would deliver the briefing to the pilots and mission planners, detailing the anticipated weather conditions for take-off and for landing up to ten hours later.

In training, Alice had sketched hundreds of charts, earning praise for her steady hand and the crispness of her lines. But now, as she sat in front of the expansive map desk, her right hand trembled, betraying her nerves. The pencil wavered, and her line strayed off course. She paused and placed the pencil down on the desk.

'You'll need a steadier hand than that, Peters,' said Elliot, his voice a blend of critique and impatience.

'It might be easier if you weren't watching over my shoulder, sir.' It was the truth, but she hoped she didn't sound petulant.

'Easier for whom?' asked Elliot. 'I'm the one who must

present this map to the aircrew at fifteen hundred hours. I need to ensure it's done right.'

'It will be done right,' Alice assured him. 'I'll redo it as many times as necessary to make sure it's perfect for you, sir.'

Elliot tapped his finger to the map. 'How about you focus on getting it right first time, Peters. We don't have time for sloppy work in this office.'

He walked away, the sound of rustling papers following him as he sat at his desk. Despite the welcome distance, Alice sensed his eyes lingering on her. She pulled out a fresh map. She refused to allow him the satisfaction of making her redo it over the tiny wobbly line caused by his overbearing presence. The map she delivered to him would be flawless.

She flexed her fingers, took a deep breath, and picked up her pencil once more.

When Alice had completed her weather chart, she took it over to Elliot and laid it across the polished wooden surface of his desk. His eyes darted over every inch of the map, his gaze intense and swift as if hunting for an error rather than taking in the details. But her isobars were smooth and even, not a single misshapen line.

He glanced up at the clock on the wall, its hands inching towards the top of the hour. 'Just in time,' he said, pushing his chair back with a scrape and striding towards the door. He yanked it open and turned back to her. 'Well? Are you coming?'

Alice hesitated, her mind racing with uncertainty about their destination. 'Shall I bring the chart?' she asked.

Elliot let out a weary sigh, as if the answer was obvious. 'I can't very well brief the aircrew without it, can I?'

Alice picked up the chart and carried it carefully, following behind Elliot as he marched out of their building and followed the narrow path skirting the runway. Ahead stood a curved metal structure, its corrugated steel surface gleaming under the pale sunlight.

'Sit in the back,' Elliot instructed as they approached the entrance. 'I'll deliver the briefing and answer any questions. You'll leave before the operational briefing begins. I'll give you a nod.'

Inside the metal room, the atmosphere was charged with anticipation. Alice handed over her weather chart and found a seat near the door. RAF personnel filled the seats on both sides, their chatter gradually tapering off as Elliot approached the front of the room. He pinned the chart to the wall and the airmen quietened down.

'Good morning, gentlemen,' Elliot began, shoulders relaxed, moving naturally as he addressed the crowd. 'Today's weather is being influenced by a high-pressure system, meaning clear skies and light surface winds at take-off. Expect to encounter some scattered cumulus clouds as you climb above ten thousand feet, but nothing dense enough to cause any turbulence. Wind speeds at twenty thousand feet are increasing, averaging around thirty knots and coming from the west so a slight tailwind pushing you along your route. Low pressure is, however, coming in behind it.'

As Elliot continued his briefing, the men paid close attention, seemingly eager to hear about their flying conditions. Some took notes, paying particular attention to cloud cover and wind speeds at cruising altitudes and the changes forecast. Despite her training, Alice couldn't help but feel a flicker of doubt. Predicting the weather six kilometres above them felt like a shot in the dark to her. Yet, it was clear that the airmen respected what Elliot had to say.

Once Elliot had finished his briefing and fielded a few questions, he locked eyes with Alice. She took his glare as her cue to leave. She stood up and slipped out of the door, leaving the hum of the operational briefing behind.

29

By the end of the week, Elliot was still double-checking Alice's data. Every hour she handed over the logbook without a word and waited for it to be returned to her with minor alterations. The changes were always to her observations. Not once had Elliot flagged an inaccurate instrument reading, and Alice intended to keep it that way.

After a week of working day shifts, Alice was set to join the meteorology assistants' roster. Her new schedule meant she would see Elliot only during day shifts. While the forecasters worked exclusively during the day, the WAAF assistants were responsible for gathering readings and observations in the evenings and during the night.

Her focus today was on getting through the shift with accurate readings and nothing but Elliot's usual minor and completely unnecessary alterations to her observations.

The challenge was the weather. Flights had been grounded all morning. A heavy fog had rolled in from the North Sea, converging with a low-pressure system from the Atlantic that had brought rain and made the fog denser.

Alice grabbed her coat and headed out into the rain; her

logbook tucked into the waistband of her air force issued skirt to save it from getting soaked.

Outside, a group of airmen sheltered under the overhang of the main building, puffs of cigarette smoke adding to the foggy air.

Seeing her leaving the office, one of them called over. 'When's this weather going to clear?'

Alice stopped and thought for a moment. She'd woken at 5.30 and the rain had begun shortly after that. *Rain before seven, fine by eleven.* She looked towards the sky, but all she saw was grey. It was wet, very wet. But there was a decent wind, and it wasn't stormy. Her expectation was that the old rhyme would call it right this time.

She blinked the raindrops off her eyelashes. Four hours for the weather system to clear plus another hour for luck. 'Maybe by eleven,' she called over to the airmen, her voice confident, even as the rain hammered the ground.

Someone cleared their throat behind her, and she spun around to find Elliot standing stiffly, flanked by two RAF officers. He glared at her.

'And where exactly did you study meteorology, Peters?' he snapped. 'There's no room for guesswork here.'

The remark earned a low chuckle from one of the officers, and Alice's face burned with embarrassment.

'Dunstable, sir,' said Alice, as she met his disapproving gaze.

Elliot's features hardened, looking even more unimpressed with her. 'They taught you to read instruments, not to forecast the weather.' He waved his hand as if shooing her away. 'Get on with it.'

'Yes, sir.' Alice turned and scarpered away towards the instrument field.

Glancing over her shoulder, she saw Elliot talking to the

airmen. He was probably telling them not to listen to her. That her job was to write down readings and draw charts only. A flicker of anger surged within her and she clenched her fists as she walked, her eyes once again on the dark sky. Perhaps she should have kept her mouth shut and referred the airmen to Elliot, but there was no need for him to ridicule her in front of others.

Rain soaked her face, and she ran through the evidence in her mind – the rain, the wind, the timings. Forecasting was about using the evidence in front of you to make a prediction. She knew little of the fancy calculations Elliot spent hours poring over, but her gut told her she was right. By late morning, the rain would relent, and the grounded flights would take off. She was sure of it.

When she arrived back in the office, she hung her coat up to dry and handed her logbook to Elliot. He said nothing as he flipped to the most recent entries, his eyes narrowed. She considered apologising to him for overstepping earlier, but thought it best not to bring it up again. Her goal was to get through the rest of her shift with as little interaction with him as possible.

She returned to her desk to wait for Elliot to step outside, double-check her readings, and alter her visual observations. The legs of his chair scraped against the floor as he stood, but instead of going outside, he sauntered towards her. She sucked in a deep breath, her mind racing over what he could possibly have spotted without leaving the building.

He dropped the logbook on her desk. 'Ready for coding,'

he said in a monotone voice before returning to his own desk.

Alice picked up the book, its pages slightly warped from the damp air. Her gaze drifted to the window where rain continued to pelt against the glass in a rhythmic pattern. It seemed Elliot only found the need to scrutinise her work on fair weather days.

She transcribed the data into the coding sheets, her fingers moving swiftly over the pages. Hours passed as she worked diligently, lost in the repetition of her tasks: coding her readings and sending them to Met HQ, then grabbing the logbook and heading outside to collect the next hourly readings.

Elliot remained engrossed in his own little bubble of concentration, shoulders hunched as he worked on one calculation after another. If he noticed the rain tapering off throughout the morning, he didn't acknowledge it.

Alice glanced up at the clock on the wall and realised it was nearing eleven o'clock. The office window was still misted over but, as if on cue, she heard the roar of a Spitfire as it raced along the runway and took off into the sky.

Shortly afterwards, the meteorology office door swung open, and an officer appeared in the doorway. He gave Alice a smile then turned his attention to Elliot.

'It seems your little apprentice there was right,' he said.

Elliot said nothing, but the officer chuckled and walked off, leaving the door wide open.

Alice cringed. The last thing she needed was for Elliot's pride to be dented by her actions. He looked up. She locked eyes with him, but it was as if he stared right through her, his mind busy working on whatever was on the paper in front of him.

She stood up, shut the door, and spread a new weather

map across the large drafting desk. As she meticulously sketched out the patterns on the map, Alice couldn't help but feel a sense of vindication. She had trusted her instincts, and it seemed they had not failed her.

She didn't need Elliot Sinclair's approval. So why was there a small part of her that still craved it?

30

THREE MONTHS HAD GONE BY, AND ALICE WAS STILL IN AWE OF her surroundings. She was alone in the office. Elliot was out for a meeting. He was still tough to work with, but even he couldn't bring her mood down today. She held a new letter from Tom, and Daphne's request for RAF Turnhouse had been approved. Today was Daphne's first day.

Alice smoothed her hand across the pages of Tom's letter and read it again, her fingers tracing the smooth lines of his signature. She smiled as she read his closing words: *With love, Tom.*

She folded the letter and tucked it in the top drawer of her desk then grabbed her coat, stepping outside for her afternoon break.

Betty and Daphne leaned against the sunlit bricks of the main building, their shadows long in the late afternoon sun. Daphne's hands cut through the air as she spoke, her gestures as animated as the story she appeared to be telling. Betty cradled a mug of hot tea, the steam swirling around her face as she listened with a half-smile.

Daphne had completed what sounded like a gruelling

eighteen weeks of flight mechanic training and had landed in Edinburgh three days ago, reuniting with Alice and Betty in their shared house not far from the base, just as Betty had predicted. Now, in her overalls, with her glossy dark hair tamed by a red scarf knotted on top of her head, she looked the epitome of a poster girl for military service.

Alice joined them, leaning against the wall with her arms crossed.

'Hey, there, Weather Watcher,' said Daphne, with a grin on her face.

'Your first day is going well, then?' Alice asked.

Daphne beamed. 'It's amazing. I thought I'd be stuck refuelling Spitfires all day, but a Handley Page Hampden limped in first thing this morning with a busted hydraulics system and an engine on the brink. I've spent the last six hours working on her. She's a beauty.' She pushed a loose strand of hair from her forehead, smearing a faint streak of grease across her skin. 'And, thanks to me, she's ready to fly again.'

Alice frowned. 'A Handley Page what?'

'A bomber,' said Daphne.

Betty raised an eyebrow over the rim of her mug. 'I'm sure the other mechanics will be thrilled to know you're taking full credit for this repair.'

Daphne grinned and waved a dismissive hand. 'OK, fine. It was a team effort.'

She reached into her pocket, drawing out a crumpled cigarette pack. As she lit one, her gaze drifted to the airmen striding out of the operational briefing room, their boots clumping against the ground. 'Imagine being up there in the sky every day,' she mused dreamily.

Alice nudged her. 'You're such a daredevil, Daph. Maybe one day you'll talk someone into taking you up.'

Betty reached out, brushing down Alice's sleeve. 'Mind your uniform,' she warned, eyeing Daphne's oil-streaked overalls. Alice glanced down, checking for grease stains and sighed in relief.

'That's Flight Lieutenant Elliot Sinclair,' said Alice, nodding her head towards Elliot as he strode from the briefing room.

Daphne's eyes widened. 'That's the weather man,' she said. 'He's cute. How do you get any work done?'

'Daphne!' said Alice.

A figure broke away from the group of airmen and strolled towards them. He was tall, with an easy confidence, his cap tucked under his arm.

'Got an extra smoke?' he asked, his voice smooth.

Daphne arched an eyebrow, a playful smile tugging at the corner of her lips. 'I might. But it'll cost you.'

The airman leaned in slightly, smiling. 'Oh, yeah? What's the price?'

Daphne inhaled her cigarette and blew a cloud of smoke between them. 'Take me up in your plane.'

The airman laughed. 'You're serious?'

Daphne handed over the nearly full packet. 'Help yourself. But any time there's an extra seat going on your plane, I want it. What do you fly?'

He took a cigarette, tapping it thoughtfully against the pack before sliding it between his lips. 'A Spitfire,' he said.

Daphne's shoulders sank and she rolled her eyes. 'Single seater.'

The airman smirked, flicking open a brass lighter and igniting the flame with a practiced flick of his wrist. 'The name's Ritchie,' he said, watching her through the golden glow of the flame as he lit his cigarette.

Daphne's eyes sparkled back at him, but then something appeared to catch her attention over his shoulder.

'The Hampden pilot,' she murmured, straightening.

A man stalked in their direction, his brow deeply furrowed, lips pressed into a grim line. His face was marked with exhaustion and simmering frustration.

'Hey, how's your plane?' Daphne called out, her voice light.

The pilot stopped, levelling her with a glare. 'I wouldn't know,' he said coldly. 'I don't intend to fly her until a real flight mechanic has checked her over.'

A tense silence settled between them. Alice and Betty exchanged glances, while Daphne simply took another slow drag of her cigarette, her expression unreadable.

'I checked her over myself,' she said, exhaling deliberately. 'She's ready to go.'

The pilot's gaze raked over her. 'Listen, girlie,' he said, his voice dripping with scepticism. 'I didn't run the gauntlet in Norway just to be downed on home turf. I've been flying since I was fifteen years old. For all I know, this is your first week on the job.'

Daphne smirked. Alice recognised that look – mischief and challenge wrapped into one.

'You've been flying planes since you were fifteen,' Daphne said, tapping ash away from her cigarette, 'and you never bothered to learn how to fix them?'

The pilot's jaw tightened. 'I know how to fix a plane.'

'Great,' Daphne said breezily. 'Then go and check her yourself. You'll see she's airworthy.'

She dropped the cigarette to the ground and pressed it out with the toe of her boot, her eyes never leaving his.

The pilot turned to Ritchie, searching for backup, but

Ritchie only shrugged, blowing out a stream of smoke. 'If she's that confident, make her go up with you.'

'What?' the pilot barked.

Betty's head snapped up. 'You can't do that!'

Daphne, however, grinned. 'Don't worry,' she said airily. 'If the plane falls out of the sky, it'll be because of the pilot, not the mechanic.'

The pilot's face darkened, but there was no backing down. He jerked his head towards the airfield. 'Let's go, then,' he said, turning and stalking away.

Daphne looked barely able to contain her excitement, but she somehow kept her composure and followed the Hampden pilot. She cast one last glance back at Ritchie, flashing him a triumphant grin.

Ritchie exhaled a soft chuckle, shaking his head. 'Who is she?' he asked.

Alice smiled, watching as Daphne strode after the pilot, chin high, shoulders squared. 'That's our Daphne,' she said, delighted that her friend's dream was about the come true.

31

With Daphne's feet safely back on the ground, she, Alice, and Betty had finished their shifts and stopped to eat in the Mess before heading home to their rented house. The scent hit them first, hot oil, salt, and something unmistakably golden. Egg and chips. Not powdered. Real yolk, real potatoes.

They hurried to join the queue, Daphne peering around the airmen in front of them, as if afraid it might all vanish by the time they reached the front.

Once they had all been served, they sat down. Alice smiled as she placed her hand above her food, watching the steam from her chips curl around her fingers.

'I can't wait to tell Tom about this,' she said. She pierced the yolk with her fork, the rich yellow spreading across her plate.

Since neither of them were able to write about their jobs, it was always good to have something new to write in a letter, even if that was just the first egg Alice had eaten in what felt like months.

Across the table, Betty rummaged through her bag. 'That reminds me,' she said. She pulled out two slightly crumpled envelopes. 'I stopped by the mailroom this afternoon and caught the late post.'

She slid the envelopes across the table to Alice.

Alice's breath hitched as she picked them up. The handwriting was familiar, broad and a little messy. She held the letters against her chest for a moment.

'They're both from Tom,' she said.

For all the censorship and distance, somehow his words still reached her. And hers reached him. Military mail seemed something of a miracle to Alice.

'I wish I had someone to write love letters to me,' Betty mused, her voice tinged with longing.

Alice smiled and reached across the table to squeeze Betty's hand.

Betty's expression brightened as she returned the smile, but a spark of curiosity flickered in her eyes. 'Did you know Nancy Pressman used to work with Elliot?'

Alice picked up a small golden-brown chip from her plate and put it in her mouth. She shook her head and crunched into the chip. 'Doing what?' she asked.

'Same as you, it sounds like,' said Betty.

'Who's Nancy Pressman?' Daphne asked.

Betty delicately sliced through the middle of her egg. 'She's the redhead on the switchboard. She connected a call to Elliot this afternoon and it came up in conversation that she used to work with him. When Nancy was out of earshot, one of the other girls told me that Nancy was just as useless in meteorology as she is on the switchboard. It was all before my time, but there was some big storm that Elliot didn't see coming.'

'We can't predict them all,' said Alice.

'This one was bad. Elliot took the blame for it, but Nancy apparently said there was a problem with her data, which doesn't surprise me.' Betty rolled her eyes. 'Her attention to detail is seriously lacking. Anyway, a plane crashed on the way back to base and, two weeks later, Nancy was moved to the switchboard.'

Alice used a chip to scoop up a small pile of coarse salt on her plate. That explained a few things about Elliot. She couldn't imagine how he must have felt. Any crash is awful, but to know his forecast was delivered based on inaccurate data must have torn him up inside. Storms are unpredictable. There's no way to know if accurate data would have changed anything, but Alice expected that wasn't how Elliot saw it.

Daphne tore her bread in two and dunked one half into her egg, the yolk clinging to the bread. 'Don't mention plane crashes to Ritchie. A Defiant turret fighter landed this afternoon,' she said, a touch of glee in her voice. 'It's a two-seater. I've told Ritchie if he takes me up in a Defiant, I'll let him take me out.'

Alice laughed and dipped a chunky chip in the runny yolk of her egg. 'It's not like he can just ask to borrow a plane.'

'Can Ritchie even fly a Defiant?' asked Betty. 'Isn't he a Spitfire man?'

Daphne waved her hand. 'He can fly anything.' She stared dreamily into space as she recalled her earlier flight in the skies above RAF Turnhouse. 'There's really nothing like it. Looking down on the world, you feel powerful and insignificant all at the same time. You have no idea what it's like to see the world from above.'

'I'm quite happy not to know,' said Betty, wiping her hands on a piece of tissue.

Alice chuckled at their banter. Despite their different backgrounds, the three of them had become firm friends. She wiped her plate clean with a chunk of bread, the last of the yellow yolk soaking into the doughy bread.

Daphne's reminiscing was interrupted by the wail of the air raid siren sounding. Chairs scraped along the floor as everyone in the Mess reacted to the sound with well-rehearsed actions.

Betty sprung up from her chair. Alice shoved the last of her bread into her mouth.

Daphne took a final gulp of her tea. 'Come on, let's go outside and take a look,' she said.

Betty shook her head. 'Are you mad? We need to get to the shelter.'

Daphne gave a small laugh and squeezed Betty's shoulder. 'You're so cute.'

'What's that supposed to mean?' asked Betty.

'We're on an RAF base. It's probably something that's been picked up on radar and will turn to nothing,' said Daphne.

'It only takes one,' said Betty. 'Better to be safe than sorry.' She turned to Alice, appealing for agreement.

Alice stared back for a moment, not sure what to decide. The only air raid she'd experienced when bombs had fallen had been the one in Millwood. There hadn't been any attacks on the base since she'd been here, and the air raid sirens usually resulted in nothing much to report. For those on the ground at least. The airmen were usually scrambled. But hearing the Spitfires roaring to life and seeing them take off in rapid succession triggered quite the burst of adrenaline.

'Just a quick look,' said Alice. She tucked Tom's letters in her bag. 'We can go to the roof and watch the Spitfires taking off.'

Betty's mouth fell open. 'Absolutely not. If the Luftwaffe are about to bomb us, I don't want to be standing on the roof.'

Alice laughed. 'Fine. Let's go to the meteorology enclosure. Elliot's gone and there shouldn't be anyone there for at least another half hour and we'll have a good view of the runway.' Alice grabbed Betty's hand and dragged her out of the building, with Daphne following behind. 'I promise we'll head straight to the shelter if we hear the slightest rumble of enemy aircraft.'

'How are we supposed to hear that above the siren?' Betty yelled as they ran alongside the runway.

Daphne reached the meteorology enclosure first, pulled open the gate, and they all hurried inside.

'Just don't touch anything,' said Alice, looking directly at Daphne, now worrying that Daphne's rebellious streak would cause her to interfere with the weather instruments and get Alice into trouble with Elliot.

'Why are you looking at me?' Daphne asked, sliding her finger down the outside of the white Stevenson Screen that protected the instruments from the elements.

'Because you're the troublemaker,' said Betty. She crossed her arms and looked around. 'Nothing to see. Can we go back inside now?'

Alice removed Daphne's hand from the Stevenson Screen and flicked her gaze towards the sky. 'Did you hear that?'

'That's not funny,' said Betty.

'I'm not joking,' said Alice. She peered in the direction of the runways.

'The Spitfires are being scrambled,' said Daphne.

The three of them stood at the fence, staring out at several aircraft taxiing the runway. Their powerful engines thundered to life, and one Spitfire after another ascended into the inky expanse of the night sky.

Alice had a lot to write about in her letter to Tom.

32

———

A WEEK LATER, ALICE CRADLED A STEAMING MUG OF TEA between her palms, the fragrant aroma curling upwards as she surveyed the bustling Mess Hall. It was that hazy hour between shifts, when the Mess Hall buzzed with chatter, and the scent of tea mingled with the remnants of lunch. She spotted Betty and Daphne huddled in the top corner. She navigated through the crowd, weaving between tables and sidestepping a few energetic pilots.

'Fancy meeting you two here,' she said as she slid into the seat beside Betty.

The three hadn't crossed paths all week, their schedules clashing with different shift patterns. Alice wiggled the logbook she'd stashed in her waistband free and set it on the table.

Betty leaned in, her voice tinged with excitement. 'Daph was just telling me she's planning to become a pilot when the war ends.'

'You've got the flying bug, huh?' asked Alice. She knew that Daphne had loved her flight in the Hampden bomber, but the idea of piloting a plane was something else entirely. 'If any woman can do it, it's you Daphne.'

Daphne grinned and opened the newspaper on the table in front of her. 'Thanks. What about you?' she asked Alice, flicking through the paper, too fast to take in anything more than headlines. 'Do you ever think about what you'll do after the war?'

Alice shrugged. 'Not really.' She put her hand on the logbook beside her. 'I do love weather, as strange as that sounds, so if there was an opportunity to stay in this field then I'd take it, but what are the chances of that?'

Betty chimed in with optimism. 'You never know. Someone had to produce weather forecasts before the war, so why not after?'

Alice shook her head and sipped her tea. 'I don't think anyone in Millwood produced weather reports. Except maybe Mrs Ferguson, but it's not a job.'

Betty grinned. 'Who says you have to stay in Millwood? Tom is a vet, he can find work anywhere, surely?'

'Betty!' said Alice, feeling a blush creeping up her cheeks.

Betty feigned innocence, her eyes twinkling. 'What? I know it's early days for you two, but from the way you talk about him and that dreamy look on your face when you read his letters, it's clear you two are meant to be.'

Alice laughed, touching a hand to her tingling cheeks. 'Maybe,' she said, hearing the hope in her voice. 'Anyway, what about you, Betty? What do you want to do after the war?'

Betty face softened, a wistful smile playing on her lips. 'I want to get married and have children. It might not be as thrilling as flying planes, but that's what I want.'

'That sounds perfect,' said Alice, giving Betty's shoulder a reassuring squeeze.

Alice lifted her gaze, her thoughts drifting to Tom as she sipped her tea. She could easily imagine a future as the wife of a country vet, their life together unfolding in a serene rhythm.

'I do so want a husband,' said Betty, sighing and breaking through Alice's thoughts.

'Look at you two,' Daphne teased, her tone light and playful. 'You need to think bigger than men.'

'Alright for you,' said Betty, 'you have Ritchie.'

'Oh please,' said Daphne, rolling her eyes. 'He's cute, but we've been on two dates, and they were both dinners here in the Mess Hall.'

Alice drained the last of her tea and set the cup down. She glanced behind her and then leaned across the table towards Daphne. 'So that wasn't Ritchie I heard snoring in your room the other morning when I returned from my night shift?'

Betty's eyes widened and she inhaled sharply, the air catching in her throat.

Daphne, without missing a beat, scooped up Alice's logbook from the table and tossed it at her with a glint in her eye. 'Don't you have work to do?'

Alice caught the logbook and flashed Daphne a mischievous grin. 'As it happens, I do. See you later, ladies.' She stood up, smoothing down the wrinkles in her uniform.

She marched from the Mess Hall, leaving Daphne to fend off Betty's inevitable barrage of questions.

～

Outside, her chunky shoes crunched on the gravel path towards the airfield's perimeter. The morning forecast had been for a calm day with calm weather predicted in the early evening. So far, everything was on track. The expanse of concrete shimmered in the low afternoon sun and Alice tilted her face to feel some heat from the sun.

A group of airmen gathered near the hangars. Alice spotted Daphne striding towards them, having apparently made a quick exit from Betty's questioning.

Alice's route along the top edge of the runway was bustling with activity as mechanics scurried about, performing last minute checks on the planes. She stopped and stared at the aircraft lined up in neat rows. What she did mattered. Pilots seemed to have a deep respect for the weather. As well they should. Their lives depended on it, and her job was to make sure they didn't get caught off guard.

She continued towards the meteorology field when another sound halted her steps. It was faint at first, a distant murmur she couldn't quite identify. When the sound echoed again through the still air, she recognised it instantly – the low, rhythmic croak of a frog.

She was about to resume her walk when a memory tickled the back of her mind. On her meteorology course, Iris had said something about frogs. Alice wracked her brain trying to remember what the story had been but came up blank. She shook her head. There were numerous soggy fields surrounding the main building so there were bound to be frogs around.

A light breeze rustled the grass that bordered the concrete runway, carrying the scent of engine oil and avia-tion fuel towards her. Alice wrinkled her nose at the strong smell. RAF Turnhouse lay on the outskirts of Edinburgh, a patch of rural tranquillity interrupted only by the rumbling of an aircraft. But right now, something felt off. It was eerily still. Birds were never welcome on the airfield, but it was still unusual not to see them flitting about, pecking at the ground.

'What would Mrs Ferguson say?' Alice mumbled to herself. 'Nature always tells you something if you listen.'

She flicked her gaze to the sky and frowned. There had been nothing remarkable in her observations the hour before. Now, cloud cover had increased. But that wasn't her concern. Her concern was the cloud types. Every cloud family seemed to be represented. It was a sign that the atmosphere was unstable. But just how big of a problem was it?

She unlatched the wooden gate and entered the secluded space that housed the weather instruments. The long grass swayed gently around her ankles as she made her way straight to the Stevenson Screen.

Opening the screen, Alice's eyes locked on to the barometer. The needles, which she had so meticulously aligned only an hour before, had separated. Four millibars in one hour. She stared at the barometer. It didn't look like a big change, but her training told her otherwise. Low pressure was moving in, and it was coming fast.

33

———

Alice quickly took the other readings, her pencil flying across the pages of her logbook as she scribbled down the figures. Once finished, she secured the Stevenson Screen door. As she looked up, the sky stretched out in a gentle blue and bright white that, to the casual observer, held no hint of the turmoil brewing above. But it wouldn't stay that way for long and whoever was up there needed to know about it.

Rushing back into the meteorology office, Alice headed straight for Elliot.

'We might have a problem, sir,' said Alice, her voice tinged with urgency.

'Might have?' Elliot lifted his reading glasses from his nose and perched them on top of his head.

The missing birds, the noisy frog, her gut – whatever it was – had told her something was wrong. But the numbers supported her feelings, didn't they? She glanced down at the data in her logbook.

'Actually, there's no might about it. We do have a problem,' she said. She thrust her logbook into Elliot's hands.

Her finger traced the freshly scribbled numbers. 'There's an area of low pressure, and I think it's moving in fast.'

Elliot scanned the numbers on the page, his expression growing serious. He stood up and strode over to the large map pinned to the wall, covered in coloured markers denoting weather patterns and fronts. His finger traced a path from where they were stationed to the likely areas affected by the approaching storm.

'We need to issue a warning immediately,' Elliot said, turning back to Alice. 'If your numbers are right, we can't afford to take any chances with this one.'

Alice nodded. 'My numbers are right,' she said, her heart pounding in her chest.

Elliot picked up the telephone. 'I'll get word to any pilots already operational. You call Drem and ask if they're seeing this too.'

The bases in Edinburgh and East Lothian, separated by thirty miles, frequently exchanged data to achieve the most accurate weather predictions for Scotland's east coast. Alice nodded and reached for the other telephone in the room, dialling RAF Drem.

Within the next hour, Alice and Elliot had done all they could do. Alice had prepared a fresh weather chart, and Elliot had given a briefing to the aircrew. Thanks to radios, the airmen already out on operation had been alerted to the worsening weather conditions for their return journeys. Now all anyone could do was wait for the planes to start coming back and hope that they could all land safely.

Alice glanced out of the window. The afternoon light had faded fast as if devoured by the towering dark clouds that had gathered overhead. The base was now shrouded in eerie shadows.

'I'll go and update the readings, sir,' said Alice. She grabbed her coat from the hooks by the door.

Elliot stood up and retrieved his coat too. 'I'll come with you.' He shoved his arms into his coat.

'You don't have to–' Alice's words were drowned out by a deafening crack of thunder that sounded as though it was directly above their heads. It was quickly followed by a blinding flash of lightning that illuminated the office.

Alice and Elliot both jumped in alarm.

'Here she comes,' said Elliot. 'Let's go before it gets any worse.'

They stepped outside into a torrential downpour that had them soaked through within seconds. They hurried towards their outdoor weather station and took the readings, Elliot shining a torch on the instruments while Alice noted down the measurements.

By the time Alice had sent the coded readings to HQ, the first of the operational aircraft was close to base.

Elliot stood by the window and peered up into the sky. He touched his hand to the edge of the window frame and Alice knew he'd be feeling the wind. The windows were not well sealed and even a light breeze in the right direction brought a draft into their office.

Elliot grabbed his coat from beside the door. 'I'm going outside for a better view,' he said.

'I'll join you,' said Alice. She picked up her coat and put her arm through the sleeve. It was still damp inside, but even a wet coat was better than no coat at all.

Outside, Alice noticed Daphne leaning against the side of an aircraft hangar. Daphne's hair was tucked under her hat, and her overalls were drenched, clinging tightly to her.

She stared intently at the sky while biting her fingernails. Alice and Elliot hurried over.

'Has anyone landed yet?' Alice asked.

Daphne shook her head. 'No. The first of them should be coming in to land any minute.' She turned to Alice. 'Ritchie's up there.'

Alice wanted to reassure Daphne that Ritchie would be fine, but how could she? It was now down to the pilot and the aircraft and Daphne knew more about planes than Alice ever would. Anything she said now would sound so hollow and uninformed. She pressed her back against the wall of the hangar and watched the sky.

'Here he comes,' said Elliot.

Daphne flicked her gaze back to the sky and Alice brought her hand to Daphne's shoulder, giving it a light squeeze. The winds howled fiercely, bringing with them the thunderous roar of the Spitfire as it approached the runway. The vibrations pulsed through Alice's legs. The Spitfire swerved and swayed in the turbulent air, and she fought the urge to squeeze her eyes shut. She felt certain the pilot would have no choice but to abort the landing and divert elsewhere.

Alice clasped her hands together, pressing them against her trembling lips. 'Come on,' she whispered. 'Calm down for just a minute.'

'It's a good plane. He can do it,' said Daphne beside her, though her voice wavered, lacking the assurance Alice would have liked.

A gust of wind slammed against the hangar's metal walls, rattling the structure around them as they huddled together, seeking shelter from nature's fury.

The Spitfire descended lower, still battling against the winds that seemed intent on pushing it off course. As the

Spitfire drew closer to the runway, Alice held her breath, her heart racing in her chest, willing the pilot to succeed against all odds.

With a final burst of power, the Spitfire touched down on the landing strip, its wheel squealing in protest. The plane bounced once before settling down and racing along the runway. A collective sigh of relief escaped their lips.

'I can't believe he did that,' Alice said.

Daphne let out a shaky laugh, her hand flying to her mouth in disbelief as she kept her eyes fixed on the aircraft.

'Incredible,' murmured Elliot beside her. Alice turned to see him gazing up into the stormy sky rather than at the Spitfire that had turned and now taxied towards them, rain streaming off its sleek metal body.

The plane came to a halt and the pilot cut the engine. For a moment, everything was still as the winds subsided. The cockpit canopy opened, and Ritchie emerged, jumping down onto the safety of the waterlogged ground below.

Daphne ran towards him, throwing her arms around his neck.

Alice felt the weight of Elliot's gaze on her.

'You have good instincts,' he said.

'Thank you, sir,' said Alice.

'How?' asked Elliot.

She turned towards him, expecting more sarcasm about her assistant training, but he had a questioning look on his face. A genuine curiosity.

'A friend taught me a few things,' said Alice, deliberately vague.

'A meteorologist?' Elliot asked.

Alice shook her head. She thought for a minute, wondering just how much she should say. Figuring Elliot already had a low opinion of her, she opted for the truth.

'A farmer friend,' said Alice. 'Mrs Ferguson. She owns a farm in Millwood. That's where I'm from. Anyway, Mrs Ferguson always seemed so on top of the weather. When I asked her about it, she said she learned it from her grandmother, also a farmer, and she agreed to teach me a few things.'

'You asked her to teach you?'

Alice shrugged. 'I was interested in how she did it.'

Elliot leaned back on the wall. She waited for him to ridicule her. But whatever he was thinking, he kept it to himself.

34

———

A week after the storm and Alice was busy typing her coded data into the teleprinter. The shrill ring of the telephone pierced through the quiet hum of the meteorology office.

Elliot picked up the receiver. 'Sinclair,' he said.

Alice glanced towards him.

His brow furrowed. 'Did you tell her civilians are not allowed on the base?'

Alice's fingers paused, hovering above the teleprinter's keyboard.

As Elliot listened to whoever was on the other end of the line, his expression shifted from annoyance to concern. His face went pale. For a fleeting moment, his eyes met Alice's before darting away.

'I'll be right there,' he said.

He stood up, chair scraping against the floor, and left the office without another word.

Left alone in the suddenly too-quiet room, Alice couldn't shake the unease that settled in her stomach.

She looked down at her coded data: a light wind and a

thin veil of fog that was already lifting. Nothing in the weather was a cause for concern. She completed her transmission and laid a crisp new map across one of the tilted tabletops. Her pencil glided effortlessly over the paper, sketching smooth, curving isobars to match the days atmospheric pressure.

When the office door opened again, Alice looked up. A cold shudder tickled her spine. There, standing beside Elliot was Mrs Ferguson, her hands clenched in front of her and a look in her eyes that drained the colour from Alice's world. Her heart raced and she sprung up from her chair.

'George?' Alice blurted out, the fear of bad news gripping her chest like a vice.

Mrs Ferguson stepped into the office. 'Why don't you sit back down?' she said, her voice uncharacteristically soft and her expression sombre as she gestured towards the chair.

Alice shook her head, feeling a mix of anguish and urgency. 'Is it my mother? Just tell me,' she said.

Elliot moved towards her, his eyes full of something too heavy.

'It's Tom,' Mrs Ferguson said, her voice catching in her throat.

No. No. No.

Alice searched Mrs Ferguson's face. *Please say "injured". Please say "critical but stable". Anything but "gone".* But Mrs Ferguson's face cracked, her eyes glistening with sorrow, and Alice knew that it was the worst possible news.

The world seemed to tilt on its axis. Time slowed, warped, distorted. Mrs Ferguson's lips moved, forming words Alice's couldn't hear over the whirring in her ears. Her legs buckled as the crushing weight of despair pulled her downwards. Elliot lunged forward, catching her before she hit the ground. She collapsed against him as sobs punched their way out of her lungs.

Grief came in relentless waves, her tears soaking through Elliot's shirt. But he didn't flinch. He just held her. She was breaking, and he let her.

As the initial shock receded, Alice pulled away, feeling dizzy and hollowed. Elliot kept his arms tight around her.

'I'm so sorry, Alice,' he whispered, before gently releasing her.

A searing ache settled in Alice's heart. She turned to Mrs Ferguson, blinking away the blur of tears. The worn lines on her friend's face were softened by compassion. She knew that Mrs Ferguson understood the pain of loss all too well.

Elliot guided Alice towards the chair and she sank into it, her shoulders trembling. Mrs Ferguson shifted another chair closer to Alice and sat beside her.

'It's quite the set up you have here,' said Mrs Ferguson, her eyes drifting around the room. 'Tom was so proud of you, Alice.'

Alice nodded. A tear slipped down her cheek, and she wiped it away with the back of her hand, trying to hold on to the strength Tom had always believed she possessed. Memories stirred within her – Tom's laughter, his gentle touch, the way his green eyes lit up when he looked at her.

Elliot reached for the pencil, and only then did she realise she was still holding it.

'Oh.' Her voice cracked. 'I've got work to do.'

She gripped the pencil tighter as if it were a lifeline. If she could just get back to the routine, she could breathe again. She could pretend.

But Elliot tugged it free from her grasp. 'I'll finish the map,' he said. 'Why don't you go and get some air? You could show Mrs Ferguson the instrument field. I bet she would like to see it.'

'But...' said Alice. *But what? What argument was she making? What was she supposed to do now?*

Before she could figure it out, Mrs Ferguson stood up and gently took her arm.

'That's a marvellous idea,' she said, her voice soft but firm.

Alice glanced at Elliot. A crease formed between his eyebrows as though it had just occurred to him that he'd invited a civilian to snoop around the base.

With a conspiratorial twinkle in her eye, Mrs Ferguson winked at him. 'Oh, don't worry, your secrets are safe with me.'

Outside, the wind pulled at them. Alice led Mrs Ferguson to the instrument field. Her feet moved by memory alone. Her legs felt wrong. As if they didn't belong to her anymore. When she reached the Stevenson Screen, she unlatched the door – but stopped.

Her hand hovered.

The ache in her chest was unbearable as her mind lost itself to more memories of Tom.

Mrs Ferguson stepped closer. 'I lost one of my sons when he was just a boy,' she said. 'And you know about my husband.'

Alice looked to her friend, her heart aching deeper than ever. 'I'm so sorry,' she said.

'It was a long time ago,' said Mrs Ferguson. 'But I found the only way through my grief was to get angry. Let it all out. Scream and shout until you can't anymore. This place is perfect for that.'

Alice swallowed hard. Her chest too tight to speak. She shook her head. 'I can't,' she whispered.

The silhouette of a Spitfire rolled onto the runway, with two more following closely behind, their engines rumbling like thunder.

Mrs Ferguson nodded towards the plane. 'That's your cue.'

The first plane surged forward, thunder filling the air. She felt its roar vibrating through her bones. She inhaled deeply and screamed. Loud. From the gut. She screamed until her throat burned and her voice cracked. The sound tore through her, uncoiling something buried too deep.

Another scream followed, and another, each one released as the planes lifted off. When the last Spitfire vanished into the clouds, Alice collapsed to her knees. The damp grass seeped through her tights, anchoring her back to reality.

'It's not fair,' she rasped.

Mrs Ferguson stood beside her, her posture upright and her voice steady. 'No,' she said. 'No, it's not.'

With gentle hands, she helped Alice to her feet and guided her along the runway's edge and back to her office.

Inside, Betty and Daphne were waiting. Their eyes were red and swollen, crumpled tissues clenched in their hands. The moment they saw Alice, their faces broke, tears spilling over.

'Oh, Alice,' Betty sobbed, rushing forward with Daphne close behind. They pulled Alice into their arms.

Alice didn't pull away.

She sank into their embrace, letting their warmth and their sorrow wrap around her, surrendering to the deep, impossible ache of goodbye.

35

HER FIRST NIGHT SHIFT SINCE RECEIVING THE DEVASTATING news of Tom's death was a sombre one. Alice pushed open the door to the meteorology office, the familiar scent of ink, paper, and cold air met her, but it offered no comfort.

Elliot was hunched over his desk, papers scattered around him like fallen leaves in a storm.

'What going on?' Alice whispered to Joan, the assistant who was just packing up to leave for the night.

Joan handed Alice the shared logbook they used and shrugged. 'I don't know. He appeared half an hour ago mumbling something about having too much work to do.'

Alice nodded, watching Joan sling her satchel over her shoulder before slipping out the door.

Alone with Elliot now, Alice took a deep breath and approached his desk. 'Can I help you with anything, sir?'

Elliot looked up. 'Elliot,' he said, rubbing the back of his neck. 'I've told you before, call me Elliot.'

'Right,' said Alice, clearing her throat. He did say that, but he hadn't seemed to mind the formal address until now. 'Elliot,' she repeated. 'Is there anything I can do to help?'

He shook his head, his focus returning to the sea of numbers before him. 'No, thank you.' He waved his hand absently over his desk. 'Just calculations. You carry on with whatever it is you normally do at this hour.'

'Right,' she echoed again, nodding slowly. 'I'll just head out to gather the instrument readings.'

She tightened her coat around her body and stepped into the night. The air was cool, a thin wind tugging at her clothing, and she tilted her head to the stars, the stillness pressing in.

By the time she returned to the warm glow of the office lights, Elliot was on his feet, his fingers wrapped around a steaming mug of tea. He looked up as she entered, a small smile on his face.

'I made you a tea,' he said, gesturing to another mug resting on her desk.

'Oh,' said Alice, quite taken aback by his unexpected gesture. 'Thank you.'

She settled into her chair and lifted the mug to her lips, savouring the warmth and comfort of the drink.

Elliot hovered a few feet away, a look of concern in his eyes as he gently cleared his throat. It dawned on Alice then that Elliot was here to keep an eye on her. He wanted to make sure she was still up to the job.

Alice shifted uncomfortably in her chair, suddenly too aware how stiff her posture was. She opened the logbook, pretending to study her notes. The lines blurred as she scanned the numbers and notes without truly registering them. Her hand stilled on the page.

A lump formed in her throat, the ache of loss threatening to spill over once more. Taking a breath that trembled on the way out, she met Elliot's gaze.

'I can still do my job,' she said, sitting up straighter and clinging to the fragile threads of composure that held her together.

Elliot didn't respond immediately. Instead, he pulled out his chair and sat down, leaning back, his eyes locked on to her. 'I know,' he said. 'But if you need to talk, I'm here.'

'Thank you,' she murmured, staring down into her tea. 'I'm going to send these readings off.'

She coded her data and moved to the teleprinter, grateful for the rhythmic clatter of the keys as her fingers flew across the keyboard.

But when the message was transmitted, the uncomfortable silence returned. The dead of night engulfed the base, only amplifying the stillness. She almost longed for an air raid to break up the tension she felt hanging in the air. She stole a glance at Elliot, who sat across from her suppressing a yawn. He slid his glasses to the top of his head and rubbed his hands across his eyes.

'You should go home and get some sleep,' Alice said.

Elliot looked up, his eyes meeting hers. 'I'm OK,' he said, though the weariness in his voice betrayed him. He fixed his glasses back into place and stretched, the chair legs scraping softly against the floor. 'Although I'm glad I don't have to do many night shifts. How do you cope?'

Alice laughed. 'It gets easier.' She leaned back slightly, letting the chair creak. 'Elliot, why are you really here?'

He hesitated, then spoke softly. 'I didn't want you to be alone.'

A surge of emotion caught Alice off guard, tears threatening to spill. Elliot's kindness was both a comfort and a torment, dredging up thoughts she had been trying so hard to bury.

'I appreciate that,' she said. 'But I live with Betty and Daphne. Some time alone is good. Besides, all I've done lately is talk about...' She trailed off, swallowing hard. 'Work is a useful distraction.'

Elliot exhaled heavily, a sigh that seemed to resonate with unspoken understanding. 'Only me being here is making you think about Tom.'

Hearing Tom's name from Elliot's lips landed hard. She flinched, and nodded slowly, unable to find words.

'Alright,' said Elliot, rising from his chair with renewed energy. 'Then let's get out of here. I want to show you something.'

Puzzled, Alice followed him out of the meteorology office and into the cool night air once more. The base was bathed in a silvery glow from the moon above, casting long shadows across the runway.

Elliot led her across the edge of the runway and towards one of the aircraft hangars. The large doors creaked open as Elliot pushed them aside, revealing the dimly lit interior.

Alice squinted her eyes. A sleek, unfamiliar plane rested inside – longer, broader, more imposing than the Spitfires that usually occupied the hangars.

Elliot gestured towards the aircraft. 'It's a Mossie.'

'What's a Mossie?' asked Alice, curiosity nudging her forward.

'Mosquito. It does photo reconnaissance.'

She reached out, her fingers grazing the aircraft's sturdy frame. It was cold to the touch.

'That's not all though,' said Elliot.

Alice felt a buzz of excitement from him as she waited for him to say more.

'This plane is flying weather reconnaissance sorties.'

'What does that mean?' asked Alice, her hand still resting on the aircraft.

'The RAF already uses Mosquitos to capture aerial

photographs of enemy occupied territory. But now, they're also capturing weather data. They even have Mossie's flying ahead of bomber squadrons to give pilots real time information on the weather conditions ahead of them.'

Alice stared at him, her breath catching. 'Oh, Elliot, just imagine what this could mean for our forecasts.'

'Exactly,' he said, grinning. 'It's all experimental at this stage, of course. But just imagine weather flights that go beyond reconnaissance. It's coming. Work is already underway to modify instruments for accurate readings at altitude. Can you imagine getting air pressure, temperature, humidity, wind speed, and cloud conditions all measured directly over the Atlantic?'

Alice gazed at the plane as if seeing it anew. 'It would be like having a crystal ball,' she said. The idea of being part of something so revolutionary sent a thrill through her. She smiled, the ache in her chest loosening.

By the time a faint sliver of dawn crept into the hangar, gilding the Mosquito in soft gold, Alice and Elliot were quiet.

'You seem lost in thought,' Elliot said, his voice gentle.

Alice blinked, returning her gaze to Elliot. 'I was just thinking about Tom,' she said. Her voice wavered but didn't break. 'He would have loved this.'

'Meteorology?' Elliot asked.

She shook her head. 'He was a vet. But he was so happy I'd found something I love. He would have wanted to hear all about it.'

Elliot smiled. 'He sounds like someone who really believed in you.'

Alice nodded.

He glanced towards the morning light inching its way

further into the hangar. 'I don't want to ruin the moment,' he said. 'But I think you have some instrument readings to take.'

Alice laughed, the sound lighter this time. 'Yes, sir – I mean, Elliot.'

36

———

By the spring, Alice and Elliot had settled into a functioning working routine. Alice mostly kept her forecasts to herself, and Elliot no longer felt the need to double-check her readings. One evening, she'd just finished typing her latest readings into the teleprinter and headed back to her desk, when Elliot threw his pencil onto his desk and exhaled.

'Something wrong?' Alice asked.

Elliot ran a hand through his hair and sighed again. 'Tomorrow's forecast isn't coming together.' He tossed his notes to the end of his desk and Alice took it as an invitation to read over his work. His notes were a jumble of numbers, equations, and weather symbols along with a hand drawn map and arrows.

'What do you think?' he asked.

'Me? I think I should stick to instrument readings.' She passed him his notebook back.

'I'm serious,' he said, sliding his notebook across the desk. 'I'd like to know what you think.'

Alice scanned the notes again. She shook her head. 'These equations. I don't know.'

'You're treating it like a maths problem,' said Elliot. 'Weather is a living thing – it moves, it breathes. You know that. Stop looking at the numbers. Look at the story they're telling.'

Alice looked up at Elliot. She'd never heard him talk like this before. It was surprising. She would have guessed he was all about the maths.

She took a breath and compared the notes on Elliot's pages with what she had seen and felt for herself. She'd been outside every hour for the last ten hours, studying the numbers, but also studying the sky and feeling the weather around her. She closed her eyes. What did her instincts tell her that tomorrow would be like?

'Well,' she began, as she opened her eyes. 'Pressure is falling so the settled weather of the last few days is coming to an end. But it's a gradual shift so the weather front that's coming is not moving fast.' She looked down at Elliot's notes and read through them again, trying to ignore the intimidating equations and look purely at the data itself. She pointed at a group of numbers. 'This is rainfall and wind speeds?'

Elliot nodded.

'Where did you get this?' she asked.

'The Navy. It's ship data.'

She raised her eyebrows. 'It's stormy.'

'That's what I'm thinking,' said Elliot. He turned the notebook around, so it was facing him. 'Look at this,' he said.

Alice dragged an empty chair around to his side of the desk, sat down, and followed his finger as he pointed at various groups of data and explained what he thought it was telling him.

Alice stared for a long time, numbers swimming in front of her eyes. 'All the signs indicate a storm is coming. My best guess is not before noon tomorrow.'

Elliot leaned back in his chair, stretched his arms up and intertwined his fingers behind his head. 'Let's look at it again in the morning and see if tomorrow's data changes anything,' he said.

'Where did you study meteorology?' Alice asked.

'Edinburgh,' said Elliot. 'It was part of my physics degree, but I also learned a lot from my grandmother.'

'Your grandmother?'

'Yes. My grandparents had a farm. My grandfather died young, so my grandmother ran the farm on her own. She was this tiny little woman, but there was no job on the farm she couldn't turn her hand to. It was an arable farm, so she was always checking out the weather to see when to plant and when to harvest. A barometer hung on the wall in her hallway and a weathervane sat atop the barn, but otherwise she relied on her instincts, honed over her decades of working the land.'

'Sounds like Mrs Ferguson,' said Alice.

Elliot nodded. 'That's what I thought when you first told me about her.'

And that's why he hadn't ridiculed her as Alice had expected him to.

The door to the meteorology office opened and her colleague, Joan, strolled in. 'Evening,' Joan said.

Alice returned the chair to the other side of Elliot's desk and began her handover, leaving Elliot to do whatever it was he did at this time of night.

Once her handover was complete, Alice grabbed her

coat just as Elliot stood up. They both said goodnight to Joan and stepped out into the cool night air.

'Are you meeting Daphne and Betty?' Elliot asked, adjusting the collar of his jacket against the breeze.

'No, just me tonight,' said Alice, buttoning her coat as they started walking.

'I'll walk you home,' said Elliot, falling into step beside her.

Alice glanced at him. 'You don't need to do that.'

'It's dark,' said Elliot, shoving his hands into his pockets as they strolled off the base together.

Alice laughed, the sound soft and easy. 'I've walked home alone in the dark too many times to count.'

'Still,' said Elliot, glancing sideways at her. 'I didn't know about those other times. I do know about this one, and I won't be able to sleep tonight unless I know you get home safely.'

Alice smiled. 'Well,' she said, 'we can't have that. You've got a storm to track tomorrow.'

As they walked, Alice slowed her pace slightly and speared Elliot for more about his grandmother and her weather forecasting skills. She sounded incredible. Another Mrs Ferguson.

Barely ten minutes after leaving the base, Alice stopped. 'This is me,' she said. She stepped towards the front door and unlocked it.

Elliot nodded. 'Have a good evening,' he said.

'You too,' said Alice.

He turned to walk away before stopping and turning back to her. 'Make sure you get a good night's sleep,' he added. 'You've got a weather forecast to deliver in the morning.'

'Me?' asked Alice.

His lips twitched into a small smile. 'It is your forecast. Goodnight Alice.'

She grinned and said, 'Goodnight Elliot,' before stepping inside her house, giddy with delight.

~

In the morning, Alice and Elliot headed to the briefing room near the edge of the runway. Alice paused just outside and inhaled deeply to steady her nerves.

'Just stick to what you know,' Elliot said.

Alice nodded. She couldn't quite believe she was about to deliver her very first solo weather briefing. Until now, her role had been behind the scenes. He'd never invited her to deliver the briefing herself. Nor did she think he ever would.

Elliot opened the door and followed Alice as she walked up the centre of the room. RAF personnel filled the seats on both sides, their chatter gradually tapering off as she and Elliot neared the front of the room. With her back turned to the now attentive audience, she focused on the large map pinned to the wall, each contour and symbol familiar yet daunting.

A bead of sweat formed on her forehead, and she dabbed it away with the back of her sleeve, hoping to mask any sign of her apprehension.

'Good morning,' said Alice, turning to face the airmen. Her voice caught a little in her throat. She put a hand to her mouth and gave a small cough. Elliot had told her there was no room for pleasantries in situations such as this, so, once her throat cleared, she launched straight into her prepared briefing.

'Our current weather is being influenced by a storm

which is moving in from the northwest, currently over the Irish Sea.'

Alice swept her hand along the map indicating the predicted path of the storm. 'Conditions are expected to remain dry for take-off,' she continued, 'with broken cloud at around eight thousand feet. Winds at the surface will be light, from the southwest at seven to ten knots. A low-pressure system will continue to deepen throughout the morning, with cloud cover progressing to nine-tenths. Winds at an operational altitude of twenty thousand feet will be from the west-northwest at forty to fifty knots by 1300 hours.'

She wasn't privy to the details of today's operation. All she knew was that there were expected take-offs and landings throughout the day. The airmen listened intently, some scribbling notes in their books presumably recording the likely weather at their designated time of operation.

'Temperatures at altitude will be minus twenty-four degrees Celsius,' she added. 'We anticipate the storm arriving at 1600 hours bringing with it significant rainfall and low cloud, making station and landmark visibility difficult. Good luck out there, gentlemen.'

There were only a couple of questions, which Alice answered with as much detail as she could at this stage. Storms could be unpredictable, especially in the skies above Scotland.

She left the briefing room, her heart racing from the adrenaline of successfully delivering her first solo briefing. If Elliot thought she'd done well, he might let her do more.

Outside, she spotted Daphne and Betty waiting for her on the corner opposite.

'Given the smile on your face, it went well?' Daphne said.

Alice nodded.

Betty's face lit up with excitement. 'Oh, Alice, I knew you'd do brilliantly!'

Alice blushed at the praise and couldn't contain her own grin. 'It was nerve-wracking at first, but as soon as I started talking, the words just flowed out of me. I really hope Elliot was pleased.'

'Are you kidding?' asked Daphne. 'You can do no wrong in that man's eyes.'

'Now who's kidding,' said Alice. 'That man hated me my first few weeks here, remember?'

'Well, he certainly doesn't hate you anymore,' said Daphne.

Alice was taken aback. 'Are you suggesting Elliot...?'

'Likes you?' asked Daphne. 'Of course.'

'No, he doesn't,' said Alice, looking to Betty.

Betty nodded. 'He does.'

'No,' said Alice, 'that can't be true. He's never shown any romantic interest in me. Quite the opposite.'

Daphne laughed. 'Oh, come on, you must have noticed the way he looks at you?'

'No. He's mellowed. Nothing more.'

'If you say so,' said Daphne.

'Do you like him?' asked Betty. 'Oh, please say you do. There's nothing more romantic than a wartime romance.'

The hairs on the back of Alice's neck suddenly prickled. Alice had already had a war time romance, and it hadn't turned out well. She wasn't about to put herself through that again. She and Elliot had developed a good working relationship over the last few months and that was how it would stay.

37

As the evening news update came to an end, Alice sank further into the comfort of her spot on the sofa. 'I'm exhausted,' she said, pulling her heavy knitted cardigan tighter around her body. 'It's bedtime for me. When I can be bothered to get up.'

Betty huddled under a blanket beside her. 'Me too,' she said, stretching her arms out in front of her, using her chin to keep the blanket in place.

Daphne sprung up from the chair in the corner. 'What happened to us?' she asked. 'I thought living together was going to be non-stop parties when we weren't on duty. Instead, we're like three old women, heading up to bed as soon as the nine o'clock news is finished.'

'We'll party next Friday,' said Alice. She stood up and flicked the wireless off, silencing the last of the day's happenings.

As part of their efforts to keep morale high, the base put on dances a few times a year. It was a chance for everyone to let their hair down and socialise. More than a few romances had sprung from these dances – some fizzled out after a weekend, but others were still going strong.

Daphne grinned. 'I can't wait. All those airmen in the same place. All looking for a dance. For a kiss, maybe.' She grabbed Alice and forced her around their small living room in an over-the-top waltz.

'Daphne!' Betty scolded. 'What about Ritchie?'

'What about him?' asked Daphne, releasing Alice from her hold. 'There's no ring on my finger. I'm allowed to dance with other men.'

'You can dance with other men,' said Betty. 'Just make sure not to kiss them. Ritchie is a nice man. He's good for you.'

Daphne laughed. 'I like to think I'm good for him too.'

'Hmm,' said Betty. 'More like leading him astray.'

'He doesn't take much persuading,' said Daphne, winking at Betty. 'But there's nothing stopping you from having a sneaky kiss, Bets.'

Betty's cheeks flushed pink.

'Goodnight, ladies,' said Alice, pushing herself off the sofa.

She opened the living room door and immediately heard a low, ominous rumble that shouldn't have been there. This close to the base, hearing military activity wasn't unusual. But this was different. The sound was uneven and unfamiliar. Her heart raced as she turned to face the others.

'Do you hear that?' she asked, her voice uneasy.

Betty shook her head. 'I don't hear anything.'

Alice stepped towards the front door. She pulled it open and was met with a gust of chilly wind.

'Oh, for heaven's sake, Alice,' Betty called from the living room. 'Shut that door! You're letting all the cold air in.'

But Alice left the door open. Her eyes were fixed on the sky above searching for the source of the noise.

A shiver ran down Alice's spine. The moon was bright, and the sky was clear.

Daphne appeared over her shoulder. 'I hear it,' she said.

Betty was on her feet now too. She draped the blanket around her shoulders and clasped it in front of her face. 'It's just a plane,' she said. 'Have you both forgotten we live within walking distance of the base? We hear planes all the time.'

Alice shook her head. 'This sounds... different,' she said. She turned to Daphne. 'What do you think?'

Daphne worked with aircraft every day and Alice hoped Daphne would tell her she was being paranoid, and it was just the distant rumble of a Spitfire lining up to land. But Daphne's skin was a little paler than it had been when they'd danced around the living room.

Daphne shook her head. 'It's not one of ours.'

A furious roar erupted, drowning out the droning of the stranger plane.

'That's one of ours,' said Daphne.

It was still dark when Alice stirred from her restless sleep. She had spent the night tangled in bedsheets, eyes fluttering open and shut, until finally deciding it was futile to stay in bed any longer. Making her way downstairs, she found Daphne already in the kitchen, work overalls on, and nibbling on a slice of toast slathered with marmalade.

'You couldn't sleep either, huh?' Daphne said, glancing up as she took another bite.

Alice shook her head, her brow furrowed. 'Knowing something awful has happened somewhere is just...'

Daphne nodded. 'Unsettling, at best. The droning seemed to go on all night. The wireless said it was a raid on the west coast.'

The vagueness of the information was intentional, Alice knew. Broadcasting details was risky with the Germans almost certainly listening in. There was no sense in telling them how successful or otherwise their attack had been.

'I'm going to work early,' said Daphne. 'Ritchie was on duty last night and I want to check on him before my shift starts.'

'Will you wait for me?' Alice asked.

Daphne nodded. Alice turned and climbed the stairs to get dressed, her mind already on the day ahead.

As she reached the top, Daphne called out after her, 'Give Betty a knock, will you?'

Thirty minutes later, Alice, Daphne, and Betty were dressed and made their way to RAF Turnhouse. They went directly to the Mess Hall, the ideal place to gather information about the previous night's raid. The scent of fried bacon lingered and there was the usual mix of people, eating, drinking, and chatting, but there was also a palpable tension in the air that wasn't usually there.

Daphne spotted Ritchie sitting on his own and rushed over to him. He stubbed out a cigarette and stood as he saw her approaching. She threw her arms around his neck, hugging him tightly. His work was perilous even under normal circumstances, but with the enemy in Scotland's skies, the danger was undoubtedly heightened, and the events of the night before had clearly rattled Daphne.

Ritchie pulled back from Daphne's embrace. His face was etched with sadness and his eyes downcast. 'There was nothing we could do. We scrambled but we're not equipped for night fighting. Besides, they left our air space quickly, so we were never the target. But the west,' he said, his voice heavy with defeat.

Daphne nodded, her expression grave. She was aware of the tactical challenges more than Alice.

'How bad was it?' Betty asked.

'Devastating from what I hear,' Ritchie said. He gestured to the stairs at the opposite end of the Mess Hall. 'If you go up to the roof, you can still see Clydebank burning.'

Alice's mouth fell open. If the fires were visible from Edinburgh, much of the town must have been engulfed in flames.

'Glasgow, too,' said Ritchie, his tone grim. 'But Clydebank took the brunt of it. They were aiming for the ship-yards, I expect, but it sounds like the town suffered the worst.'

Ritchie grabbed a heavy-duty jacket from the back of his chair and put it on. 'I'm off to Clydebank today. It's apparently chaos over there and they've put out a call for extra help. Teams from Glasgow are already on site, and more crews are heading over from Stirling. A bunch of off-duty guys have volunteered to join them.'

'You've been on duty all night,' said Daphne. 'Have you even slept yet?'

Ritchie shook his head, rubbing a hand over his eyes as he tried to muster a reassuring smile. 'I'll be fine,' he said, though the dark circles under his eyes suggested otherwise.

He picked up his mug, but barely took a sip before setting it down again.

Daphne slipped her hand into Ritchie's. 'Is it safe?' she asked, her brow furrowing.

Ritchie leaned in, brushing his lips softly against Daphne's. When he pulled back, Daphne managed a small smile, but the deep crease between her eyebrows betrayed the anxiety she must have felt. Alice noticed it too; Ritchie hadn't actually answered the question.

'Alice?' a voice called out, snapping Alice out of her thoughts.

She spun around to see Elliot approaching, a steaming mug of coffee in his hand. 'What are you doing here? I thought you weren't here until this afternoon.'

'I'm not supposed to be,' said Alice.

He raised an eyebrow and waited for her to explain.

'The air raid,' she said, her stomach knotting. 'I wanted to see if there was anything I could do.'

Elliot took a gulp of his coffee, his fingers drumming against the tin mug. 'I hear buses are on the way to start evacuating civilians.'

'Evacuating civilians,' Alice said slowly. That wasn't the usual response to an air raid. 'Why would they need to do that?'

'Well,' said Elliot, shifting on his feet. 'The damage is extensive.'

Alice's throat went dry. She turned to Daphne and Betty who stood in tense silence. 'How bad could it have been?' she asked, though she wasn't sure she wanted the answer.

Ritchie stepped forward, keeping his voice low. 'From what we're hearing, more than two hundred German bombers leaving tens of thousands of civilians with no homes to go back to.'

Alice grabbed a nearby chair to steady herself, her fingers tightening around the frame. She shook her head furiously, her voice laced with disbelief. 'That's impossible,' she said.

Elliot stood beside her, his hand gently resting on her back. 'Are you alright?' he asked.

She turned to Ritchie. 'I could go with you,' she said. 'Just for the morning.'

Ritchie shook his head. 'You'd never make it back in time for your shift.'

'You're going to Clydebank?' Elliot asked.

Ritchie nodded. 'I'm off shift now. I'll help wherever I can.'

Elliot took another mouthful of his coffee and then stared into his mug as if searching for the answer to whatever question rattled around his mind. He glanced around them, checking for anyone who might overhear and then leaned closer to Ritchie. 'The forecast is for a calm, clear night.'

'Meaning what?' asked Betty, looking from Alice to Daphne.

The Germans had been ruthless, showing no mercy to the people of London. They returned night after night with relentless bombings that left behind utter devastation. Clydebank wasn't London, but it was home to a shipyard and the re-purposed Singers' munitions factory, which made it a strategic target. It was highly likely that the Germans were not yet finished with Clydebank.

Daphne stepped closer to Ritchie and wrapped her arm around his waist, pulling him closer. 'Meaning there's a good chance the Germans will be back tonight,' she said.

38

———

The Germans did come back. Clydebank and Glasgow faced a second night of relentless bombing. In the end, more than a thousand people lost their lives. Life on the base felt different after that. Everyone was on edge. Waiting for the next raid.

Alice looked up as she ambled along the edge of the runway to collect her instrument readings. The moon was mere days away from being full and it lit up the airbase with sparkling clarity.

Suddenly, the jarring scream of the air raid siren rang out. Alice froze mid-step, peering into the endless expanse of starlit sky, listening for the rumble of aircraft engines. But all she heard was that heart-stopping wail. A surge of goosebumps prickled along her arms, and an icy shiver ran down her spine. Where she'd once associated that alarm with the thrill of watching the Spitfires scramble, it was now an ominous sign that life for someone somewhere might be about to change forever.

Ahead, two dark silhouettes rushed towards her. Their

outlines, etched sharply against the night, unmistakably identified them as airmen.

As they neared, one of them shouted with urgency, 'Alice! Get inside!'

She recognised Ritchie's voice among the rapid footsteps pounding on the concrete runway. 'What's going on?' she asked.

'The Germans are coming,' said Ritchie, passing her.

Alice felt her breath fully leave her body for a moment and she gasped for more air.

'Take care up there,' she yelled after Ritchie and his comrade as they sprinted past her on their way to their aircraft.

Alice stepped back from the runway, but, despite her nerves, didn't go inside. Her eyes fell on the aircraft hangar where she knew Daphne was working the nightshift. Four figures emerged from the shadows inside the hangar, moving with co-ordinated precision as they hurried to the parked Spitfires. They wasted no time in darting underneath the planes, removing the heavy chocks from the wheels.

At the same time, Ritchie and the other airman climbed into the cockpits of their respective planes and fired up the powerful engines. The roar momentarily overpowered the lingering shriek of the siren. Their aircraft taxied to the runway, skimming across the surface before surging forward in a sleek, determined take off into the inky sky.

The siren fell silent as soon as the planes were in the air. Alice rushed towards the flight crew on the ground. Spotting her approaching figure, Daphne stepped away from the others, meeting Alice halfway.

'Are you OK?' Alice asked.

Daphne put a brave face on everything, but Alice knew

that her friend worried whenever Ritchie was scrambled. 603 Squadron's primary role was daytime defence. Daily sorties, though dangerous, had become routine, but unplanned nighttime flying meant confirmed threats, and since Clydebank, Daphne had been in a state of anxious anticipation until Ritchie landed safely.

With a sudden burst of enthusiasm, Daphne said, 'We've got a brand-new Spitfire in the hangar.' Even in the glow of the moonlight, Alice could tell Daphne's smile was forced. 'Guess who delivered it?'

'Who?' asked Alice, happy to allow Daphne to change the subject and think about something other than Ritchie.

'Rita!' Daphne said, her tone rising with what sounded more like genuine enthusiasm.

'Who's Rita?' asked Alice.

Daphne shrugged with an animated gleam in her eye. 'I have absolutely no idea,' she said. 'But she's a woman, and she flew that Spitfire all the way from Liverpool.'

'Ah,' said Alice, understanding Daphne's excitement. It wasn't about Rita herself. It was the idea that a woman had been trusted with piloting a Spitfire. When the RAF realised they couldn't spare male pilots for non-combat flying, women took over. The ladies of the Air Transport Auxiliary now delivered new, damaged, and repaired aircraft wherever they needed to go in the UK.

'I can't wait to take flying lessons,' said Daphne, with a hint of wistfulness in her voice.

Alice smiled. 'So, you'll be the one soaring in a Spitfire someday?'

Daphne shook her head, her gaze drifting towards the sky. 'No. Even if I started now, I doubt they'd allow me to join the ATA. But after the war, I'll be up there.'

Alice smiled at the rare mention of a future beyond the

clash of war. These days, no one seemed willing to plan beyond the next week. Including her.

'I've got to go,' said Daphne, heading back to work to no doubt distract herself with aeroplane maintenance and a shiny new Spitfire.

It was as good a plan as any and Alice set off once more to take her readings, hoping it would be distraction enough. The thought of the Luftwaffe prowling above made her feel ill. Bile rose in her throat. She swallowed hard and glanced at the starlit sky, whispering a prayer that Ritchie and the others could repel the Germans and return safely.

In the morning, Alice sat at breakfast in the Mess Hall with Daphne and Betty, who had just arrived to start her shift. The room buzzed with the quiet murmur of RAF personnel exchanging tired greetings. Daphne kept her gaze fixed on the door, her shoulders hunched until Ritchie finally appeared. He came in, gave Daphne a quick wave, and headed straight for the coffee pot. He poured himself a mug of coffee, adding three heaped spoons of sugar, and then dropped into the empty chair beside Daphne. She shifted closer to him with a gentle nudge, her shoulder brushing his as if silently expressing her relief at his safe return.

'We think they were heading back to Clydebank,' Ritchie said, his voice heavy with the weight of what he must have witnessed. 'Some of them made it, but we managed to intercept others, forcing them to scatter. They still dropped their bombs though. Everywhere from the borders to Arbroath. Nothing on the scale of Clydebank, but still. Leith was hit.'

Alice's heart sank. The others sat in silence. The news of any raid was grim, but it felt extra devastating when the raids were so close to home. Her heart ached for Ritchie. She could hardly fathom the horror of witnessing a Nazi raid from the sky, trying desperately to fend off the attack yet knowing it wasn't enough to stop innocent people on the ground from perishing.

Ritchie took a long sip of coffee. 'We made it tougher for the Luftwaffe, no doubt, but we need better night defences.'

Daphne pressed a kiss to Ritchie's shoulder, and he smiled. A gesture for her benefit only, Alice suspected.

'I want to help,' said Alice. 'I'm off shift now. I'm going to Leith.'

Ritchie nodded. 'I'll drive us.'

'I'm coming too,' said Daphne, straightening up in her chair.

'No,' said Ritchie. 'If this is anything like Clydebank, they're coming back tonight. We need you here. Every plane we have needs to be flight ready. And there's no one I trust more to do that.'

Daphne looked at Ritchie for a long moment. She glanced at Alice, before leaning forward and kissing Ritchie on the lips. 'You better bring her back.'

39

———

RITCHIE DROVE AS CLOSE TO THE BLAST SITE AS HE COULD before finding somewhere safe to leave the car. Alice reached into the back seat and grabbed the first aid kit she'd brought from the base along with the tin helmet she'd received as part of her uniform kit. Once outside, she put the helmet on and buttoned up the mechanics overalls that Daphne had insisted she wear. They walked towards the flames ahead of them. Leith's tenements were still burning. The Luftwaffe had apparently missed their target – the ship-yard in Leith Docks – and had instead wiped out several hundred homes.

'It was a parachute mine,' said Ritchie.

Alice nodded. She wasn't entirely sure what that meant. She could guess, but didn't see the point in dwelling on what had caused the damage when the people in front of her needed help.

'They wouldn't have heard it coming,' Ritchie added. 'It would have floated down to the ground silently and the first anyone would have known is when it landed on top of them.'

The air was thick with dust and ash, the acrid tang of smoke catching in Alice's throat. Fire engines and ambulances were stationed on every corner. Uniformed figures darted through the rubble like pieces of a desperate machine, each doing their part to keep things from falling further apart.

Alice took a deep breath and steeled herself for the task ahead.

'We'll meet back at the car at seven,' said Ritchie.

She glanced down at her watch, rubbing her fingers across the glass face. 'Seven o'clock,' she said.

'And be there,' Ritchie said, his voice firmer. 'I'm on shift tonight and Daphne will kill me if I don't bring you back with me.'

She and Ritchie made their way to what appeared to be a makeshift co-ordination point among the smouldering debris. A first aid tent had been erected nearby and Alice took a moment to scan the landscape around her, trying to get her bearings.

She spotted a young girl huddled beside a burned out building, tears streaming down her soot-streaked face as she clutched a tattered doll to her chest.

'I'll start there,' said Alice, pointing to the girl.

Ritchie's attention was focused on the opposite direction. A group of firefighters were frantically trying to extinguish a blaze in a nearby building. Multiple jets of water flew through the air, but it didn't seem to be enough.

Ritchie gave her shoulder a brief, firm squeeze. 'Be safe,' he said, before hurrying towards the fire crews.

Alice approached the girl and knelt beside her, offering a gentle smile and a steady hand. 'I'm Alice. Can you tell me your name?'

The girl looked up, eyes glassy and filled with a silent kind of terror. Alice's heart cracked. She reached out, gently placing a hand on the girl's shoulder.

'Let's take you to the first aid station,' said Alice. 'The doctor will check that you're OK and then we can find your family.'

The girl let herself be led away. As they walked, Alice kept her voice soft.

'Do you live with your mother?' she asked.

The girl nodded.

'Do you know where she is?'

The girl's mouth twisted as tears welled again. She shook her head.

'Don't worry,' said Alice, forcing a confidence into her voice. 'We'll find her,' she said, hoping that was true.

At the first aid station, Alice handed the girl over to a nurse with a quick summary. Just as she finished speaking, a man barged into the tent, crashing into a trolley lined with metal instruments. He reached out his hand and caught the trolley before it tumbled to the ground.

'Can anyone help?' he yelled. 'We've got someone trapped beneath a collapsed staircase at Largo Place.'

Three men jumped up from seats that lined the tent wall and hurried after the man.

Alice knelt in front of the girl. 'The nurse is going to look after you now. OK?'

The girl nodded.

'You've been very brave,' said Alice.

Alice straightened up and looked to the nurse.

'Don't worry,' the nurse said. 'I'll take care of her from here.'

Alice nodded her thanks and hurried from the tent. A

young woman crossed her path, and Alice thrust out a hand to stop her. She wore navy trousers and a navy casual jacket. Dark red curls poked out from beneath her tin hat, the letter W painted on the metal, marking her out as an Air Raid Precautions Warden.

'Which way to Largo Place?' Alice asked.

'Follow me,' the woman said urgently.

'Are you ARP?' Alice asked as they walked.

'I am,' said the woman. 'And you?'

'WAAF from RAF Turnhouse. I'm Alice.'

'I'm Jude.' She stared at the destruction around them. 'Can you believe I've been an ARP Warden for six days and this happens?'

'Were you on duty last night?' Alice asked.

'Not officially,' said Jude. 'But you hear the sirens, and you go. That's Largo Place up ahead.'

The three-storey tenement building was a smouldering shell, its charred walls marked with black streaks. The roof had partially collapsed, sagging precariously at the edges, while the homes inside almost certainly reduced to ashes and twisted metal. A line of people scrambled among the rubble. They frantically passed rocks and wooden planks to each other, working with feverish urgency to reach the person trapped beneath the debris.

Alice and Jude joined the effort, their hands moving in a blur as they caught and tossed aside whatever rubble was handed to them. The ground around them was a chaotic mess of scattered bricks and splintered wood, and each movement sent more debris cascading down, releasing choking clouds of dust that stung Alice's eyes and filled her lungs.

Suddenly, a loud crack echoed through the ruins, and a

shower of bricks rained down like a ferocious hailstorm. One of the bricks struck Alice's helmet with a jarring thud, and she silently thanked Daphne for reminding her to bring it, her heart pounding with relief.

'Give me a hand here,' someone yelled from inside the building.

Everyone stopped what they were doing, watching and waiting to see what happened next. Alice flicked her gaze to the smoke-clogged sky and offered up a prayer.

There was a commotion at the front and an elderly man appeared atop the rubble, flanked by two men. They lifted the man up and carried him cautiously away from the building. The man's leg looked badly mangled, and he had a deep gash on his forehead, but he was alive.

A young boy, his grandson Alice guessed, followed behind him.

A warden walked beside the boy. Alice caught a snippet of their conversation as they passed her.

'You did well,' the warden told the boy, brushing soot from his hair. 'You stayed with him. That helped.'

Alice blew out a deep breath and turned away from the building. Debris littered the railway embankment and track, a jagged scar blasted into the side of the embankment.

She turned to Jude. 'What's next?'

'There were no incendiaries,' said Jude. 'The main fires seem to be under control now, so I guess we can help most at the first aid station.'

Jude set off, Alice following.

'Do you have a sense of the scale of damage yet?' Alice asked.

Jude nodded slowly. 'Three churches, hundreds of homes, hundreds of shops. And you saw the chaos at the first aid station earlier. Those injured are in the hundreds too. Mercifully few fatalities, so far. But that won't bring their families any comfort.'

'No,' said Alice. 'No, it won't.'

Her heart ached for the families left behind. She knew how hard that was. She hadn't asked exactly how Tom died. Nothing good could come from knowing. She preferred to remember him as he had been, not be haunted by how he died.

Alice and Jude arrived at the first aid station, their eyes widening at the scene before them. The number of people needing help had swelled from only an hour or so ago. A long line of patients stretched out, most of them clutching makeshift bandages fashioned from torn shirts and towels pressed against deep, bleeding wounds.

Alice scanned the frenzied environment, her gaze darting from one overwhelmed volunteer to another, seeking someone who might direct their help where it was most needed.

Her attention was abruptly drawn to a man staggering in her direction, his face pale and contorted with pain. A dark, wet stain spread across his abdomen, blood seeping through his shirt in a menacing bloom. Alice reached out instinctively to steady him.

'Let me find somewhere for you to sit,' she said. 'Then I'll get someone to help.'

The man's arm slumped heavily around her shoulders, and just as Alice braced herself to support his weight, his knees buckled. He collapsed to the ground with a thud, pulling Alice down alongside him in a tangle of limbs and desperation.

Alice scrambled up, kneeling beside the man. 'He's losing blood fast,' she said to Jude. 'Can you find me some bandages or a towel? Anything we can use to stop the bleeding.'

Jude darted off while Alice scanned the people around her, searching for a medic. 'Can anyone help?' she called out.

Seconds later, Jude returned with a pile of bandages in her hand. Alice lifted the man's shirt. The wound was significant, gaping, with blood pooling on his skin. She placed the bandages over the wound and pressed down, applying as much pressure as she could, trying to stem the flow of blood. The man was still. Silent.

Just then, a doctor arrived at their side, his presence a welcome relief.

'Maintain pressure on the wound,' he said, examining the patient. 'Does anyone know what happened?'

Alice shook her head. 'He came in alone.'

A crowd formed around them.

'Does anyone know this man?' Alice asked.

No one answered.

The doctor's expression was grave as he assessed the situation.

'Coming through,' someone yelled.

The crowd parted, making space for another medic pushing her way through. She carried a stretcher, which she laid beside the patient.

'I'll take over,' she said to Alice.

Alice and Jude moved aside, watching as the two medics lifted the man onto the stretcher and carried him away. They turned to each other, both more than a little shaken.

'Let's find somewhere for you to wash up,' Jude said.

Alice looked down at her bloodstained hands and nodded, grateful for Jude's suggestion.

They quickly made their way to a nearby water pump, where they both scrubbed the blood from their hands. As they finished cleaning up, another commotion caught their attention. A woman this time, moaning as she stumbled along, pressing a bandage to a wound on the side of her head. She was being led by a nurse.

'Can we help?' Alice asked the nurse.

The nurse pointed behind her. 'In the next tent. It's triage and they need help cleaning and dressing wounds.'

Alice and Jude hurried towards the triage tent, where they were immediately put to work.

As the sun dipped low, and the light turned golden through the smoky haze, Alice and Jude sank down onto the ground outside the triage tent. Alice dropped her helmet beside her. Her overalls were torn and smeared with ash and other people's blood. Her hair matted with sweat and soot.

'Do you live around here?' Alice asked.

Jude nodded. 'I lived on Largo Place.'

Alice winced at Jude's use of the past tense. 'I'm so sorry,' she said. 'Are your family all OK?'

Tears sprung to Jude's eyes, and she blinked furiously as though refusing to allow tears to fall. 'My mother and sister were injured. I was checking on them when you first saw me. They'll be OK.'

Alice's own heart clenched with empathy, feeling the weight of Jude's pain in each word as she shared her story. Three of her neighbours had died and many more were injured, and now homeless. Alice's hands clenched into fists. She wanted to be angry. She wanted to scream and cry and lash out at the Germans who were inflicting such pain on the world. Instead, her fury drained, leaving only a hollow exhaustion as she sat silently wondering what it would take to end this nightmare.

40

––––––

By the time Jude and Alice had parted ways, Jude had reunited with her mother and sister. It was a tight-knit community, and grief hung heavy in the air. Everyone mourned those who had died and remained on edge in case the Germans returned that night.

Alice glanced up at the sky, imagining the parachute drifting gently down like a weather balloon. Only instead of data, this one had delivered devastation.

The streets buzzed with activity as those who no longer had homes gathered to plan their next steps. Alice wandered among small groups huddled in the rubble, people clutching the few belongings they'd managed to salvage from the wreckage.

She ran a hand through her damp hair, tying it into a ponytail and savouring the cool air on the back of her neck. A few more steps brought her to the scorched remains of Leith Town Hall. The once-proud sandstone facade was now blackened and blistered, though the columns still stood tall. Smoke curled around them like ghosts, yet their classical beauty lingered, defiant.

Something beckoned her forward and Alice stepped inside, weaving through broken glass and splintered beams. Dust floated in the shafts of light streaming through the holes in the ceiling. Shattered tiles crunched beneath her boots as she moved deeper into the ruins, passing scorched portraits and bent brass plaques.

A corridor led her towards Leith Theatre.

The heavy doors creaked as she pushed them open. The theatre beyond was a cavern of silence, where golden light filtered through the high round windows, catching the particles in the air. The lower seating was mangled, rows of plush chairs torn open and burned to their springs, the floor beneath warped by fire and water. Scorched curtains dangled from their rails.

Alice stepped onto the stage, her boots echoing across the wooden boards. She walked slowly to the centre stage, feeling both entirely out of place and yet inexplicably drawn to it.

Perhaps it was the theatre's quiet that appealed to her, a strange kind of sanctuary amid the day's chaos. The space was broken, yes, but it was also still. She tilted her head to the light, letting it warm her face through the sweat and grime on her skin.

Then a sound cut through the hush.

A voice. Faint but calling her name.

Her eyes scanned the auditorium, picking out the silhouette of someone standing in the doorway below. A tall figure, hand raised to shield against the light. Her breath caught. It was Elliot.

A whirlwind of emotions flooded through her – surprise, confusion, and a hint of something else she couldn't quite place.

Before she could reply, a loud, splintering crack rang out

from above. She looked up, just in time to see a jagged section of the roof collapse.

She threw herself to the side. The stage shuddered as a beam crashed down, splintering on impact and sending shards of wood flying. Dust exploded in a cloud around her.

'Alice!' Elliot shouted.

He ran, boots pounding across the debris strewn aisle and up the side stairs. She coughed, brushing soot from her eyes as he appeared above her.

'Are you hurt?' he asked, crouching beside her.

'I'm–' She started to speak, but before she could finish the word, he pulled her into his arms and held her tight, pressing her close.

'Don't ever do that again!' he said.

She stiffened only for a second. Then she sank into the embrace. 'It's not like I did it on purpose.'

She heard his heart pounding in his chest, his grip on her tight, anchoring her in place amidst the pandemonium.

When the dust settled, Elliot loosened his grip on her. 'When Daphne told me where you'd gone,' he said, hoarsely, 'I was desperate to get here. But I've been on shift all day. I came as soon as I could. I found Ritchie, but I've been looking for you everywhere.'

'I just needed a moment,' she murmured, voice muffled against his collar.

'You could've been–'

He couldn't bring himself to finish the sentence, but Alice was certain she knew what was on his mind. Her arms tightened around him.

They stayed there on the stage for a long moment, wrapped in each other, framed by ruins and golden light.

~

They finally stood, dust and splinters clinging to their clothes. Elliot brushed ash from Alice's shoulders, his hands lingering as though afraid she might vanish if he looked away too long.

'Come on,' he said gently. 'Let's get Ritchie.'

They stepped cautiously through the wreckage, back out into the war-ravaged streets of Leith. A few firemen were coiling hoses by the side of the road, and a warden gave them a tired nod as they passed. The worst of the chaos had subsided.

Ritchie was leaning against a lamppost, his sleeves rolled up, face streaked with soot and sweat. He held a cup of tea in one hand, and his shoulders sagged with the kind of exhaustion only a day like this could bring.

Relief bloomed in Alice's chest at the sight of him.

He looked up and smiled when he saw them, raising his mug in greeting. 'Thought you'd got lost in there,' he said.

'I nearly did,' said Alice, her voice dry.

Ritchie's eyes narrowed slightly as he studied her, then he nodded to Elliot. 'Are you taking her home?'

Elliot gave a small smile. 'Yes.'

'I can't go yet,' said Alice. She scanned the streets still full of people. 'There's more I can do.'

Ritchie shook his head. 'You look like you're about to collapse where you stand.'

Elliot shook his head. 'You worked a nightshift before you got here. You need sleep.'

'I can manage,' she started, but Elliot was already steering her gently by the elbow.

'The worst is over,' said Ritchie. 'Everyone has been accounted for. In one way or another,' he added.

Alice nodded. Her hand drifted towards her heart as she thought of the people who had lost their lives.

'The wardens have it all under control now,' said Elliot.

'I'll see you back at base,' said Ritchie.

Alice managed a smile and waved as Ritchie turned back towards the wreckage, his figure slowly disappearing from view.

Alice practically fell into Elliot's car, her legs suddenly feeling leaden. The car was quiet, the hum of the engine the only sound between them for a time. Alice leaned her head against the cool glass of the window, eyelids heavy. The ache in her body had become a constant thrum, every joint and muscle stiff.

Elliot's gaze darted between the road ahead and Alice sitting beside him. The weight of the day's events and the unspoken emotions between them was heavy, tension palpable in the air.

'When Daphne told me where you'd gone,' Elliot said, eyes fixed ahead, his voice barely above a whisper. 'I was... '

'Furious?' Alice suggested.

Elliot shook his head. 'Terrified.'

He kept one hand on the steering wheel and reached out with the other one, his hand finding hers. The warmth of his touch stunned her – it wasn't dramatic or sudden, just steady. Familiar. But it sent a ripple through her chest all the same.

'I couldn't bear the thought of losing you,' he said, voice raw.

A lump formed in her throat, thick and unexpected. She squeezed his hand. A rush of emotion surged through her and an overwhelming sense of connection that she hadn't ever experienced with Elliot.

Leaning back into the soft fabric of her seat, she turned to look at him. He smiled, and in that instant, she felt as if the ground beneath her had shifted, silently and without warning.

She closed her eyes. Her hand stayed in his, anchoring her and unravelling her all at once.

The realisation crept in, like a fog rolling in from the North Sea.

She cared for him. More than she was ready to admit.

And that terrified her more than anything.

41

A MONTH LATER AND IT WAS THE TURN OF GREENOCK. Everyone said the two nights of raids hadn't been as devastating as those in Clydebank. The shipyards and key infrastructure had survived. That was good, but there were still hundreds of people dead and thousands of people homeless.

Alice sat alone in the meteorology office, grateful to have work that distracted her. She leaned over her desk and, with a steady hand, drew pressure lines on the map in front of her, curving around in long flowing lines. It was almost soothing. The isobars, evenly distributed like rows of gentle waves, indicated stable atmospheric pressure meaning Elliot could assure the pilots of calm weather at their morning meeting. Only that wasn't especially good news these days. The Nazis also liked to fly in calm weather.

Elliot cleared his throat and moved to sit on the edge of his desk. His eyes didn't leave her. 'Are we really going to pretend nothing happened between us?' he asked.

Alice looked up from her drawing, her heart suddenly pounding in her chest. 'We were exhausted,' she said. The pencil trembled between her fingers. 'And emotional. That's all it was.'

Elliot tilted his head, watching her carefully. 'Was it?'

She dropped her gaze and began drawing again, though the lines blurred beneath her vision.

'I know you feel this too,' said Elliot.

She stiffened. A quiet panic rose in her chest. 'There's a war on, Elliot,' she said, forcing the words out. 'This, whatever this is, it doesn't matter.'

But even as she said it, the lie settled heavily on her, like a towering thunder cloud pressing down.

It *did* matter. That was the problem.

She had loved once before, and the war had taken him. How could she begin to explain to Elliot that she couldn't do that again? A wave of guilt rolled over her. Every stirring of emotion within her felt like both a new beginning and a profound betrayal.

'It matters to me,' said Elliot. The rawness in his voice made her chest tighten further.

Before she could speak, the telephone rang. The sound jolted them both, snapping the moment in two. Elliot reached for the receiver. 'Yes?'

She exhaled slowly, glad of the interruption.

His conversation was brief. He replaced the receiver with a soft click.

'Elliot,' she began, not even sure what she wanted to say.

But he was already reaching for his jacket. 'I have to go,' he said, not meeting her eyes as he strode out of the office.

Alice sat frozen, the pencil loose in her hand now. She stared down at her unfinished weather map. The lines were smudged and senseless. She scrunched the paper into a tight ball and reached for a fresh map.

Minutes later, the door to the meteorology office banged

open, the handle clattering against the wall. Daphne strode in, her overalls opened at the front, breathless with excitement. Behind her, Betty followed at a more measured pace, her arms folded across her chest, a frown settling between her brows.

They both stepped inside, and Betty closed the office door behind them.

'Where's the weather man?' Daphne asked, her eyes darting around the room as if Elliot might be hiding somewhere.

'He's been called away,' said Alice, setting her pencil down with a soft tap against the wooden desk. She leaned back in her chair, stretching out her fingers, loosening the stiffness in her grip.

'I bet I know why,' said Daphne, practically vibrating with energy.

Alice sighed. Yet again she was about to be the last to hear some juicy bit of information. Betty and the other switchboard operators liked a good gossip about what they'd overheard. The airmen seemed to talk just as much as the switchboard ladies, and were decidedly less discreet, so Daphne also overheard things she wasn't supposed to know.

'Well,' said Alice, raising an eyebrow. 'Spill it.'

Daphne grinned and plonked herself down in Elliot's chair. 'It's big,' she said. 'Really big.'

Betty sighed and dragged a chair over from beneath one of the meteorology desks. She sat down with a huff, glancing up at the large clock on the wall.

'She's been like this all the way here,' Betty said. 'I only went to the Mess for a cup of tea, but Daphne intercepted me and insisted we come here first.' She checked the time again, her lips pressing into a thin line. 'I doubt I'll even have time for tea now.'

Daphne waved a dismissive hand. 'What I've got to tell you will be worth missing a cup of tea for,' said Daphne.

'If it's not the end of the war, it's not worth it,' said Betty, shifting in her chair.

Daphne shrugged. 'It's not the end. But it's possibly the beginning of the end.'

'Really?' asked Alice, trying not to get her hopes up.

Daphne pulled off her hat and ran her fingers through her hair, scratching at her scalp. 'I hate that bloody thing,' she muttered.

'Daphne!' said Alice, prompting her friend to get on with it.

Daphne rolled her eyes and placed her hat on the edge of Elliot's desk. 'Fine. An unidentified plane was spotted coming over land from the North Sea. Plotters quickly labelled the flight Hostile and tracked it as far as Northumberland before it disappeared. Our boys were scrambled to intercept.'

'That's not news,' said Alice. RAF Turnhouse was primarily a fighter station, so planes were regularly scrambled when enemy aircraft appeared near the coast.

'No, they weren't scrambled from here,' said Daphne. 'We first scrambled a Spitfire from Acklington or somewhere like that and then a Defiant from Ayr, I think it was.' It was just like Daphne to know which aircraft had been scrambled but less certain of where they had come from. 'The Defiant was only a few miles from the bandit when the pilot bailed out and the plane crashed into a field.'

Betty sighed dramatically. 'My tea break is almost over. Is there a point to this story?'

'Why yes,' said Daphne. 'The point is that the downed pilot asked to speak to one person and one person only.'

'Let me guess,' said Betty. 'He had delusions of grandeur and insisted on being taken to Churchill himself.'

Daphne shook her head. 'Nope. Someone a little closer to home.'

Alice and Betty exchanged a glance. 'Who?' they asked in unison.

'None other than the Duke of Hamilton.'

'The Duke of Hamilton,' said Betty. 'Our station commander?'

'The very one,' said Daphne. 'Apparently the Duke set off early this morning to visit the pilot in hospital.'

'Well,' said Betty, standing up and brushing her hands down her skirt. 'As exciting as that tale was, I have to get back to work.'

Daphne's grin widened, a flicker of mischief in her eyes. 'That wasn't the exciting part,' she said.

Alice and Betty exchanged a glance. 'What's the exciting part?' asked Alice.

Daphne leaned back in Elliot's chair, crossing her arms behind her ahead as if savouring the moment. 'Rumour has it, the pilot was Rudolph Hess.'

A heavy silence fell over the room.

Alice's breath hitched in her throat. 'Hess?' she asked. 'Vice Chancellor of the German Reich?'

Daphne nodded, her lips curling into a knowing smile. 'That's right,' she said. 'Hitler's deputy is in Scotland.'

42

ALICE SAT ON THE BUS AS IT TRUNDLED ALONG COUNTRY roads, twisting and turning its way to Millwood. Scotland had been through a lot in the weeks since she'd last been home. Thousands of people were dead. Tens of thousands of people were homeless. If Rudolph Hess had come to Scotland to broker a peace deal, then he had failed. The war raged on, and Hitler had publicly declared Hess as mentally ill.

The Luftwaffe continued to attack Scotland, but something had changed. The RAF were better at fighting them off. Two weeks ago, three German bombers had been shot down in the North Sea. And only a night ago, a raid had resulted in the Germans offloading their bombs into the fields of rural Aberdeenshire. Enemy bomber crews seemed increasingly reluctant to take chances in Scotland's skies and that meant their bombs were doing less damage. Taking fewer lives.

Alice's heart began to beat a little faster as the familiar sights of her hometown came into view – quaint cottages with flower-filled gardens, the rolling green hills, and Mr Nobleman's car parked up outside of the local pub, where it seemed to spend much of its time. Everything looked the same, yet she knew that beneath the surface, everything had shifted.

When the bus came to a stop, Alice retrieved her small suitcase and stepped onto the pavement. A cool breeze greeted her, and she took a deep breath of fresh country air, steeling herself for what lay ahead. A visit to Violet was never without its challenges. But right now, with Elliot, RAF Turnhouse also had its challenges.

Waiting on the street outside her home stood Violet, Peggy, and Mrs Ferguson. Her throat tightened, and she swallowed hard, surprised by the wave of emotions that washed over her.

Peggy stepped forward first, enveloping Alice in a hug that smelled of lavender and starch. Alice closed her eyes and let herself lean in, just for a second longer than necessary.

'Oh, how I miss you,' Alice murmured, her voice catching.

She was grateful her mother had retained Peggy as their housekeeper. Peggy had been a constant presence in Alice's life, becoming like family over the years. And it was good for Violet to have company since Alice was away.

'Welcome home, Alice,' said Peggy warmly, cupping a hand to Alice's cheek. 'You're so skinny.'

Alice laughed. 'The cooks in the Mess are not a patch on you,' she said, which wasn't actually true. The women in the kitchen always made sure those on the base were well fed, with hearty portions, even if variety was sometimes limited.

Mrs Ferguson smiled at Alice and gave her a nod. 'You

look well. Professional weather watching seems to be good for you.'

Alice smiled. 'It has its moments.'

Then Violet stepped forward and put her arms out. 'I'm so proud of you, darling,' she said, her voice gentler than Alice had been expecting.

Alice leaned into her mother's arms. Tears welled up in her eyes and rolled down her cheeks. Everything she'd been holding in for weeks hit her at once, each suppressed feeling clamouring for release. She surrendered and sank deeper into her mother's embrace.

As Alice composed herself, she wiped away tears and took deep, steadying breaths. 'I'm sorry,' she said, wiping her face with her sleeve. 'I don't know why I'm crying. I just missed you all so much.'

Violet clapped her hands together. 'Shall we go inside? Peggy has prepared the most marvellous lunch for us all.'

Alice followed her small welcoming party into the dining room where a modest spread had been laid out on the table: a small platter of neatly sliced sandwiches, a pie with a dark, flaky crust and, beside it, a golden quiche, its surface speckled with herbs.

'The pie is rabbit,' said Mrs Ferguson, with a trace of pride. 'Polish soldiers are stationed near the farm. I let them hunt on my land, and they always bring me something in return.'

'The eggs in the quiche also came from Mrs Ferguson's farm,' added Peggy. 'But the herbs and the vegetables came from your garden.'

Violet steered Alice towards the dining table with a hand on her back. 'Come and sit down, and you can fill us in on your adventures.'

They all sat down. Alice helped herself to a cheese sandwich. Mrs Ferguson sliced a generous piece of pie, the flaky crust crackling under the knife. She slid it across the table towards Alice, sending with it a rich, meaty aroma.

Over lunch, Alice kept her stories light. She painted a picture of her daily routine, talking about instruments and readings, and about Daphne's obsession with planes and the gossip Betty overheard working on the telephones.

'And what about air raids?' Violet asked, leaning forward, her eyes clouded with worry. 'You're so close to the city.'

Alice paused, holding another cheese sandwich halfway to her mouth. She took a bite, chewing slowly before replying. 'One or two,' she said lightly, hoping it would be enough to give her mother the reassurance she seemed to be craving.

Going into any details of the air raids at the base or the time she'd spent in Leith would help no one.

Once they'd finished eating, Peggy cleared away the plates, Violet following close behind her.

With the room quiet, and Mrs Ferguson sitting across from her, Alice asked a question that had been playing on her mind.

'Mrs Ferguson,' Alice started tentatively. 'After your husband died, did you ever... find someone else to love?'

Mrs Ferguson's eyes softened, a distant look appearing in them as she recalled memories from the past. The seconds stretched. Finally, she exhaled, the sound quiet but heavy.

'No,' she said. 'I was never lucky that way.'

Alice hesitated. 'You think it would have been lucky? Not some kind of betrayal?'

Mrs Ferguson shook her head. 'Goodness, no. That's the

thing about love. Real love. You only ever want what's best for each other. If you can't be there to love them, then it's a blessing when someone else steps in. Someone good. That's not betrayal.'

The words landed with Alice, rippling through her chest.

Before she could say anything more, Peggy returned carrying a tray of tea with four cups and saucers and a plate of shortbread biscuits. Violet carried a plate of scones and a sugar dish.

'I'm afraid that's all the sugar we have, so go easy,' she said, looking at Alice as she placed the dish in the centre of the table.

Peggy placed a milk jug beside it. 'That's all the milk, too.'

Violet sighed as she poured tea for everyone. 'I can't wait for this war to be over. Then we can all return to our old lives.'

Alice smiled, but it was hollow. A strange weight settled in her chest, growing heavier with every passing moment. Like everyone else, she wanted the war to end.

But the life she once knew was gone. Tom was gone. And the girl who had loved him had died with him. Still, she had clung to that version of herself, holding on to guilt and sorrow as if they could somehow keep her whole. Instead, they only tied her to the past. And the truth was, she no longer wanted her old life.

Mrs Ferguson's words echoed in her mind.

If you can't be there to love them, then it's a blessing when someone else steps in.

Her mind shifted to Elliot, and the look on his face when she'd told him that whatever had happened between them in Leith was because they were tired and emotional. It wasn't true. And, despite the hurt in his eyes, he knew it wasn't true either. There was something real between them.

Alice stirred her tea in silence, her heart whispering a question she wasn't ready to answer. Could she allow herself to be loved again?

43

THE SKY ABOVE WAS STREAKED WITH LOW GREY CLOUDS ON the day Alice arrived back at RAF Turnhouse. She breathed in the cold, oil-tinged air as she headed to the meteorology office. It smelled of routine. Of duty. And she loved it.

She was an hour early for her shift, but she had to be sure she'd catch Elliot before he finished for the day. She had rehearsed the words she wanted to say over and over; on the bus, in the mirror, even to the chipped ceiling above her bed. *"I do have feelings for you, Elliot. I just don't know if I'm ready. But I want to try."*

Nerves fluttered in her stomach. She hadn't realised how hard it would be to say them out loud.

Alice pushed the office door open, relieved to find Elliot at his desk, sleeves rolled up, the usual stack of reports fanned out before him. He looked up as she entered, and then quickly stood.

'Alice. You're back.' He tugged at the collar of his shirt and Alice got the impression he was somehow as nervous as she was. 'How was Millwood?' he asked, his voice held an unusual edge she didn't recognise.

Alice glanced around the small office, checking they were alone. 'Strange,' she said, forcing a smile. 'Familiar and different all at once.'

'Good to have you back.' He gestured towards the chair opposite him. 'Please. Sit.'

She lowered herself onto the hard wooden seat, folding her hands in her lap. Her throat tightened. Now or never.

'Elliot, there's something I wanted to–'

He cut across her, reaching into his desk drawer. 'Before you say anything, I need to give you this.'

He slid an envelope across the desk. Her name was written on the front in thick black ink.

Alice blinked. Her fingers trembled slightly as she picked it up. She broke the seal and unfolded the paper inside.

Royal Air Force Orders: Aircraftwoman A. Peters is to report to RAF Felixstowe for temporary assignment, effective immediately. Duration: two months.

Alice looked up, stunned. 'Felixstowe? Why?'

Elliot cleared his throat. His knuckles whitened as he gripped the edge of his desk.

'It's a temporary transfer,' he said. 'There's a project down there. Classified. Meteorological work. They needed someone with experience, and I... I recommended you.'

She gasped, momentarily stunned. The words she had rehearsed shattered into shards of confusion.

'*You* recommended me?' she said, slowly. '*You* arranged this?'

Elliot hesitated. His gaze flicked to the window where raindrops were beginning to spatter the glass. 'Yes,' he said.

Silence stretched between them, thick as the overhead clouds.

Alice swallowed. 'Right. I see.' She stood too quickly, the chair scraping against the floor. 'Well, that's that, then.'

'Alice–' said Elliot, standing up but respecting her space.

'You didn't have to send me away, Elliot,' she said, her voice low and brittle. 'If you've changed your mind, if you don't want me...'

'No!' His voice cracked like thunder in the small room. He took a step towards her, then stopped himself, his jaw tightening. 'That's not what this is.'

She turned to face him, fists clenched at her sides.

'Then what *is* it? Because I came in here ready to tell you how I feel.' She stopped herself, teeth pressing into her bottom lip. 'But clearly you've made your decision.'

'Alice, listen.' He ran a hand through his hair. 'It's not about pushing you away. It's the opposite. This assignment is important. They need good people down there, and you're the best I know. It's the kind of thing you should be part of. I thought you'd want it.'

Her chest tightened as if someone had pressed a hand against it. Perhaps he thought his words would flatter her, soften the blow. But all she felt was the distance growing between them.

'Maybe next time,' she whispered, her voice cracking, 'you could ask me what I want.'

She turned towards the door.

Elliot called after her. 'Alice, please, come back.'

She paused at the door, hand on the frame. Her voice came quieter still, more vulnerable. 'I wanted to tell you that

I do feel something. For you. I just...' She swallowed hard. 'I'm not sure I'm ready. But I wanted you to know.'

Elliot's face softened, but he said nothing.

She stepped out into the corridor before the ache in her chest could break her open.

PART III

44

The sea wind bit at Alice's face as she stood in the grounds of Felixstowe's Golf Club. The club had been taken over by the Royal Navy and served multiple military purposes. For Alice, it was the home of Operation Outward – a naval operation that her meteorology skills had been loaned to. Overhead, gulls swarmed and shrieked, their cries lost in the vast sky. Below her, the choppy waters of the estuary. She'd swapped the smell of engine oil for salty sea air and the tang of seaweed.

Her two-month temporary transfer was now in its sixth month. Her final month, or so she'd been promised.

Working with her Royal Navy colleagues, Alice stood with a clipboard in hand, scarf flapping against her coat. She was ready for the latest release of balloons.

'Ready for launch, ma'am,' a voice called out behind her.

Alice turned to see Jane Wallace, a slender, red-cheeked young woman, gesturing towards the oversized hydrogen balloon bobbing beside her. Jane had been a Wren for more than a year, but this was her first week working with Alice.

Alice stepped forward, checking her notes.

'Balloon 71. Wind trajectory easterly, estimated travel time five to six hours. Target zone: Northwest Germany.' She paused, then looked up. 'Payload primed?'

'Yes, ma'am. Steel wire payload. Fuse set.'

The slow burning fuse was calibrated to drift across the Channel and bring the balloon down over Germany. This launch used trailing steel wire, designed to snag on power lines and disrupt electricity supplies. Other launches attached incendiaries, calibrated to ignite over Germany. Alice had seen the impact that even small incendiaries could have. It wasn't something she felt good about, but she knew that it was needed.

She gave the instruction. 'Proceed.'

Jane moved briskly and released the tether. The balloon, a little over two metres in diameter, floated upwards, slow and majestic. Alice stood still, following its climb until it was little more than a speck in the sky.

'Isn't there a danger that the Jerries will retaliate and do the same to us?' asked Jane. She removed her gloves and wiped her palms down the front of her uniform.

'Maybe,' admitted Alice. 'But it's harder for them. Winds at high altitudes tend to blow from west to east, giving us the advantage.'

Jane shook her head and gave a small laugh.

It *was* such a strange idea. Weaponised balloons sent drifting on the winds to wreak havoc deep inside enemy territory. And yet, it worked. Forest fires. Power outages. Rail disruptions. The balloons did their job, quietly and unpredictably. There was something both ingenious and slightly mad about it.

Of course, linking individual launches to specific incidents of disruption was impossible. Still, the powers that be seemed pleased with the operation, and the Navy were on track to launch over a thousand balloons a day.

Jane slipped her hands back into her gloves and leaned closer to Alice. 'Is it true that Churchill came up with the idea after some runaway barrage balloons made it across the North Sea and caused chaos in Sweden?'

Alice smiled. 'So they tell me. Prepare the next balloon please.'

At the end of Alice's three-hour launch window, she tucked her clipboard into her launch kit. She walked back towards the operations hut, the wooden floorboards inside creaking under her boots, drawing glances from her naval colleagues. The room was warm, filled with maps and instruments and the low hum of quiet voices. Weather charts lined the walls, and radiosonde instrument packages jostled for space beside their ground-based receivers and stacks of classified weather reports.

It was a far cry from Turnhouse and her hourly weather readings and observations. Here, she was analysing someone else's data and writing the weather reports. She was making the decision to launch or not.

It was satisfying work. And it mattered.

She had wanted to hate being here. Believing that Elliot had sent her away to be rid of her. But on her first day in Felixstowe, she understood she'd been wrong. Elliot had seen this as an opportunity for Alice. And he had been right.

She sat down at her assigned desk and opened her top drawer, pulling out a faded notebook. Its edges were worn, the cover slightly bent from frequent handling. Her hand trembled as she picked up her pen, hovering it over the page as she read the faint ink of words she'd written months ago. *Dear Elliot.* She'd tried to write this letter so many times, but the right words always eluded her. She didn't know how to feel something for Elliot and make peace with the part of herself that still heard Tom's voice on quiet nights.

She snapped the notebook shut and moved to the window, just as another balloon lifted into the sky. It looked so harmless up there, floating on the wind like a child's toy. But Alice knew better now. The most innocent of things could conceal something deadly.

45

––––––––––

Felixstowe – Three weeks later

Alice removed her flash-proof hood and let it hang around her neck while she waited for the next batch of balloons to be brought to the launch site. She scanned the grey horizon. The wind was strong, and she felt in the pit of her stomach that today's launches, her final launches, would end early.

'I think we're done after this round,' she said to her colleague.

Squadron Leader Thorn was a fellow Scot who had spent the early years of the war in Balloon Command in Edinburgh. He'd been a pilot in the first world war and had rejoined the RAF at the outbreak of the second war.

Thorn tugged his own flash-proof hood away from his face and peered down at his notes. 'Agreed. Pity. Don't want you leaving with unfinished business.'

'To tell you the truth,' said Alice, 'I'll be glad to get back to weather balloons. There's something soothing about watching a balloon ascend into the upper atmosphere knowing its purpose is collecting data.' She watched as the teams in front of her attached their explosive payloads. Another eight balloons were almost ready to launch. 'There's nothing soothing about these balloons.'

Thorn nodded. 'I know what you mean. Barrage balloons are the same. It's tough going to get them off the ground, but once they're up, their purpose is protection, not destruction.'

Barrage balloons were ten times the size of the balloons in front of them. Launching them had been a man's job in the early months of the war. But, as with so many other jobs, WAAFs had quickly stepped in when the men were needed elsewhere.

These balloons acted as a shield above key targets, making it more difficult for enemy aircraft by forcing them to fly at higher altitudes. This reduced their bombing accuracy and increased their vulnerability to Britain's air defences. Barrage balloons didn't harm anyone. At least they weren't designed to. A few planes had collided with the steel cables that tethered the balloons, and the planes hadn't fared well.

A sharp gust of wind came off the sea, scattering grit into Alice's face. 'This isn't what I expected summers by the seaside to be like,' she said.

'Almost makes you miss the fog of Turnhouse, huh?'

Alice smiled. She missed a lot more than the fog at RAF Turnhouse. 'You heading back to Edinburgh soon?'

Thorn shrugged. 'I go where they tell me to. And, for now, they're telling me to be here.' He repositioned his flash-proof hood.

Alice blinked hard and stared down her portable

anemometer. The tiny vane quivered. She frowned. 'Cross-winds are unstable. We'll need to recalibrate the launch angles. If they pull the balloons too low...'

'They could drift back into our own airspace,' Thorn finished grimly. He didn't work in meteorology, but as a pilot and his work with barrage balloons, he understood the hazards of launching in erratic weather.

Alice turned towards the next balloons being prepped. Balloon number 43 was next. Wren Jane Wallace was already in her protective gear, a flash-proof jacket and hood, and fire-proof gloves. She attached the incendiary unit to the jittering balloon.

Alice pulled her hood back into place, the fine gauze covering her face. Working with incendiaries was hazardous. There was no room for complacency.

A dull gleam came from the small, metal incendiary unit swinging like a pendulum beneath the balloon. A fierce payload in a tiny package.

Suddenly, a sharp whistle cut through the air.

'Fuse on 43 just activated,' Wallace yelled. 'Timer's off. Prepare for premature ignition!'

Alice spun on her heel. Balloon 43 jerked violently in the wind, the cable tether twisting. The incendiary unit's indicator light glowed solid red. A telltale warning that the mechanism had triggered early.

'Launch it now!' Alice shouted.

But Wallace was already moving, frantically trying to release the balloon. 'It's stuck!' she yelled, her gloved hands fumbling, and her voice tight with panic.

The balloon was rising, but not fast enough. There was no way it could reach open water. And they couldn't allow it to go off while still within their range.

Alice hesitated, her heart pounding. There were twenty people on the ground. Twenty potential casualties. There was only one choice. She reached for the wire-cutting snips from her launch kit and ran towards the balloon. Every instinct screamed at her to stop. But she didn't.

The balloon pitched dangerously in the wind. She dived beneath the tether and dropped to one knee, clamping her clips to the already frayed cable with all her strength.

'Get back!' Alice yelled.

Come on, come on, come on.

The snips clamped down harder and the cable finally snapped. The balloon jerked skywards with a violent tug.

Five heartbeats later, the device exploded.

The thunderous roar echoed across the estuary. A searing plume of orange flame lit up the sky. Alice pitched backwards, arms instinctively rising to shield her face as a burst of heat washed over her.

Then silence.

Only her own ragged breath in her ears.

She pushed herself up slowly. Wallace was at her side in an instant, helping her to her feet.

'Bloody hell! Are you alright?' asked Wallace.

Alice nodded, her vision shimmering. She peeled off her gloves and hood, wincing as a curl of smoke drifted up from the scorched mesh.

Wallace exhaled heavily, hands on her knees. 'You nearly caught fire. You know that, right?'

Alice didn't answer. Her heartbeat still thundering in her ears.

Later, in the quiet of the operations hut, she sat hunched over a chipped mug of steaming tea. She couldn't bring herself to drink. Her hands trembled as she cradled the mug.

If Wallace hadn't called out in time. If the snips hadn't worked. If she hadn't acted quickly enough.

She shut her eyes and thought of Elliot.

And Tom.

And how thin the line was between life and loss.

46

____

RAF Turnhouse

Alice was at her desk in the meteorology office flipping through squares of coloured fabric. Daphne sat opposite her. Betty had roped them in to making decorations for the dance and, for the past week, Alice and Daphne had spent every teatime making bunting from coloured paper and random swatches of fabric.

Their companionable silence was interrupted when Betty flung open the door, her cheeks flushed and eyes bright with excitement.

'I have the best news!' Betty announced, voice high with glee.

Daphne barely looked up from the strips of fabric in her lap. 'The war is over?' she asked, her tone dry and teasing.

Betty gave a theatrical sigh. 'OK, maybe not the *best* news, but it's still great news.' She marched over to Elliot's chair and sat down behind his desk.

Daphne perked up. 'We don't have to cut out any more

of these fabric triangles?' she asked, tossing her scissors onto the desk and rolling out her shoulders.

Betty shook her head and handed Daphne back her scissors. 'Keep cutting. I have a date for the dance tonight.'

Daphne burst out laughing. 'A *date* for the dance. That's your news?'

'Oh, be quiet, Daph,' Betty said, huffing now, a faint pout forming. 'You'll be going with Ritchie, so why shouldn't I take a date too?'

'Because you were supposed to keep Alice company since Elliot is away,' said Daphne. She shrugged. 'But I guess I can do that, since Ritchie is playing in the band anyway.'

Alice sat, scissors in hand snipping a blue square in half. Her eyes were on the fabric, but her ears were strained to every word.

She hadn't seen Elliot since she'd returned, and she couldn't help but feel that was deliberate on his part. He'd spent the last three weeks on Tiree, a small island in the Inner Hebrides. They'd added a dedicated weather station to the RAF base there and had a meteorological observer squadron flying daily sorties over the Atlantic to capture weather measurements.

'That brings me to my second piece of news,' said Betty, practically vibrating now. 'I may have overheard some weather-related chat this morning. It sounds like Elliot is coming back *today*.'

Alice's fingers paused mid-snip. A flutter spread through her chest, but she quickly smothered it.

'Have you got a speech prepared?' asked Daphne.

Alice shook her head, lips tightening. 'No speeches this time.'

From the corner of her eye, she caught Daphne and Betty exchanging a glance.

'Anyway,' Alice said briskly, pushing aside the sudden lump in her throat. 'Who are you going to the dance with, Betty?'

Betty leaned in as if sharing state secrets. 'He's called Joe Southwood, and he has the *dreamiest* blue eyes I've ever seen.' She glanced behind her and leaned even further forward, whispering now. 'As soon as I saw those eyes I thought our children would be just darling!'

Daphne snorted. 'You don't have to whisper,' she said. 'There's no one here, Mrs Southwood.'

Betty grinned, scooping up some of fabric triangles and sorting them into a neat pile. 'That *does* have a certain ring to it.'

'And, seriously,' added Daphne, her tone softening. 'I'm happy for you. Given all the effort *you've* put into decorating for the dance, I'm glad you'll get to enjoy it.'

'It does look great, doesn't it?' Betty said, missing the sarcasm in Daphne's voice. 'When the other girls first asked me to join the decorating committee, I had to wonder what the point was. But with the middle tables cleared away to create a dancefloor, and the amount of bunting we've made, the place is transformed.'

'*We've*?' asked Daphne, arching an eyebrow.

Betty rolled her eyes and plucked the scissors from Daphne's hand. 'Joe's visiting from London,' she said, picking up a swatch of pink printed fabric and snipping its frayed edge. 'I don't actually know what he does. Something top secret, and civilian since he's not in uniform. He was in our office yesterday and someone mentioned the party. Today he came back and asked me if I'd save him a dance.'

'And let me guess,' said Daphne. 'You told him he could have all of your dances because you weren't going with anyone, and he asked you to go with him.'

Betty's mouth dropped open, her cheeks turning scarlet.

'Oh my goodness,' Daphne cackled. 'I'm right!'

Betty cleared her throat, eyes darting towards Alice for backup. 'That's not exactly what happened.'

'Sounds like you have a nice, handsome man to whisk you around the dancefloor tonight so that's all matters,' said Alice, finally letting a smile slip through. She pointed to herself. 'Plus, a single friend to whisk you away if he turns out to be a terrible bore.'

Just then, the office door swung open. Elliot stood in the doorway, his kit bag slung over his shoulder.

Daphne leaned forward, whispering under her breath. 'Next time, Betty, try to share your gossip a little earlier.'

Alice stood, her heart leaping into her throat. 'Elliot,' she said, the name feeling strange on her lips after so long. 'How was Tiree?'

'Wild and windy,' he said, with a tired grin. He dropped his kit bag on his desk. 'But it was amazing. You would've loved it.' He glanced at Daphne and Betty. 'I'll tell you more later.'

'Top secret weather chat,' said Daphne. 'That's our cue to leave. Come on, Mrs Southwood.'

Betty stood up and thumped Daphne playfully on the arm. She tucked the chair back under Elliot's desk.

Alice's skin tingled and the room hummed with energy. Like a blend of nerves, hope, and something else she couldn't quite define.

Then a voice came in the hallway.

'Aircraftwoman Peters? Is that you?'

A man in a flight suit stepped out from behind Betty, and Alice's mouth dropped open. She knew that grin instantly.

'I can't believe it,' Alice said. 'Pilot Officer Harding!'

She moved around the desk, caught in a swirl of old

memories from her training days in Dunstable. 'What are you doing here?'

'I was with Elliot on Tiree,' Harding said. He dropped the kit bag he carried on the floor and drew her into a warm, brief hug. He turned to Elliot. 'I didn't realise *your* Alice was also *my* Alice.'

'You two know each other?' Elliot asked, a faint edge in his voice.

'We trained together,' Harding said. 'When this one was little more than a secretary in a uniform.'

Daphne's eyes narrowed. 'A what?'

Harding put up his hands in surrender. 'Hey, I'm man enough to admit I was wrong.' He turned to Alice, eyes sincere. 'You're getting quite the name for yourself in meteorology. I heard about your work in Felixstowe. Bombs on balloons. Impressive.'

Alice stiffened. Elliot had talked about her. To *him*.

'Yeah, well,' said Alice, eyes darting to Elliot. 'Did you hear I almost set myself on fire? Not quite as impressive.'

Betty gasped as her hand flew to her mouth. 'Oh, Alice!'

Alice waved it off. 'It was nothing really. An incendiary that detonated early. I had to cut the balloon free.' She pointed towards the ceiling. 'It exploded right on top of us.'

'Wait,' said Harding. He put a hand on Alice's arm. 'That was you?'

'You heard about that?' Alice asked.

Harding nodded. 'A lot of people heard about that.'

Alice groaned and hid her face with her hands. 'It's not quite the way I wanted to end my time in Felixstowe.'

Harding prised her hands away from her face. 'Why not? You saved the day. That's what I heard, anyway.'

Elliot spoke for the first time in minutes. 'How did *you* hear about it?'

Harding smirked. 'Got a girl down there. Wren Jane Wallace. Cute little thing.'

Daphne let out an exasperated grunt. 'You're quite the charmer. I can't imagine why Alice never mentioned you.'

Harding chuckled, slinging his arm around Alice's shoulders.

'Alice and I had something special,' he said. 'But some things are better kept to ourselves.'

Alice shook her head and laughed. 'How long are you here for?'

'I leave tomorrow morning,' said Harding.

'Great,' said Betty. 'You can join us for the dance tonight.'

Elliot cleared his throat. 'Right, let's get that tour started,' he said to Harding, his tone brusque but not unfriendly.

Elliot and Harding shifted their bags to the corner of the office.

Alice reached out, laying a gentle hand on Harding's arm. 'I can't believe I'm saying this, but it's good to see you.'

'You too, Peters,' said Harding. 'Save me a dance.'

Alice nodded, watching as they disappeared out the door.

'That was surreal,' said Alice. And she'd learned that Elliot had been talking about her while she'd been away. She wasn't sure if that was good or not. 'I think Elliot's mad at me. He seemed... off.'

'He seemed jealous,' said Daphne.

'Jealous? Of what?' Alice asked.

'Maybe the number of times you and Mr Tall, Dark, and Handsome touched each other,' Daphne teased. 'Did something happen between you two?'

'No!' Alice said, a little too quickly. 'He was just the cheeky guy on my training course. We sat next to each other.'

'That's probably not what's running through Elliot's mind right now,' said Daphne. 'Just split your dances between Elliot and Harding equally tonight,' she added with a cheeky smirk.

Alice tossed a pencil at her. Daphne ducked, laughing as the pencil clattered to the floor.

Betty scooped it up, replacing it back on Alice's desk. She gathered up the bunting. 'Come on,' she said to Daphne. 'You can help me with these. Alice has some thinking to do.'

'Do I?' asked Alice.

'Or you can keep circling around your feelings for Elliot,' Daphne said. 'Whatever works for you.'

They swept out the door, leaving Alice alone.

She stood still for a moment. A storm churned in her stomach. Confusion, guilt, hope, fear. It was too much.

There was only one place that made sense right now. She grabbed the logbook and her coat, seeking refuge in the comfort of her instrument readings.

47

———

LATER THAT EVENING, THE PARTY WAS WELL UNDERWAY. ALICE had just replenished the bottles of beer on the refreshments table when Daphne appeared carrying a large glass bowl of punch, a ladle tucked under her arm.

She set the bowl down and plunged the ladle into the orange liquid, swirling it around to disperse the apple slices bobbing on the surface. 'Want a taste?'

Alice screwed up her nose and laughed. 'No need. The alcohol is seeping into my body just standing here. How much vodka did you put in it?'

'Enough,' said Daphne. She turned and flicked a strip of bunting that was pinned neatly to the wall. 'Our hard work paid off, don't you think?'

The thin paper streamer swayed gently, catching the flickering light from the overhead bulbs.

'The place actually looks festive,' said Alice, her gaze sweeping the transformed Mess Hall. British flags hung proudly, half-obscuring the usual stains and scuffs on the walls, and clusters of paper lanterns dangled from the ceiling like chandeliers.

The band played cheerful live music on a makeshift stage in the corner – Ritchie strummed a guitar with practiced ease while two of his airmen buddies accompanied him, one with a jaunty fiddle and the other pumping lively notes from an old accordion.

'Will Ritchie get a break so you can dance?' Alice asked, tilting her head towards the stage.

Daphne shrugged, a crooked smile tugging at her lips. 'I'll find someone to dance with regardless.' She opened a bottle of beer and took a long swig.

'I'm sure you will, despite the outfit,' said Alice, giving Daphne's grease-streaked overalls and heavy boots the once-over with mock judgement.

'We don't all have fancy frocks in our wardrobe,' Daphne shot back, grabbing Alice's arm and forcing her into a twirl.

Alice raised an eyebrow. 'You forget I've seen inside your wardrobe.'

Alice had chosen a midnight blue dress with a knee-length hem and short sleeves. The colour made her auburn hair, pinned up in a loose twist, stand out. As she smoothed the fabric, a memory surfaced. This was the same dress she had worn to George Ferguson's house.

'I hope this dress isn't bad luck,' she said, fingers grazing the hem. 'The last time I wore it was to George Ferguson's dinner party.'

'Ooh, the fiancé,' said Daphne with a grin. 'I still can't believe your mother had you engaged behind your back.'

Alice laughed, a genuine, throaty chuckle.

'What are we laughing at?' Betty burst in, appearing as if from nowhere. Her cheeks were flushed pink from dancing, and she made a beeline for Daphne's beer, snatching it without hesitation and taking a hearty gulp.

'Alice's fiancé,' said Daphne dryly. 'And help yourself.'

Betty's eyebrows knitted together as she lowered the bottle. 'Sorry, I was gasping. But fiancé? Did I miss something?'

Alice shook her head. 'No. The last time I wore this dress was to dinner with George Ferguson.' She reached across the table behind her and passed Daphne a fresh beer.

'Oh,' said Betty. She gently touched Alice's arm. 'Are you OK?'

Alice smiled. 'Thanks for the concern, but honestly, I'm fine. It just reminds me of how far I've come. Marrying George would have been the easy choice, but I didn't. I walked away. Maybe that doesn't sound like much, but for me, that took courage.'

Daphne nodded towards the entrance. 'The question is,' she said, her voice suddenly low and pointed, 'how much of that courage do you have left?'

Alice followed Daphne's gaze to the entrance where Elliot and Harding strolled in. Both men wore dark trousers and light shirts, Harding's open at the neck, while Elliot's was neatly buttoned up and accented by a dark green tie. Elliot's eyes immediately locked on to hers with an intensity that made her breath catch in her throat. He leaned towards Harding and said something. Harding turned his head, his eyes bright with mischief. He flashed Alice a smile.

'Here they come,' said Daphne.

'Have you got your dancing shoes on, Alice?' Betty teased.

Alice's stomach fluttered. The crowd seemed to part slightly as the two men strode across the hall.

Harding held his hand out to Alice. 'Care to dance?' he asked.

Alice smiled, sliding her hand into his warm palm. She

caught Elliot's eye briefly. He offered her a small, unreadable smile and stepped aside to let her pass.

Behind them, Ritchie and his fellow musicians kicked the tempo into high gear, launching into an upbeat, rollicking tune. The fiddle took centre stage, the accordion playing along in harmony as Ritchie's guitar strummed out a rapid beat that had the room pulsing.

Alice laughed, breathless, as Harding whisked her around the dance floor. Her blue dress flared as he spun her, her shoes skimming the wooden floor.

Two songs later, the band gave the dancers a little respite. They eased into a slower tune, the kind that made couples draw closer, hips swaying in sync.

Alice breathed deeply as Harding pulled her gently towards him, one hand clasped in hers, the other resting respectfully at her waist.

'I was sorry to hear about your guy,' he said, his gaze soft but steady. 'Tom, right?'

Alice looked up, startled. Her grip on his hand tightened slightly. 'How did you hear about Tom?'

Harding gave a gentle smile. 'Elliot told me.'

She looked away for a moment. The dance floor shimmered with motion and light, but her thoughts drifted elsewhere.

'And now you're wondering what else Elliot has told me about you,' Harding added, a knowing glint in his eye as he leaned in just slightly.

Alice smiled. 'That thought did cross my mind.'

'He's a good man, I think,' said Harding, his tone sincere.

Alice nodded. 'He is.'

Harding glanced around the Mess Hall then back at her. 'There's not much else to do on Tiree, so people tend to talk.'

Alice felt heat creep up her back. The idea of the two men discussing her was more than a little unnerving. She bit her lip, trying not to imagine the details.

'What exactly are you doing on Tiree?' she asked.

Harding's lips curled into a wide grin. 'Flying meteorological sorties over the Atlantic.' His voice carried a hint of pride.

Alice blinked and shook her head.

'You never pictured me for a weather man, huh?'

'No, I didn't,' said Alice. Her eyes narrowed teasingly. 'And Jane Wallace. You know she's too good for you, right?'

Harding threw back his head and laughed, the sound full and genuine. 'Oh, I know.'

When the song faded into silence, Harding released her, stepping back with a small, gallant bow. 'Thank you for the dance.'

They wove their way back towards the refreshments table. Daphne and Elliot stood huddled in conversation. Elliot looked up and handed over two cold bottles of beers.

Alice took hers, feeling the cold seep into her hand. She lifted the bottle to her lips and sipped, wincing at the cool bitterness. 'Where's Betty?' she asked, still slightly breathless.

Daphne arched an eyebrow. 'She ditched us to dance with Joe Southwood, but we saw them sneak out of the door a few minutes ago, so goodness knows what they're up to.' She laughed. 'Although it's Betty. She probably has him fetching another box of decorations.'

Harding turned to Daphne. 'Can you dance in those boots?'

Daphne rolled her shoulders back. 'Well enough to push you around the dancefloor, Harding.'

Harding laughed, passed his beer to Elliot, and held out his arm. 'Let's see about that.'

'Harding,' said Alice. She nodded towards the band. 'Just so you know, Daphne's boyfriend is the guitar player.'

Harding winked at Alice. 'I'll be on my best behaviour.'

'I won't be,' said Daphne. She grabbed him by the shoulders and yanked him backwards onto the dancefloor. 'Let's see what you've got, Harding.'

Alice turned back towards Elliot, feeling a flicker of awkwardness. She placed her beer, still mostly full, on the table.

'Would you rather have punch?' Elliot asked, gesturing towards the large glass bowl Daphne had placed there earlier.

Alice wrinkled her nose. 'Have you tried it? Daphne made it. It's probably ninety percent vodka, ten percent juice.'

Elliot laughed. 'That sounds about right.'

She watched Daphne spinning Harding around the floor with surprising grace given her clumpy footwear.

Elliot set his bottle down on the table. 'Do you want to launch a weather balloon?'

Alice's eyes lit up. 'Yes!'

As they made for the door, Alice glanced back to the dancefloor. Daphne was laughing, one hand in Harding's as she twirled. Betty was still nowhere to be seen. The band had picked up the pace again and the joy in the room was a tangible thing.

Alice smiled. During war, it was these moments, imperfect and alive, that she wanted to hold on to.

She turned to Elliot, walking just ahead of her, his stride steady. Not so long ago, she was busy doing what everyone else expected of her. Now, she was slipping out of a party to chase a weather balloon into the night with a man who once intimidated her. There was still a conversation to be had, but for now, she was happy.

Really, properly happy.

She reached up and tucked a loose strand of hair behind her ear, then quickened her pace to match Elliot's.

As the door swung shut behind them, Alice took one last look over her shoulder. She caught Daphne giving her a wave before the door sealed, muffling the music and laughter inside.

Courage. How much courage did she have left? That's what Daphne had asked her earlier.

Outside, under the stars, she was about to find out.

48

———

ALICE STOOD WITH ELLIOT IN A CLEARED PATCH OF GRASS near the instrument field. They had to be far enough away from any buildings or trees for the balloon to climb freely. Any snag could bring it down, and with it, their chances of data. The balloon inflated slowly. The hiss of the hydrogen tank was the only sound between them.

A low moon glowed through scattered clouds, casting long shadows. Alice's fingers were steady as she tied the radiosonde transmitter to the base of the balloon with a thin cord. It was a delicate piece of kit, a small box no bigger than a loaf of bread. If all went well, the sensors inside would measure the invisible layers of the sky and transmit real time temperature, humidity and pressure data to a ground receiver tuned to the same frequency.

'Looks good,' Elliot murmured, crouching beside her to double-check the connections. 'So, you almost blew yourself up?'

Alice laughed. 'There was a bit more to it than that.' She shook her head. 'It still amazes me that meteorology is playing such a significant part in this war. A balloon filled with nothing but gas and wires, and yet it could change the course of a mission, even the course of the war.'

'That's the beauty of it,' said Elliot, straightening up. 'Fighting with facts and figures. Meteorology is what will *win* this war.'

'How do you mean?' Alice asked.

'Think about it,' he said. 'To win, we need Allied boots on the ground. To do that, we need to cross the Channel. But the Channel is treacherous. Tides. Fog. Wind. The only way we'll ever get enough troops over there is if the weather lets us. And it's the meteorologists who will tell command when that is.'

The balloon was fully inflated now, trembling like an excitable dog waiting to be unleashed.

'You ready?' Elliot asked.

She held the thin string tight in her hands. 'I'm ready.'

The balloon tugged gently. She let go.

It soared skywards, a pale blur against the dark sky, the radiosonde trailing behind like a silver thread.

Elliot was close now, not touching her, but solid and warm beside her.

'Still afraid to love me?' he asked.

The air seemed to vanish from her lungs. She had avoided this conversation for too long. She had hidden behind work, behind fear, behind the grief of losing Tom. But in this quiet field, stripped of walls and war, there was nothing left to shield her.

'Yes,' she said. 'But I'm more afraid of never trying.'

He turned to her. His face was soft in the moonlight, his eyes unguarded. 'Then try.'

She didn't move at first. The wind lifted strands of hair

across her cheek and Elliot reached out, brushing them away with tender fingertips. She stepped forward. Her lips met his with certainty, firm and deliberate, leaving no room for hesitation or doubt.

When they parted, the balloon was long gone, somewhere high above them, already sampling the upper winds.

Elliot smiled, his eyes shining. 'Come on,' he said. 'Let's find out what's happening up there.'

They headed back along the edge of the runway. Harding was leaning against the wall outside the Mess Hall, a cigarette in hand.

'Where's your dance partner?' Alice asked.

Harding smiled. 'She ditched me for a musician.'

'Want to track a weather balloon?' Alice asked.

Harding took a long drag of his cigarette. 'Not tonight. There's another beer in there with my name on it.' He tossed the end of his cigarette to the ground, and pressed his foot to it, extinguishing its glow. 'Maybe I'll see you on Tiree some time, Peters.'

Alice smiled. 'You never know.'

She watched Harding return to the dance and then slipped her hand into Elliot's. He leaned towards her and kissed her, his grin wider than she'd ever seen before.

Once in the office, Elliot moved to his desk, switched on the radiosonde receiver, and pulled an extra chair over.

Alice sat beside him, watching as he adjusted the tuning knob, his focus sharp.

'You know,' said Alice. 'There was never anything between me and Harding.'

Elliot turned to look at her. 'I didn't think there was.'

'Oh,' said Alice. 'That's good. It's just, Daphne thought. Well, it doesn't matter. I just wanted you to know that.'

'Harding's all bluster. Besides, you were with Tom at that time.'

The receiver chirped, then gave a steady ticking tone as the radio signals came in. Elliot turned away, reading the tiny dials and meters. 'Here we go,' he said.

His gaze flicked back and forth between the receiver and the conversion charts on the desk in front of him as he interpreted the data being received.

'Altitude two thousand metres.' His brow furrowed as he concentrated. 'Temperature negative three point six.'

Alice picked up a pencil and scribbled down everything he said. They'd launched the balloon for fun, but any data they could collect was still valuable and should be recorded.

'Pressure seven hundred and ninety-four millibars,' Elliot continued. 'Relative humidity sixty-five percent. Wind from two hundred and forty degrees, speed twenty knots.'

Once Alice had finished writing, Elliot plucked the pencil from her fingers and slid the notebook towards him.

'I'll write, you read,' he said.

Alice concentrated hard, desperate not to miss a thing. 'Altitude three thousand metres. Temperature negative seven point eight. Pressure seven hundred and one millibars. Relative humidity fifty-eight percent. Wind from two hundred and thirty degrees, speed thirty-two knots.'

'That's a strong gradient,' said Elliot.

It took two hours for the full data set to be received and interpreted.

Finally, Elliot flicked the receiver off with a decisive click. 'It's after midnight,' he said. 'You should go home.'

Alice rolled her shoulders back, feeling the tension ease as she stretched out her neck. The soft glow of the desk lamp cast warm pools of light around them. 'Elliot?'

He looked up, meeting her gaze with attentive eyes. 'Yeah?'

She leaned forward, bridging the space between them, and pressed her lips to his once more, the gesture tender and lingering. 'Thank you for waiting,' she whispered.

Elliot's smile grew, slow and sincere. 'As long as it took.'

49

THE MORNING AFTER THE PARTY, ALICE WAS ON THE EARLY shift. It was still dark as she took her first readings and made her way back to the meteorology office. A patch of low pressure had rolled in overnight, and thanks to a thick fog, no planes would be taking off that morning.

Once she'd coded and sent off her data, she sat on top of the drawers by the office window, waiting for that first chink of light. Her uniform jacket was draped over her shoulders, and her hair curled slightly at her temples from the damp air. Outside, the airfield shimmered with puddles, but the quiet was soothing.

The office door creaked opened, and Elliot approached without a word, holding out a mug of tea. He handed it to her and leaned against the wall on the other side of the window, close but not crowding.

'Flights will be back on this afternoon, I expect,' he said.

'Mid-morning,' she replied softly. 'The skies will clear soon.'

A gentle smile tugged at Elliot's lips, and they both sipped from their mugs, savouring the momentary peace.

She glanced at him over the rim of her mug, studying the lines near his eyes, the steadiness in his expression. Something had changed, not just between them, but within her own heart. She patted the space beside her on top of the drawers, and Elliot sat down, his arm pressed against hers.

'It doesn't feel the way I thought it would,' she said suddenly.

'What doesn't?' he asked, his eyebrows knitted together in curiosity.

'Letting someone in again.' She rotated the mug in her hands, tracing its edge with her fingertip. 'I thought it would feel like a betrayal. Of Tom. Of everything we didn't get to have.'

Elliot didn't speak right away. He waited. He never rushed her, always allowing space for her thoughts to unfold.

'And now?' he asked.

She turned to the window, where a slender beam of sunlight pierced through the grey clouds and spilled across the runway.

'Now it feels like... breathing,' she said. 'Like coming back to myself.'

Elliot curled his fingers around hers with gentle reassurance. She nestled her head against his shoulder, feeling the warmth and steady rhythm of his breath. He softly kissed the top of her head.

'The war's not over,' she said. 'But we're here, together. And for now, that's enough.'

They sat that way for a while longer, watching the sky together – forecasters by trade, but for once, not trying to predict what came next.

~

The sun had pushed fully through by mid-morning, just as Alice had predicted, a quiet triumph in a world where so little felt certain.

She found Daphne in the hangar, half-swallowed by the belly of a Spitfire. Only her legs stuck out in worn overalls smeared with oil. She was humming something cheerful and off-key.

'You'll never believe this,' Daphne called out without looking. 'My next job is to polish this baby from nose to tail. Either the war's ending or someone important is visiting.'

Alice smiled, shoving her hands into the pockets of her coat to warm them.

Daphne slid out from under the plane, blinking in the light. Her hair stuck out in wisps from under a headscarf, and one eyebrow was streaked with grease. She wiped her hands on a rag, then stood up, sizing Alice up like she was inspecting an engine. 'Alright,' she said, narrowing her eyes with mock suspicion. 'What's going on? No one ever visits me here.'

'Nothing,' said Alice, a little too quickly.

Daphne pointed the dirty rag at her. 'I don't believe you. I haven't seen a smile like that on your face since. Well, since forever.'

Alice tried and failed to suppress a grin. 'I smile all the time.'

'Not like that you don't.' Daphne stepped closer, tilting her head. 'You look like you're trying not to float off the ground. What happened? Something in the forecast lift your spirits? Or someone?'

Alice flushed, glancing away, her shoes scuffing the hangar floor. She didn't say anything, but the silence seemed to speak for her.

'So,' Daphne said, folding her arms and cocking her head, 'Elliot or Harding?'

'Daphne!' Alice protested, heat creeping up her neck.

'Ah,' Daphne said with a smug grin. 'Elliot, then.'

Alice hesitated, then tilted her head. 'What do you think?'

Daphne slung an arm casually around Alice's shoulder. 'You deserve something good, Alice.' She'd dropped the teasing for something gentler. 'Hell, we all do. But you most of all.'

Alice leaned into her friend. 'Thanks, Daph.'

'Now get out of here before someone asks you to help change a tyre.'

Alice laughed. She walked away with the sound of Daphne's laughter echoing behind her, and for the first time in a long time, the day ahead felt like a beginning.

50

───────

One Year Later

There was no such thing as a weekend when you did war work, and two days off together had become a rare luxury. Alice had chosen to spend her two days in Millwood. Elliot had dropped her off the day before, but he'd had to return immediately to Turnhouse for a top secret meeting. Everyone was on edge. Planning for the invasion was well underway, only no one seemed to know if it was happening next month or next year.

Over the past year, Elliot had visited Millwood with Alice three times, charming Violet a little more with each visit. It helped that he was handsome, carried the impressive title of Flight Lieutenant, and had been happy to be paraded around the village with Violet on his arm. Her mother was quite taken with him. As was Alice. They had managed to navigate both their relationship and their work without letting one interfere with the other.

Now, on a quiet Tuesday morning, Alice sat at Mrs

Ferguson's well-worn wooden table, listening intently as she read aloud her latest letter from George. Soft light filtered through the kitchen window, casting a gentle glow over the room.

'I'm so happy to hear that George is well,' said Alice.

Mrs Ferguson nodded her head. 'I know I shouldn't say it, but war has been good for him. It's made him grow up and get out from under the influence of his mother.' She paused, glancing at the letter in her hands. 'He writes about the camaraderie he's found with his fellow soldiers, how they've become like brothers to him. It's given him a sense of purpose and responsibility that he's never had before.'

'He's becoming his own man,' said Alice.

Mrs Ferguson smiled. 'That he is.'

Alice sipped her tea, glancing down at the chips in the mug. War was a strange thing. For so many people, including her, it was devastating and liberating all at once.

Mrs Ferguson folded the letter and tucked it back in its envelope. 'Now, tell me, what's new with you?'

Alice's mind buzzed with the enormity of it all. The fleet of weather ships and the number of weather reconnaissance flights had expanded rapidly. The Met Office was now working directly with their counterparts in the Royal Navy and the US Army Air Forces. British meteorologist, Group Captain James Stagg, had become the chief meteorological adviser to General Eisenhower, the man responsible for leading the Allied invasion. Meteorology was a pivotal factor in the war's progress and Alice was right in the thick of it.

Despite the thrill of her work, it was sometimes frustrating to keep it all to herself. But she understood why that had to be the case. She shrugged and said, 'Not a lot.'

Mrs Ferguson laughed and stood up. 'When this war is over, I'm looking forward to hearing all your stories. Something that isn't a secret, however, is Jocelyn. She's pregnant again.'

Alice laughed. 'Oh no! Did Mr Nobleman's fence break again?'

Mrs Ferguson tutted. 'Silly man. But no. This one was planned.' She counted the towering stack of sandwiches.

'That's an awful lot of sandwiches you've got there.'

'They're for the soldiers,' said Mrs Ferguson.

'The Poles?' asked Alice, recalling that Polish soldiers were billeted near the farm. They had become something of a permanent presence in East Lothian. Working alongside the British, the Poles supported the defence of the east coast of Scotland and were now regularly seen in and around the village.

Mrs Ferguson shook her head. 'New ones,' she said. 'They're on Gullane beach. They've got these massive trucks that drive right out of the sea and onto the sand.'

Alice was aware of a military exercise in progress. There had been a steady stream of ships navigating to and from the port at Leith all last week. The rumours at Turnhouse suggested it was a rehearsal for landing in France. But she was surprised to hear that anyone could get close enough to witness the action given the secrecy and security that must have surrounded the operation. On the drive here, she and Elliot had been rerouted, diverted along several different roads and nowhere near the beaches.

'And you've seen this?' Alice asked, curiosity piqued.

'Not officially, of course,' said Mrs Ferguson, her tone conspiratorial. 'They've got roadblocks up, and guards are stationed everywhere to stop people going near the beach. But these boys think with their stomachs. As long as I don't go empty-handed, I can usually find someone who'll let me sneak past.'

Alice laughed. That sounded about right. She'd known many an airman who could be swayed by food, and it seemed the army was no different.

With the sandwiches neatly wrapped, Mrs Ferguson picked up a flask and began filling it with steaming coffee. 'I'll just fill this flask, and we'll head off and take a peek,' she said, her eyes twinkling with a sense of adventure. 'You can pop those mugs into the bag on the counter, if you like.'

Alice stood up and placed half a dozen tin mugs into a bag, wondering just home many times Mrs Ferguson had sneaked her way down to the beach.

They arrived at the road leading down to Gullane Bents, where a young soldier stood guard at a makeshift roadblock. He looked barely old enough for military service, his face smooth and unweathered, but there was a weariness in his eyes, one that suggested a long morning of monotony rather than the strain of battle. He stretched out his arms and yawned.

'Coffee was a good idea,' Alice murmured.

Noticing them approaching, the soldier quickly stifled his yawn. 'I'm sorry, folks, this road is closed,' he said.

Mrs Ferguson stepped forward. 'Oh, don't worry, son, we know,' she said, her tone warmer than Alice had ever heard it before. 'We're only here to give you boys something to eat. We've seen how hard you've all been working this past week.'

She rummaged through her bag and produced a small, neatly wrapped paper parcel. Presenting it to the soldier, she added, 'Rabbit pie. Freshly made this morning.'

The soldier straightened at once, as if buoyed by the

mere thought of a meal. He reached for the parcel. With careful hands, he unwrapped the pie, lifting it close to his face and inhaling deeply. 'It smells incredible,' he said. 'I haven't had rabbit for months.'

'We country folk like to take care of our boys on the frontline,' said Mrs Ferguson. 'Coffee?'

'Yes, please, ma'am,' he said.

Alice handed him a tin mug, and the soldier accepted it with an eager grin.

Mrs Ferguson unwrapped the platter of sandwiches while Alice passed the soldier a napkin.

'Some sandwiches for later?' Mrs Ferguson asked in a soft, sweet tone.

The soldier wrapped up the pie, tucking it into his pocket, then placed his steaming cup at his feet and helped himself to two hearty sandwiches. 'Thank you,' he said. 'This is much better than what the army have been feeding us out here.'

Mrs Ferguson nodded. 'You're very welcome. Now, which way should we go to hand out the rest of these?' she asked.

The soldier took a bite of his ham sandwich, chewing thoughtfully before gesturing behind him, through the roadblock. 'Just down that way,' he said.

They moved on, passing another half a dozen soldiers, handing out sandwiches and draining the flask of coffee. By the time they were done, they had reached Main Street – a stone's throw from an open view of the beach.

Ducking down the side street, they stopped on the grassy slope above the bay at Gullane. From their vantage point, Alice gazed out into the shimmering water. Anchored in the Firth of Forth was a large Navy ship, its dark silhouette imposing on the horizon. Surrounding it, smaller boats

– amphibious trucks – bobbed on the waves as they made their way to the sandy beach.

White-capped waves lapped against the side of the vessels. Just as Mrs Ferguson had described, the boats seamlessly transformed into trucks and emerged from the surf, driving smoothly onto the beach.

Men leapt from the vehicles with practiced precision, swiftly unloading crates of weapons onto other waiting trucks. The scene was a flurry of motion, yet it appeared carefully choreographed.

War had come to East Lothian and Alice felt a flicker of relief that the soldiers assembling on the beach were their own.

'What do you think?' asked Mrs Ferguson, pulling Alice from her thoughts. 'Do you think their plan will work?'

Alice looked back at the Navy ship on the horizon, her mind racing. If this was the plan for landing in France, every detail would matter. And Elliot was right. The weather would be crucial. The Navy would need low tides and calm seas, while the RAF would need a full moon to guide the supporting air crews. But if the weather was too stable, the Germans would see them coming.

While her inner doubts whizzed around her body, one of the trucks, now fully loaded, rumbled to life and drove off the beach below. A soldier nearby collapsed to his knees and vomited, his body convulsing as the contents of his stomach erupted, no doubt churned by the waves in the North Sea. Waves that, from land, seemed so gentle.

When he had nothing left to expel, the man pushed himself upright, kicked sand over the mess, and ran back towards the amphibious trucks.

Alice swallowed hard. 'Yes,' she said finally. 'Their plan will work.'

Mrs Ferguson exhaled, as if he had been holding her breath, and nodded. She dusted her hands. 'Let's get back to the farm,' she said. 'You can say hello to Bernie.'

Tearing their gazes away from the shoreline, they turned for home, collecting the now-empty tin mugs along the way. But Alice couldn't get the images from the beach out of her mind. No amount of preparation could guarantee success. If the operation failed, what would happen next?

51

6 June 1944

'This is D-Day. This is not a practice. This is D-Day.'

The voice burst across the Tannoy system, cutting through the low murmur of midnight. In the mess hall, conversations stopped, and utensils clattered against plates. For a moment, everyone sat frozen, glancing at one another to confirm they had truly heard what they thought they had.

The officers were the first to react, pushing back their chairs and marching with speed and purpose. Alice sprang to her feet, abandoning her half-eaten meal, and hurried towards the meteorology office. Elliot was already there, standing in the centre of the room, his expression serious. He raised a hand to signal to Alice and the other meteorology assistants filing in behind her to wait.

All leave had been cancelled for the past two months, and meteorology assistants had been doubled up on shifts for the last week. Everyone had known the invasion was coming, but no one had known exactly when. That task fell to Group Captain James Stagg, who had been tasked with finding the ideal conditions for the Allies to cross the Channel.

Alice took a seat by the window and stared out into the night sky. The full moon shone brightly, its edges blurred by a veil of cloud cover. She ran her finger down the glass, tracing a zigzag line as if connecting the dots of rain still clinging to the other side. The gale-force winds had eased, but the driving rain lingered.

By sunrise, everyone would know what had happened. The Nazis would know, too. The fight back had begun. And one way or the another, the end of the war would be in sight.

Once everyone had reported for duty, Elliot cleared his throat. 'Our job for the next twenty-four hours is to monitor weather activity and send continuous reports to HQ.'

Excitement crackled in the air, but Elliot tempered it with a raised hand. 'Before we begin,' he said, his voice quieter now, 'let's take a moment to close our eyes and offer whatever kind of prayer means something to you for the boys out in the Channel.'

Alice had seen the rehearsals – amphibious trucks landing on the beach at Gullane. Similar exercises had reportedly taken place up and down the Scottish coast and Ritchie had spoken of the RAF drills over the Firth of Clyde. For weeks, American troops had flooded into bases across the country. The signs had been there. Everyone had been waiting for this moment.

Now that it was here, the announcement over the Tannoy felt like a relief. Rumour had it that bad weather had already delayed the operation by a day. But everything was in place. Tens of thousands of troops were in the Channel. Elaborate deceptions were at play to confuse the Nazis.

The full moon and low tides were essential elements, and they wouldn't last long. Months of intricate planning and costly rehearsals had led to this. The only thing that could still disrupt it was the weather.

And another delay would be disastrous. Massive troop movements couldn't remain undetected for long.

Alice wasn't privy to classified information, but she had learned to read Elliot as clearly as the weather. She had seen the anguish on his face over the last few days as he read the hourly weather reports. He had paced the edge of the runway, and scanned the sky as if he could will the thick, grey clouds to break apart. He hadn't left the base at all over the weekend.

Alice glanced out of the window again. It seemed Stagg and his team had correctly predicted a break in the weather. The storm was clearing from the west and, as cloud drifted away, the moon shone brightly once more.

She closed her eyes and said a quiet prayer for the men risking their lives at that very moment. Many of the men who had passed through RAF Turnhouse in the last few years would be out there. And she prayed they all made it back.

When she opened her eyes, Elliot asked, 'Who's first on instruments?'

Alice's hand shot up. 'I'll do them.'

Elliot nodded, and she grabbed the weather logbook.

Outside, the air was thick with moisture, the scent of damp earth mingling with the tang of aviation fuel. She moved along the runway's edge, heading towards the meteorology enclosure. The operation was already underway, paratroopers had likely landed, and soon the naval and aerial assaults would begin.

It was too late to turn back, whatever the weather.

Still, her orders were clear: monitor, encrypt, and report on every weather instrument they had available to them. Accurate forecasts would be just as critical in the battles ahead as they were for today.

She entered the enclosure and carefully opened the Stevenson Screen, the instruments inside glistening with condensation. Right now, the lives of tens of thousands of men depended on the weather matching its forecast.

Alice set the notebook down and recorded the instrument readings.

By the time morning came, Alice barely registered the hard surface of the desk beneath her forehead. Her whole body was drained, her mind foggy after hours of coding, transmissions, and prayers. Her eyelids fluttered, heavy as lead, and exhaustion pinned her down like a weight.

A long yawn escaped her lips, and she forced herself to sit up, smiling at Elliot who looked just as weary. Dawn had broken, casting weak, pale light through the office window.

Just then the door burst open.

Daphne and Betty rushed in, the sharp clip of Betty's heels against the floor shocking Alice back into alertness. Daphne looked as frazzled as Alice felt, her hair limp and overalls stained with grease and far too much oil, clear signs that she too had worked through the night. Betty's shift hadn't yet started. She was as pristine as ever, her uniform pressed, her hair styled in smooth waves. She looked well-rested and smelled faintly of lavender soap.

'Turn on the wireless,' said Daphne, panting. 'The official announcement is about to go live.'

Elliot groaned as he stood, rolling out the stiffness in his shoulders before reaching for the dial. The wireless crackled to life, static hissing.

Alice rubbed the heel of her palm against her tired eyes. She moved to Elliot's side and reached for his hand, fingers intertwining in an unspoken need for comfort.

They all bowed their heads, breath held, as the wireless crackled again. Then, at last, the voice of the BBC news announcer broke through:

'Communique number one. Under the command of General Eisenhower, Allied naval forces, supported by strong air forces, began landing Allied armies this morning on the northern coast of France.'

Elliot gave Alice's hand a small squeeze. 'Well, it's official,' he said.

The room remained silent for a moment longer, each of them absorbing the enormity of it.

The invasion had begun. The sun had fully risen, and the world was waking up to a new chapter in history.

52

—————

A year later and the war in Europe was over. Alice stood at the edge of the aircraft hangar, her eyes trained on the sky. For once, she wasn't watching cloud formations or measuring wind speeds. She was on the lookout for a single plane, carrying its most precious cargo yet.

Daphne.

The late afternoon sun painted the horizon in hues of gold and blush pink. Alice squinted as she scanned the sky.

'Do you see them yet?' she asked, shifting her weight from foot to foot.

Betty raised a hand to her brow, shielding her eyes from the glare. 'No. I still can't believe she's actually doing this.'

'Me neither,' said Alice, hugging her arms to her chest. 'Flying over Edinburgh as a passenger is one thing, but taking the controls is... I don't even know the word for it.'

'Terrifying,' Betty offered.

'Magical,' Alice countered. 'That will be Daphne's word.'

Around them, the base thrummed with life – mechanics shouting over the roar of an engine, the distant bark of a commanding officer, and the steady thud of boots on concrete. Despite the rest of Scotland still riding the wave of VE Day celebrations, work at RAF Turnhouse had continued at its usual relentless pace. War still raged in the Pacific, and until demobilisation notices arrived, life in the Women's Auxiliary Air Force remained business as usual. With the one exception that RAF pilots were being granted permission to take some WAAFs on special flights over Europe as a gesture of gratitude.

Of course, Daphne had been desperate to go, but with no flights leaving from Turnhouse, it had seemed impossible. Then Ritchie had worked his magic, securing a small Tiger Moth, a nimble trainer aircraft with dual controls and an open cockpit, and offered Daphne her first flying lesson.

Betty squinted towards the horizon. 'Is that them?'

Alice looked up. A speck had appeared in the sky, growing larger by the second. Then the familiar shape of the Tiger Moth emerged, its yellow fuselage catching the light as it dipped gracefully towards the airfield.

Alice barely breathed as she watched the landing. The plane's wheels kissed the ground, bounced slightly, then settled into a smooth roll across the runway. The engine sputtered and whined as it powered down.

Daphne leapt from the plane and pulled her leather helmet off. Her long hair was a wild tangle and her grin stretched from ear to ear. She bolted towards Alice and Betty, her boots pounding the ground, laughter bubbling from her.

Alice barely had time to brace herself before Daphne flung her arms around them both, squealing into their ears.

'Well?' asked Alice, breathless from the force of the hug.

Daphne stepped back, her eyes wide with exhilaration. She tilted her face to the sky, as if she was still up there. 'Magical,' she whispered, as if the word itself contained all the wonder she felt.

Alice grinned at Betty, who only shook her head and laughed.

'Turns out the Tiger Moth is the plane for me,' said Daphne. 'Not only did I get to take the controls, but with the open cockpit, I could see for miles! I felt...' She pressed a hand to her chest, exhaling. 'I felt free.'

Behind them, Ritchie strode towards the group, having handed the plane over to the ground crew. 'Who's going up next?' he asked, amusement dancing in his voice.

The girls all laughed, and Ritchie shrugged. 'The offer's there.'

'Aircraftwoman Peters?'

Alice turned, her stomach flipping at hearing her name so formally.

A clerk from the mail room strode towards her. She thrust a letter into Alice's hands. 'Congratulations,' said the clerk, smiling, before she pivoted and walked away to deliver the rest of her mail.

Alice blinked, her heart hammering.

'What is it?' Betty asked, leaning in.

Alice slid her thumb along the envelope's seal and pulled out the crisp paper inside. Her stomach dropped as she read the title.

Notice of Demobilisation.

She swallowed hard. 'I'm being demobbed.'

Betty inhaled a sharp breath. 'When?'

Alice forced her eyes back to the letter, scanning the neatly typed words. 'November.'

A lump formed in her throat. The clerk had obviously

thought she was delivering good news. And for many women, it was good news. Plenty of them were counting the days until they could return to their old lives.

But Alice didn't want to go back.

Her old life had become somewhere she enjoyed visiting, not somewhere she belonged.

She folded the letter carefully, her fingers firm around the edges. Then she lifted her gaze to Ritchie.

'Ritchie,' she said, her voice steady. 'I think I will take that flight.'

53

A WEEK STRETCHED BY BEFORE ALICE AND RITCHIE'S schedules aligned, and the Tiger Moth was free. Elliot tugged on the straps of Alice's parachute, checking and rechecking until he was satisfied it was securely fastened. A gentle breeze teased loose strands of her hair, and she tilted her face to the open sky, heart quickening.

'Please be gentle with me,' she whispered.

Elliot, standing in front of her, smiled. He pressed his lips to hers and kissed her firmly before he too cast a glance towards the sky.

Beside him, Betty's complexion was ashen. She gnawed at her fingernails, her eyes darting between Alice and the waiting plane. 'You don't have to do this,' she said.

'Shush,' Daphne murmured, giving Betty a gentle nudge. 'She *wants* to. You should be going up too. Time is ticking away for all of us. When will we ever get another chance?'

They had all now received their demobilisation orders. Betty was the only one relieved by the prospect of leaving. She had no plan beyond returning to her parents' house and was looking forward to no more late-night shifts, no more war. The uncertainty of what came next didn't seem to bother her. Alice almost envied her ability to let go so easily.

Ritchie strode over to Daphne, pressing a quick kiss to her cheek. 'You jealous?' he teased.

'Nah,' Daphne said breezily. 'She can have you.'

Ritchie laughed and continued towards the Tiger Moth, the same plane he'd given Daphne her first flying lesson in.

Elliot clasped Alice's hand in his. 'You ready?' he asked.

Alice exhaled sharply. 'Is it possible to be ready and terrified at the same time?'

Daphne's lips curved into a knowing smile. 'I think that's the perfect way to feel.'

Betty stepped forward, hesitating. Alice caught Daphne throwing her a warning glare, as if silently pleading with her not to say anything that might plant doubt in Alice's mind.

Betty squared her shoulders. 'Keep calm and carry on,' she said, her smile tight and forced.

Alice pulled them both into a hug, holding on for a moment longer than necessary. Wherever she ended up next, it wasn't likely to be anywhere near Daphne or Betty. She and Elliot hadn't discussed their future either. The thought had gnawed at her for weeks, a dull ache that she was refusing to confront.

'Ready when you are,' Ritchie called, gently hurrying Alice on.

She took a steadying breath and stepped towards the plane, its bright yellow fuselage gleaming under the late morning sun. Ritchie extended a hand, and she grasped it, her grip tighter than she intended. The moment her foot touched the metal step, a thrill of nervous anticipation surged through her. She swung her leg over the side and eased herself into the narrow front seat. Before her, the cockpit held unfamiliar dials and levers, a world of machinery she had no intention of touching.

She pulled the heavy leather helmet over her head, the snug fit muting the surrounding sounds. The chinstrap was firm against her jaw.

Ritchie secured himself in the back seat.

'Ready?' his voice crackled through the intercom.

'Ready,' said Alice.

The world outside blurred as the engine roared to life, drowning out everything else, her doubts, her fears, even Betty and Elliot's worried expressions. She cast one last glance down at Daphne, who was grinning, as she watched.

The propeller spun to life and the plane lurched forward. The vibrations pulsed through Alice's body as the Tiger Moth gained speed along the runway. Wind rushed against her exposed face, sharp and exhilarating, stealing her breath. Then, with a smooth, powerful lift, they were airborne.

The ground fell away beneath them, the base and airfield shrinking into miniature. Alice closed her eyes for a moment, surrendering to the weightless sensation of ascent.

When she opened them again, a breathtaking panorama unfolded. The city of Edinburgh tucked behind them, and patchwork fields stretching ahead in a mosaic of greens and golds. Across the estuary, the Forth Bridge appeared, spanning the water like a steel serpent, its intricate lattice glowing fiery red in the sunlight.

She craned her neck, but could no longer see RAF Turnhouse. The long hours spent there tracking weather data, studying wind speeds and cloud formations, and coding reports had given her a sense of purpose. It had been challenging, but she'd loved every minute of it, and it had shaped her in ways she never could have imagined when she'd first entered Alderbrae recruitment office.

A sense of peace washed over her as she gazed at the world spread out beneath her. Demobilisation did not have to mean the end of her adventures. There was nothing but endless possibilities on the horizon.

Ritchie's voice crackled through the intercom again. 'Well, what do you think?' he asked.

Alice smiled.

'Marvellous,' she said, loud enough for him to hear over the droning engine. Then, quieter, more to herself than anyone else, she said, 'I think the future can be anything I want it to be.'

An hour later, the Tiger Moth's wheels screeched on landing, throwing up a swirl of dust, as it rolled to a stop. Alice sat still until Daphne reached up and extended a steady hand to help her climb out.

'What did you think?' Daphne asked as Alice dropped down to the ground. Daphne leaned in and unfastened Alice's chin strap.

Alice pulled her helmet off and let out a breathless laugh. 'It was everything you said it would be.'

Elliot stood a few paces behind with his hands in his pockets, waiting until Alice had stripped out of her flying gear. Then he stepped forward and took her hand. 'You're not about to throw up, are you?' he teased.

Alice laughed and shook her head, the roar of the engine still echoing in her ears. 'No, I'm not.'

He moved closer and pressed his lips gently against her cheek, making her pulse drum that little bit faster.

Ritchie jumped down from the plane in one smooth move.

'Thanks again, Ritchie,' Alice said.

'My pleasure.' Ritchie tugged off his helmet. He wiped the sweat from his brow and then nodded towards the plane and its polished fuselage. 'Hey, Daph. How would you like to own one of these?'

Daphne laughed.

'I'm serious,' Ritchie said. 'War's over, and the Tiger Moth is considered a surplus military asset so they're selling them off cheap.'

Betty, standing well back from the plane with her arms folded, cleared her throat. 'Isn't it too soon to be offloading military assets?'

Ritchie shrugged. 'Tell that to the Ministry of Supply. There are some hoops to jump through, paperwork, security clearance, that kind of thing. But it's just a formality for us, I would think.'

Daphne's grin spread wide. 'You're serious?'

Ritchie nodded and leaned back, casually resting against the body of the plane. 'You up for it?'

Daphne's fingers trailed across the Tiger Moth's smooth fuselage. Alice could see her mind at work. 'Let's open a flying school. I'll be your first trainee. You fly, I'll fix.'

Ritchie raised his palm, and Daphne slapped it with a triumphant high-five, her face shining with pure joy.

Betty brushed dust from her uniform. 'I've had enough excitement for one day. While you two plan your future, I'm off for lunch. Anyone want to come?'

'I will,' said Elliot. 'I heard there's rhubarb crumble.' He wrapped his arm around Alice. 'You coming?'

Alice nodded. As they set off towards the Mess Hall, Alice wiggled free from Elliot's hold and strode ahead.

'What's the hurry?' Elliot asked, increasing his pace to match hers.

'Oh, no,' said Betty, now trailing behind. 'You *are* going to throw up, aren't you?'

Alice turned and laughed. 'Why does everyone think I'm going to throw up?'

'Well, why the hurry?' asked Betty.

They filed into the Mess Hall, the rich savoury smell of stew greeting them. Alice made a beeline for the newspaper rack. Scanning the titles, she pulled a copy of The Daily Telegraph free from the stand and held it up. 'This is why.'

Elliot furrowed his brow. 'You want to read the news?'

Alice shook her head. 'No. I want to read the job adverts.'

Elliot and Betty exchanged bemused looks. 'Why?' asked Betty.

'Because,' said Alice, spreading the newspaper out on a nearby table, 'getting demobbed doesn't mean going back to Millwood. I am a woman with choices.'

She flicked to the Situations Vacant pages, scanning through the list of jobs advertised. Bookkeeper. Cashier. Clerk. Domestic Help. Typist.

'Not great choices,' said Alice. 'But choices all the same.'

54

November 1945

The sun hung low in the morning sky, a bright gold that promised to chase away the chill of the winter air. But it did little to warm Alice's mood. It was almost eight o'clock and she strolled alongside the runway, instrument logbook in hand, for the final time.

In just two hours, she'd be on a train bound for Lancashire, where she would be officially demobilised. After five years of dedicated service, she would be released with a handful of clothing coupons and a civilian ration book. It felt like too small an ending for something that had defined her so fully.

She unlatched the Stevenson Screen, tapped the barometer's glass, and carefully noted the readings. Structure and routine had been her life for so long. She couldn't go back to Millwood without at least a plan.

Readings collected and observations noted, Alice made her way back to the meteorology office, passing the Mess

Hall on the way to snag a newspaper from a collection near the door.

Elliot was standing by the window when she walked in. He turned as the door clicked shut behind her.

'All done?' he asked.

She held up the logbook. 'Do you want to check my figures one last time?'

He smiled, rather sheepishly, and Alice laughed.

Once her data was submitted, she sank down into her chair. Betty had been demobbed in September and had counted down the days until her last shift. Even Daphne, who had another week to go, was looking forward to it, eager to start the next chapter. She and Ritchie were now the proud owners of two Tiger Moths and Daphne was itching to take to the skies again.

'We should leave in an hour,' said Elliot, nodding towards the clock on the wall. 'You'll want plenty of time before the train.'

Alice nodded, her gaze fixed on the second hand ticking forward. 'It's hard to believe I'll be back in Millwood tonight.'

'And you're certain you don't want to come and stay with me in Edinburgh?' Elliot asked gently.

She smiled at him. 'Of course I want to. But not like this.'

Moving in with Elliot was too close to a life of domesticity. She wanted a husband and a family, but she wanted the timing of that to be on her terms, not because she had nothing else to do.

She unfolded the newspaper across her desk and turned to the job adverts, scanning down the listings.

'Anything?' Elliot asked, removing his glasses to polish them with the edge of his sleeve.

'More bookkeepers,' she murmured. There was a time

when she would have jumped at the opportunity to apply for a bookkeeper post. But now, that felt like moving backwards.

'You'll find something,' he said, holding his glasses up towards the window to check the lenses were clean.

She knew he was trying to be supportive, but his platitudes were not helping. It had been months and nothing remotely interesting had been advertised. It was easier for him. He'd been retained by the RAF, his future neatly mapped out in forecasts and flight paths. For her, the horizon was murky.

She turned the page. *Situations Wanted – Men.*

Her brow furrowed. It was surprising that they even had to advertise. Men were returning from military service and walking into jobs, often reclaiming their old positions, while the women who had filled in for them were being encouraged to return to domestic life. It made sense, she supposed. But that didn't make it fair.

Then her eyes landed on something different.

Deputy Forecaster – Civil Aviation.

Her pulse notched up a gear as she read through the advert. The Air Ministry were recruiting someone to provide weather briefings at London's new civilian airport. Applicants had to collect an application form in person with interviews in December, ahead of the airport opening in the spring. *Preference given to applicants with prior service in the RAF's meteorological branch.*

She read the advert again. Every word of it was something she could do. Something she *had* done.

'Elliot,' she said, her voice sharper than she had intended.

He looked up from his desk.

'How would you feel about me working in London?'

A crease formed on his forehead, and he stood up, crossing the room. She pushed the newspaper across the table towards him and tapped her finger to the advert.

He scanned the lines of text, his eyes darting back and forth across the page. After a moment, he slid the paper back towards her and crossed his arms over his chest. 'I hate to point out the obvious.'

Alice's heart sank. 'I know. I'm not a man.'

He perched on the edge of Alice's desk and stared at her, his eyes looking deeper into hers as if searching for the answer to a question he hadn't yet asked.

'London,' she said again, quieter now. 'Whether it's this job or another one. How would you feel?'

Elliot looked away. His jaw clenched, the pause stretching between them. When he finally met her gaze again, his expression carried a mix of emotions she found impossible to decipher. 'Those six months when you were in Felixstowe were the hardest six months of this war for me,' he said.

Alice reached for the pencil on her desk, rolling it beneath her fingers. 'Those months were hard for me too. But we weren't together then.'

The separation had been difficult, and now that they were a couple, she couldn't help but wonder if any future separation would be easier or infinitely harder. Would knowing exactly what she was missing make the distance more unbearable?

Elliot reached out, pressing her hand gently to the desk. She stilled the pencil, her fingers tightening under his.

'I love you, Alice,' he said simply.

She looked up at him, a smile flickering at the corner of her mouth. 'I love you too. Is there a "but" coming?'

He shook his head. 'No buts. I love you. That's it. And

whether it's this job or another one, I can't say how I'll feel about it. All I can promise is that I won't stand in your way. Just promise me we'll talk about it. That we'll decide together.'

It wasn't a guarantee that they'd be able to work something out, but neither of them could predict the future beyond the weather. But, still, it felt hopeful, and she smiled, wider this time. 'I promise,' she said.

He turned the newspaper back towards himself, his eyes narrowing as he scanned the advert again. He shook his head slowly. 'There's nothing here you can't do,' he said, echoing her own thoughts.

Alice leaned back in her chair, a confident grin spreading across her face. 'I know.'

Over the past five years, she had repeatedly proven her worth to countless sceptical men, overcoming her own doubts in the process. And she could do it one more time.

Elliot studied her, curiosity etched on his face. 'What are you thinking?'

Alice glanced towards the window where a Spitfire rumbled into view. 'I'm thinking I'm not going to Millwood tonight,' she said. 'I'm going to London.'

55

Alice's breath fogged in front of her as she looked down at the note in her hand, checking the address for the third time. It matched. The building before her was a rather nondescript civil service block tucked away in central London, functional and forgettable. A far cry from the future London Airport where she hoped to be working soon. The site was still transitioning from RAF base to civilian hub. For now, tight security arrangements likely meant interviews for Deputy Forecaster candidates were best conducted off-site.

She stepped inside and was directed to the third floor. Her heart raced in her chest, a mix of nerves and the exertion of the climb. At the top, she paused, exhaling as she slipped her coat off. It was a thick woollen jacket, charcoal grey, chosen for warmth as much as appearance. Outside, the sky had been low and colourless, with a biting wind that carried the promise of sleet by nightfall. A weak high-pressure system was holding the worst of the rain at bay, but temperatures in the city remained firmly at the lower end of the seasonal average.

She'd agonised over what to wear. In the end, she'd settled on a pair of high-waisted black trousers and a simple white blouse. Smart, but not overstated. Her black leather handbag held her carefully prepared notes. She smoothed a hand down her shirt, making sure each button was in place, then opened the door.

'Good morning,' said the receptionist, seated behind a large wooden desk.

Alice smiled. 'Good morning. I'm here for the Deputy Forecaster interview.'

The woman eyed her curiously before lifting her pen. 'Name, please?'

'Al Peters.'

A flicker of amusement passed over the receptionist's face. She struck a line through the list in front of her. 'You can take a seat over there,' she said, pointing to a row of chairs along the back wall. 'Mr Baker will be with you shortly.'

'Thank you.'

Alice settled into a seat, draping her coat over her knees. She unzipped her handbag and glanced inside, weighing whether she had time for one last review of her notes. She'd prepared a detailed weather forecast that covered both ground and upper-level conditions for the coming days, with additional commentary on possible flight paths over Europe. She'd even factored in passenger experience – turbulence, visibility, and the thrill of seeing snow-capped mountains from above. Elliot had helped her access up-to-date data, and she'd made good use of it.

Still, she zipped her bag shut and rested it in her lap.

There wasn't anything more she could do. Now she just had to hope Mr Baker wouldn't turn her away the moment he realised that *Al Peters* was, in fact, a woman.

The sound of a door opening cut through the quiet. Heavy footsteps thudded ever closer. A man entered the corridor and strode towards her. He was clean shaven, with thick black hair, peppered with grey at the temples. A pair of dark-rimmed glasses perched on top of his head.

'Mr Peters?' he asked, glancing at the empty chairs beside her.

Alice stood up. 'It's Miss Peters, actually.'

He looked her up and down, then peered at the application form in his hand.

'Al Peters?' he said, uncertain.

'That's right.' She felt it unnecessary to explain that Al was short for Alice.

'I'm Mr Baker.' He removed his glasses from his head, putting them on and studied the paper again. 'There must be some mistake. This is the interview for a Deputy Forecaster.'

'That's right,' said Alice again. 'I've worked in meteorology with the RAF for the last five years. Most of that time at RAF Turnhouse, where I not only took responsibility for the weather instruments, but I also regularly prepared forecasts and briefed the aircrews. I also completed a six-month posting in Felixstowe.'

Mr Baker's posture shifted subtly. She'd mentioned Felixstowe briefly on her application, leaving the specifics off so as not to stray into classified territory. But from his reaction, she sensed that Mr Baker was well aware of Felixstowe and its meteorological connection.

He held the application form out towards her. 'This is you?' he asked.

Alice nodded, a calm smile on her lips. 'It is, sir.'

He pushed his glasses back on top of his head and extended his other hand. 'Then it's good to meet you,' he said, shaking her hand. 'Follow me. The interview panel are waiting for us in room seven.'

He turned and led the way. Alice caught the receptionist's eye. The woman gave her a grin.

'Good luck,' she said quietly as Alice passed.

Alice followed Mr Baker, the tap of her heels echoing against the linoleum floor. Room seven was a modest conference room with a long table and several chairs arranged around it. Three men in dark suits sat waiting, watching Alice intently as she entered.

'Miss Peters, please take a seat,' Mr Baker said, gesturing to the empty chair at the head of the table. He introduced the men by name only, offering no indication of their roles or meteorology expertise.

After some preliminary questions about her background and experience, one of the men cleared his throat. He was a middle-aged man with a stern expression and Alice took a discreet deep breath.

He leaned forward, folding his hands on the table. 'Miss Peters, we're impressed with your experience thus far. Now, to test your skills, we'd like you to provide us with a weather forecast for the upcoming week.'

Alice felt a surge of adrenaline at the challenge. *This* was what she had prepared for.

She smiled. 'Certainly,' she said, and launched into the most detailed weather briefing of her career so far.

EPILOGUE

Spring 1946

The sun was bright in a sky brushed with wispy clouds as Alice gazed out over Mrs Ferguson's farm. The fields were too dry. Not for long though. Pressure was falling and she expected rain by morning. She shook her head, struggling to comprehend how much time had passed. It had been more than five years since she first set foot on the farm. The land hadn't changed, but her life was unrecognisable.

The gentle chime of metal on glass pulled her from her thoughts. She turned to see her mother standing on the grass with a glass of sparkling wine in her hand. Elliot strolled over and slipped an arm around Alice's waist.

'Ready to be the centre of attention?' he whispered, kissing her cheek.

Alice smiled, glancing at Violet's small audience. Mrs Ferguson was there, of course, along with George and his now wife Dorothy James. She'd kept her own name, and Alice loved her just a little bit more for that.

Violet cleared her throat.

'Thank you all for coming today to see Alice off as she heads to London. And a special thank you to those who travelled far to be here.'

Alice glanced over at Daphne and Betty. Betty was already dabbing a tear from her cheek.

'We are so proud of Alice,' Violet continued. The "we" was a quiet nod to Alice's father. He had spent the final months of the war in the Pacific and returned just before Christmas. But he was away again now, as he so often had been in his military career. At least this time, it was for months, not years. He'd arranged leave to visit Alice in London soon, and she could hardly wait.

'It's no secret I wasn't thrilled when Alice enlisted,' Violet said, turning towards Alice. 'But I see now you knew best. We're all going to miss you, darling. London. I still can't quite believe it. But we wish you every success in this new venture. To Alice!'

'To Alice!' the small crowd echoed, raising their glasses.

Alice turned to Elliot. 'That wasn't so bad,' she murmured.

'Alice, I–'

Whatever he was about to say was cut off by Daphne and Betty who rushed over and flung their arms around Alice, sending wine sloshing to the grass. Betty squealed in her ear.

Daphne grinned, releasing her. 'So, civil aviation forecaster, huh? Sounds fancy.' She tapped her glass to Alice's. 'They're lucky to have you.'

'I can't believe you're going to London,' said Betty.

'And I can't believe *you're* getting married,' said Alice, tugging Betty's hand to admire the diamond on her finger.

Betty beamed. 'I know. Isn't it exciting? You're both invited, of course.' She turned to Elliot. 'You too.'

Elliot smiled and nudged Alice with his elbow. 'Thank you. I'll leave you ladies to catch up. Mrs Ferguson wants to introduce me to some cows.'

Alice laughed. 'Don't stand behind Jocelyn. I hear she's cranky these days.'

Once Elliot had gone, Daphne asked, 'Can you believe we're all together again?' It was the first time since their demobbing six months earlier.

Betty smiled. 'And can you believe this one is a pilot?'

'Actually,' said Alice. 'I can. How's it all going?'

Daphne shrugged. 'Like flying a plane.'

'And Ritchie?' Betty asked. 'What's it like working together?'

'It's pretty great,' said Daphne. 'He does his thing. I do mine. He would have come today, but he's off buying a plane.'

'Another one?' asked Alice, eyebrows raised.

Daphne nodded. 'This one makes five. Plus, we store planes for other people, so we've got nine in total. I handle maintenance. Ritchie runs the flying school.' She nodded towards the sky. 'And we both get to spend as much time up there as we want.'

'Sounds idyllic,' said Alice. 'I'm happy for you.'

'Me too,' Betty added.

Alice glanced towards Elliot who seemed to be listening patiently to whatever story Mrs Ferguson was giving him.

'What's going to happen when you leave?' Daphne asked gently.

Alice sighed. 'Neither of us have brought it up yet. I just don't know what to say.' There were rumours the squadron at Turnhouse might be disbanded, but it wasn't yet clear what that would mean for Elliot. They had spent the last few months seeing each other at the weekends. But tomorrow, Alice would be in London and Elliot would be in Edinburgh.

'Long distance romances can work,' said Betty, her tone bright with forced cheer.

'I guess,' said Alice.

'Do you love him?' Betty asked.

Alice smiled. 'I really do. But I also love meteorology. This is a rare opportunity, especially for a woman. I can't turn it down.'

'And you shouldn't,' said Daphne. 'You and Elliot will figure it out.'

Elliot returned, carrying a bottle of wine. 'Anyone ready for a top up?'

Daphne and Betty held out their glasses and Elliot poured.

'Shall we go say hello to Alice's mother?' Betty asked.

Daphne rolled her eyes. 'Subtle, Betty.'

'What?' asked Betty, all innocence.

'In case you missed it,' said Daphne with a playful glint in her eyes, 'that was Betty's code for *let's leave these two alone to talk about the future.*'

'Daphne!' said Betty, horrified.

Elliot laughed, and Alice reached out and gave Daphne a playful shove.

Daphne swiped the wine bottle from Elliot. 'I'll take that.'

'How were the cows?' Alice asked, still delaying the inevitable conversation.

Elliot smiled. 'Charming. I met Bernie, the cow you and Tom delivered.'

Alice smiled and snuggled into Elliot's side. 'Tom delivered him. I just watched.'

That was one of the many things she loved about Elliot. He never shied away from talking about Tom. He understood that Tom, though gone, had been an important part of her life, however brief, and he respected that.

'We do need to talk,' he said, kissing her gently on the top of her head.

Alice straightened. 'I suppose we do.'

He reached into his jacket pocket and pulled out a letter. He unfolded it and handed it to her.

'What is this?' she asked, her eyes scanning the page.

'A transfer. To London,' Elliot said. 'I didn't want to say anything until it was official. And I won't come unless you want me to. But I wanted us to have the option.'

Alice stared at him. 'Elliot. I don't know what to say. You'd move to London for me?'

He folded the letter again and tucked it back in his pocket. 'I love you, Alice. And I'm proud of you. You've earned this opportunity, and I would never ask you to give it up. I just need to know if you see me in your future.'

Setting her glass down, Alice ran a hand through her hair, stunned that Elliot would uproot his entire life for her.

'You'd really come to London?' she asked, needing to be sure.

Elliot nodded.

Her heart leapt in her chest. She threw her arms around his neck, squealing with joy.

'Is that a yes?' he asked, laughing. 'Are we going to London together?'

'Yes!' Alice cried out. 'It's a yes!'

He kissed her, then lifted her off her feet and spun her around.

She grabbed the nearby bench to steady herself as Mrs Ferguson appeared, handing Elliot an empty bottle.

'There's another one in the kitchen,' said Mrs Ferguson.

'On it,' said Elliot, flashing Alice a grin before heading off.

Mrs Ferguson watched him go, then turned to Alice. 'Tom would have liked him.'

Alice smiled. 'I think so too.'

The low rumble of a plane overhead drew their eyes skyward. The once feathered clouds were now swelling with moisture.

'You leave tomorrow?' Mrs Ferguson asked.

Alice nodded. 'I do.'

Mrs Ferguson offered a gentle smile, her eyes crinkling at the corners. 'Take a coat.'

Alice mirrored her smile. 'I know,' she said. 'It's going to rain.'

THANK YOU FOR READING

Thank you so much for reading *The Weather Watcher*. This story was such a joy to write. I had the best time diving into the fascinating world of meteorology and discovering the critical role it played in World War II.

If Alice's journey kept you turning the pages, I'd be truly grateful if you left a quick rating or review. Hearing from readers is both a thrill and a little nerve-wracking, but reviews help other readers stumble across my books too.

Word of mouth makes all the difference to authors like me, so I'm truly grateful for your help in spreading the word about my books.

Thank you again for reading.

Claire x

ABOUT THE AUTHOR

Claire Anders was born and raised in a seaside town in Scotland. She now lives in Edinburgh with her husband and daughter. When she's not writing, you can usually find her walking her dog in the nearby woods or with a book in one hand and chocolate in the other.

The Weather Watcher is Claire's third historical fiction novel. Claire also writes contemporary feel-good fiction with a touch of romance. All of her books feature strong friendships and supportive communities with a secret or two thrown into the mix.

www.claireanders.com

 facebook.com/claireandersauthor

ALSO BY CLAIRE ANDERS

Historical Fiction

Between Moons

The Clover Girls' Network

The Weather Watcher

~

Contemporary Fiction

Sunrise in Thistle Bay

New Beginnings - A Thistle Bay Short Story

Snowfall and Second Chances